N

Detective Jackson Mysteries

The Sex Club

Secrets to Die For

Thrilled to Death

Passions of the Dead

Dying for Justice

Liars, Cheaters & Thieves

Rules of Crime

Crimes of Memory

Deadly Bonds

Agent Dallas Thrillers

The Trigger

The Target

Standalone Thrillers

The Baby Thief

The Gauntlet Assassin

The Lethal Effect

The Target

An Agent Dallas Thriller
By L.J. Sellers

THE TARGET

Cover art by Gwen Thomsen Rhoads

ISBN (ebook): 978-0-9840086-6-7
ISBN (print): 978-0-9840086-7-4
Published in the USA by Spellbinder Press

Chapter 1

Monday, July 7, 1:35 p.m., Phoenix

Jamie Dallas sat in the open doorway of the plane, resisting the urge to grip the sides. The wind roared like a freight train as she glanced down at the earth ten thousand feet below. A dark shape plummeted under her, about twenty yards behind the plane. She could catch him, but she had to go now. Fear, queasiness, and excitement rolled up into her throat. She crossed her arms and leaned forward, letting herself fall into space.

A rush of cold air stunned her and she fought to remember her training. Slow count to three to clear the plane. Arms back and head down. She leaned right, aiming at her target. The earth rushed at her as she plummeted through space, the noise deafening, like the world's biggest storm rushing by in an endless stream.

Her target was upright but still free-falling. To escape, he wouldn't open his chute until the last minute. Neither would she. But could she catch him? So much was riding on this.

Her stomach roiled after a minute of headfirst descent. She'd made many jumps but had never gone into a nosedive before. Her FBI training hadn't prepared her for this. Nothing had. It was the craziest thing she'd ever done.

But she was gaining on him, closing the gap with every second. For a moment, she closed her eyes to calm her nerves and think through her next moves.

When she opened them, she and her target were dangerously close to the patchwork fields below. But he was almost within reach. Another two seconds and she would have him.

A thousand and one, a thousand and—

He reached for his ripcord. *Shit!* She had to make contact now or get the hell away. Dallas threw her arms forward, and her fingers brushed his. *Yes!* She'd done it.

She arched her back to right herself, with feet down. Another pause to create space between them, then she grabbed her ripcord. The chute opened, jerking her body upward. The floating began, a peaceful conclusion to an exhilarating adventure. But she wouldn't get to enjoy it for long. They were close to the earth, and she braced for a hard landing. She couldn't wait to gloat about her victory. Not only did Sam owe her a hundred dollars, but for the next week, he had to call her "sir" and give her sex whenever she wanted it.

He'd bet that she couldn't catch him in a free-fall, counting on her being too nervous to try a headfirst dive or too scared to stick with it long enough to pull it off. Hah! Sam obviously didn't know her well yet and probably never would. With any luck, she'd pick up another undercover assignment and get out of Phoenix for the rest of the summer. If she were gone long enough, their relationship would fizzle, and that was just fine. Her job was too rewarding to let a guy interfere with it.

In the hangar, while Sam was still packing their equipment— part of his dues for losing—she peeled off the flight suit, then checked her phone. She'd missed a call from Special Agent Gossimer, her supervisor. So much for her afternoon off. She'd been working overtime on a fraud case involving a convenience store owner and food stamp cards, so she'd earned the time off. But the deskwork, sorting through transactions, had been so deadly dull, she'd started plotting crimes in her head just to feel alive.

She stuck in her earpiece and returned the call. "It's Dallas. What's up?"

"An agent in San Diego is dead, and his office is asking for you."

Travel! And maybe an undercover assignment. Her body started to hum. Then she realized an agent was dead, possibly murdered, and remembered that her job was sometimes more dangerous than her hobbies. Dallas headed for the exit. "Why me? I don't have homicide experience."

"We'll talk when you get here."

"Hey, wait." Behind her, Sam hurried to catch up.

She'd momentarily forgotten him. It almost made her laugh. Straight-faced, she turned back. "Sorry, but I have to return to work."

"What about our movie date?" The disappointment on his face didn't detract from his looks. She'd met him here at the airport on her last jump, and they'd been dating only a month.

Why did guys get so invested? "It'll have to wait. My boss is sending me out of town." She kissed him before he could respond, then whispered, "Think how great the sex will be when I get back. Absence can be good."

He pulled away and locked eyes with her. "How long will you be gone?"

"I don't know yet." She didn't want to discuss it, but she needed an escape plan. "We don't have a commitment. You're free to do what you want while I'm gone." And so was she.

Dallas headed for the door.

Chapter 2

Two days earlier, San Diego

Carla River had only been to one other funeral, her mother's, and that had been long ago. Now she stood in a crowd of FBI agents, mostly men in suits, listening to a eulogy for a man who'd changed her life—twice. Tears ran down her face, blending with the light drizzle that dripped from the sky. It almost never rained in San Diego, but today, maybe because sunshine wouldn't have been appropriate, the sky was as dark as the suits around the grave.

The first time she'd met Joe Palmer, he'd come to her childhood home and arrested her dad, then led the investigative team that had dug up the bodies under their house. Her serial-killer father had gone to prison, and a year later her mother had killed herself, leaving River homeless as a teenager. But she'd hung onto the business card Joe had given her and remembered his offer of help if she ever needed it. After a year on the streets, she'd finally called and asked for that assistance. He and his wife had taken her in and supported her through high school, then helped her access grants to attend college. River had later joined the bureau, modeling her life after Joe's, but she'd never really had an opportunity to repay him. Now he was dead, and her heart ached with loss.

After the service, she sought out the only person in the crowd she knew. Flanked on both sides by agents as she walked to her car, Jana Palmer looked surprisingly stoic. As River approached, her heart fluttered. She had changed so much since the last time Jana had seen her. Would Jana even recognize her? She glanced at the other agents, older men near retirement age, then touched Jana's arm. "Can we have a moment alone? I'm Carla River with the Eugene office." This moment could be awkward, and she'd already taken her share of grief from coworkers, mostly men who didn't understand.

The other agents walked away, and the widow stared at her, eyes puzzled. "Carl River? Oh my god."

"I had the surgery a year and a half ago. I'm sorry I didn't tell you and Joe. I didn't think he would understand." River was still five-ten and broad shouldered, but her face had softened and her sandy hair had grown to her shoulders.

Mrs. Palmer opened her arms and pulled her in for a hug. "Joe wouldn't have, but I do. Thank you for coming. It's so good to see you."

More tears threatened to spill, so River pulled back, self-conscious of her thick, androgynous body. "What happened? I didn't even know Joe was sick."

The widow repressed a shudder. "It was very sudden. And they still don't know exactly what he died of, but it was most likely an infection. He had a cut on his hand that became red and swollen." She grabbed River's arm and steered her away from the nearby group. "I want you to investigate. There's something going on at the company I work for. I told Joe about it and two weeks later he died."

"What are you saying? You think Joe was murdered?"

She sighed. "I don't know. But someone has to find out."

River was torn. "I'd like to look into it for you. I owe both of you. But I don't think the San Diego bureau will want me involved."

"I don't care. I want you to do this, and I think you'll need my help. Those stuffed suits can just get over it."

There was the spunk she'd come to love all those years ago. Mrs. Palmer had gone to bat for her many times when River was a teenage boy, taking on school administrators and social workers with equal zest.

"Come to the house," she continued. "And I'll tell you what I know and show you Joe's notes. It may be nothing, but someone has to investigate."

The Palmers' home sat on a gentle slope in the Mission Hills area, with a peek-a-boo view of the ocean. The property was a step up from the small tract house she'd shared with them twenty-five years earlier. River climbed from her car and instinctively turned west. The clouds had cleared, and the sight of the ocean filled her with a homesickness she hadn't expected. She waited while Mrs. Palmer parked in the garage, then followed her inside.

"Make yourself comfortable on the terrace," Jana said. "I'll bring Joe's notes and some iced tea."

River stepped outside and sat in a plush patio chair. The air was warm, damp, and unusually still for San Diego. She took off her jacket and tried to relax and enjoy the gorgeous view. But Joe Palmer was dead, possibly murdered. And Jana wanted her to stay in town to investigate. River owed it to her mentor, but she also loved her private, rural home outside Eugene, Oregon, and she was already eager to return.

Jana came out with two glasses of tea and a folder tucked

under her arm. Her long-ago foster mother seemed shorter and softer than she remembered, but her face hadn't aged much, and her hair was dyed dark brown.

"Where do you work now?" River didn't have the heart to make small talk. Grief still gripped her, and, if Joe had been murdered, she had to get moving before the leads disappeared.

"TecLife. It's a medical device company that's doing some innovative things."

"What's going on that made you want Joe to investigate?"

"It's not so much what's happening at TecLife, but what's been happening to another company." Jana took a long sip of tea. "First, our main competitor had a warehouse full of magnet-based migraine devices destroyed by a fire. It's a new product, and the fire delayed the launch, which was a financial setback." She leaned toward River, her voice more intense. "Our company's lead product is an electrical stimulator that treats migraines."

Probably coincidence. But River would humor her for a while. After spending her life with an FBI agent, Jana had probably come to be overly suspicious.

Before River could respond, Jana added, "A security guard died in the fire. They think he'd been drinking and fell asleep."

"Maybe he started it accidentally."

Jana shook her head. "They suspected arson but never found an accelerant."

Probably a pyromaniac with no connection. "There must be a reason you think the fire is connected to your company."

"I overheard a snippet of conversation between the two cofounders. They were in a conference room, and I was in the adjacent copy room. Here's what I think I heard." Jana opened the folder and read from the top paper. "ProtoCell's delay buys us time to expand our market share, but they'll rebound quickly if we don't escalate this."

Aggressive, but not conclusive. "Who was talking?"

"I think it was Max Grissom, the CEO, but I can't swear to it. The copy machine was running."

"And the other person?"

"Higher pitched, so maybe Cheryl Decker, the president, or Curtis Santera, head of R&D."

"When did that conversation take place?"

"Feb 17th, two days after the fire. But I'd heard them talking about ProtoCell's product before the fire too."

River grabbed a notepad from her bag and jogged it down. "You said *first.* What else happened?"

"In April, ProtoCell's health tattoo started causing skin infections and had to be pulled from the market while they looked into the problem. The PR was horrible, and the sales of all their other products plunged."

River felt old and uninformed. "What's a health tattoo?"

"It's a thin skin patch with electrodes that monitor vital signs." Jana looked over her glasses at River. "Guess what TecLife's newest product is?"

Interesting. "A health tattoo?"

"Yep. Ours transmits data to the wearer and/or their doctor's smartphone, so it's more advanced, but being second to market is always a disadvantage." The widow sighed. "I hate to think badly of TecLife, but it's struggling. We have innovative products in the pipeline, but the development has been slow and expensive. The company may not have enough cash-flow to continue, and I think the founders are feeling desperate."

"You think these executives committed acts of sabotage?"

River heard the skepticism in her voice.

Jana frowned. "Not personally, no. But I think they might have hired someone."

"These are serious accusations. Tampering with medical devices could be lethal." River thought about Joe's sudden death from a possible infection. Had they killed him with lab-grown bacteria?

"That's why I told Joe about my suspicions. He was skeptical, but he agreed to investigate." Jana's eyes misted over. "I never thought he'd end up dead."

River shifted in her chair, planning how she would handle this. "Did Joe take this to the bureau?"

His widow shook her head. "He wasn't convinced, so he decided to look into it on his own until he had something solid. But there's another development."

River picked up her pen again.

"The real profit is in wide-scale prescriptions. So both companies are developing weight-loss devices with biologicals. ProtoCell, our competitor, will soon release a weight-loss implant, and TecLife is working on a similar product they've been very secretive about. It's potentially a billion dollar market."

Stunned by that number, River reached for the black folder. "Let me see Joe's notes."

The paperwork was thin, but it included a copy of the fire marshal's report of the warehouse blaze, which had been ruled inconclusive. Joe had also talked to the head of security at ProtoCell, but the conversation had been brief, and Joe had noted: *Failure to follow sanitation protocols.*

"I know what you're thinking," Jana said, standing up. "But I'm not crazy, and I have something else to show you."

She came back a minute later with a plastic evidence bag

and handed it to River. Inside was a translucent one-inch square of plastic film, with fine black lines intersecting through it.

"I found it in Joe's coat pocket yesterday. It's a PulseTat, one of the recalled ProtoCell health tattoos. What if it killed him somehow?"

Was it possible? River's gut knotted into a ball of dread. She had no choice but to put her life on hold and pursue this. Her boss in Eugene would be supportive and transfer her cases to other agents. But the San Diego bureau might not welcome her intrusion in their jurisdiction. She took long slow breaths to release her tension. She would push past any resistance, as she had before. When she'd gone through the change from male to female, she'd been assigned to Portland, and some of the men—people she'd worked with for years— had given her a hard time, pressuring her to quit. She'd finally transferred to Eugene for a fresh start where everyone knew her as Carla from day one. But none of that mattered now.

Getting inside TecLife would be the key to solving this. Even if Joe hadn't been murdered, the bureau still needed to stop the sabotage before innocent people were hurt. Could she infiltrate the company? She looked up at Jana. "Are you still in the human resource field?"

"I'm the HR director at TecLife."

"Can you get me hired? I need access to investigate." Another flash of dread rippled through her. Undercover work was not her strength. Her favorite mantra came to mind. *I can only do my best and control my part in this.*

Jana's brow creased. "I don't know. The founders like to hire young people."

Ouch. She was barely forty. Still, River felt relieved, and a better idea came to mind. Agent Jamie Dallas. Young, talented, and quick at gaining access. River had worked with her before to stop an eco-terrorist. Now she just had to convince the local bureau to work with her and Dallas in handling the investigation. She would start by calling the Phoenix director.

Chapter 3

Monday July 7, 3:07 p.m., Phoenix

For a minute, the air conditioning in the Phoenix FBI office felt fabulous, cooling her skin after the short but unbearably hot walk from the parking lot. But as she trotted upstairs, Dallas pulled on her business jacket to keep the refrigeration at bay. She entered Gossimer's office on the third floor and promptly sneezed. *Damn.* She'd been too late with the jacket. When her skin cooled rapidly, she started sneezing. Stopping the outburst was nearly impossible.

She sat down and sneezed again.

"How many more you got?" Gossimer asked. "Should you come back later?" He was old enough to be her father but still attractive. She'd come to like short gray hair on men, after being surrounded by it in the bureau for years.

"I'm fine." Dallas pinched the cartilage between her nostrils. Sometimes it helped. Her record was twenty-six sneezes, and it had happened right here in this building just a few months on the job. She'd grown up in Flagstaff, and after her training at Quantico, she'd requested a position in Arizona to be close to her aunt and her best friend. Because no other agent in their right mind wanted to live in Phoenix, she'd landed her first-choice location. Every July and August, she regretted that decision. "What have you got for me?"

"Special Agent Joe Palmer of the San Diego bureau died earlier this week. He'd been sick for a few days, then went into septic shock in the ER. He had a nasty sore on his hand and his blood count indicates an infection, but the autopsy was inconclusive." Gossimer's eyes were troubled. "But that won't be your focus."

Curiosity was killing her, but Dallas nodded and waited, holding back a sneeze.

"Palmer's wife, Jana, works for TecLife, a medical device business. She thinks the company is engaged in corporate sabotage against its competitors. She asked her husband to look into it, and two weeks later he was dead."

Dallas' pulse quickened. She finally had a glimmer of her role in the case. "Did he have an open file?"

"No. Palmer was looking into it on his own and only had some personal notes."

"The bureau wants me to get inside the company and see what I can find."

"Jana Palmer works in HR and can get you an interview."

Yes! Dallas lived for undercover work. Yet this one made her nervous. "I don't have enough science or tech background to pose as a researcher, so it would have to be an administrative job."

Gossimer smiled. "They have an opening right now for an assistant to the president. I take it you're interested in the assignment?"

"Of course. If someone in the company killed one of our agents, I want to help get the bastard." As soon as she said it, she realized what it meant.

Her boss raised an eyebrow. "You're sure? If they murdered one agent, they might try to kill another."

She swallowed a lump in her throat. "I'll be careful. They won't suspect someone from the inside." Dallas wondered what Palmer had done to flag their attention.

"On the upside, none of this is a given. The wife could be wrong about the company, and Agent Palmer could have died of an infected spider bite."

"What makes her think TecLife is conducting corporate sabotage?" The bureau wouldn't send her out to San Diego unless they had something solid.

"One of their competitors had a warehouse fire, in which a guard died, around the same time Mrs. Palmer overheard the executives talking about the competitor's product. A month later, another device company had to recall its new product, some kind of skin patch that monitors blood pressure." Gossimer scowled and handed her a file. "These are medical devices, and tampering with them endangers lives. Which is why we're taking the allegation so seriously."

"Who's my contact in the San Diego office?"

"It's a little complicated. Carla River, from the Eugene office, knew Palmer years ago when she lived in San Diego. She came down for his funeral and asked to investigate. She also requested you for the undercover assignment."

Dallas' apprehension eased. She'd worked with River in Oregon and liked her style. "Why is it complicated?"

"Politics." Gossimer gave a small shrug. "Agent River is the one who talked to the wife, heard her concerns, and located Palmer's notes, so she will be your contact. But the SD director appointed someone to head the investigation into Palmer's death."

"So they're treating them like separate cases?"

Her boss offered a phony smile. "Yes, but they kept Palmer's investigation in the white collar unit, and they'll share information."

"Good to know." She hoped the politics wouldn't undermine her role in the case. Undercover work required a 24-7 support team. "When do I leave?"

"As soon as you can. I'll get the UC people started on your new ID and background right away."

Who did she want to be this time? It would be her first undercover role that required her to show up for work. "If I'm going to interact with people in an office, I should stick with something familiar. What about J.C., the initials, for a first name?"

"What goes on the driver's license? The motor vehicles people don't like initials."

"Why not Jamie? Jamie Hunter. No one is going to see my license." She'd had a dog named Hunter, a black lab, when she was a kid. Her father had run over him in a drug-induced rage. But what she liked best about the name for this assignment was its obviousness. She'd already used the FBI acronym as her initials, as well as SOB. "I'll introduce myself as J.C. or Jace." In the bureau, everyone called her Dallas, and she preferred it. "What about my background?"

"It's probably not as important this time, but let's brainstorm anyway."

Her last UC assignment had required her to infiltrate a group of survivalists, and the background had been critical to getting accepted. "What do we know about TecLife's founders?"

"Max Grissom and Cheryl Decker both went to Stanford, so we'll add that to your résumé." Gossimer glanced at his notes. "They both also worked for other medical technology companies, which are now their competitors."

"I need a history in the industry, but one they can't check

out too thoroughly. Maybe a tech company that's gone out of business." Dallas tried to recall headlines from the business section of the *Times*, but she typically focused on computer and digital technology, as well as financial news.

"We'll have our background people work on it." Gossimer gave her a sly smile. "We have some new toys and tactics you might get to try out."

Another shimmer of pleasure. "Like what?"

"Dime-sized tracking devices that slide into purses or pockets and the ability to activate webcams on computers without the users' knowledge."

Dallas resisted the urge to rub her hands together. *Damn,* she loved spying. "I assume I'm targeting both founders. Anyone else in the company worth checking out?"

"Curtis Santera, the head of R&D, owns fifteen percent of the company's stock, so he has a lot to lose if TecLife goes under."

Pumped and ready, Dallas couldn't sit any longer. "I need to start packing and prepping."

"We'll have your new paperwork by noon tomorrow, so you can get to the DMV and buy a plane ticket. Once you hit San Diego, you can trade in your new driver's license for a local issue."

"Where will I stay?" Dallas grabbed her tablet computer from the desk, realizing she'd been too excited to take notes.

"Agent River is working on that. She knows the area and will call you tomorrow."

Dallas would have more questions later, but right now she had to move. "I'll be in touch."

"Good luck. Keep me posted."

She hurried out, eager to transform into J.C Hunter. Slipping into the skin of another person made her neurons sing. It wasn't the same heart-thumping thrill as skydiving, but the challenge—and delicious deception—lasted for weeks or months. The high was far better than any drug or short-term adventure. She'd discovered the thrill as a teenager, after taking acting lessons and practicing characters on strangers.

The classes had been just one of the many activities her sweet Aunt Lynn had enrolled her in to keep Dallas from thinking about, or copying, her drug-snorting, good-for-nothing parents. All of those endeavors—archery, tennis, piano lessons, language classes—served her well now and helped her fit in almost anywhere. But it was the acting skills that made her an excellent infiltrator.

She practically skipped out of the building, feeling lucky to have a job she loved. Undercover work was a license to lie, cheat, and spy—all for the good of her country.

On the drive to her condo at the edge of Scottsdale, she called her landlord to let him know she'd be gone again for a while. After parking her Rav4 at the back of the lot where it would get some shade, she hurried upstairs, mentally planning her next steps. Inside, she kicked off her shoes, liking the feel of the hardwood floors on her feet. Her friend Stacie had urged her to buy rugs or artwork, but Dallas loved the bare walls and open spaces. Clutter made it hard to breathe and sent her running from a room.

But for UC assignments, she kept a box of fake family photos and knickknacks in the hall closet. She would ship them tomorrow when she had an address in San Diego. The personal items would make her temporary apartment look lived in, just in case someone stopped by or she brought a guy home for a hookup. The thought excited her. Seduction was often a bonus in her undercover roles, even though the bureau technically didn't allow sexual encounters with a target. But she was good at extracting information during prolonged foreplay.

Not knowing how long she would be gone, she packed two suitcases to the hilt, choosing mostly office clothes in shades of beige, gray, and black. Her blond hair looked best against neutral colors, but she was thinking of dying it red for the assignment. She owned a couple of sexy date dresses in teal—the only real color she wore—and they would look good with crimson tresses. If she had to stay on the job more than a month, she'd have to buy more feminine office clothes. Through college, she'd worked mostly as a waitress, preferring the constant movement and cash tips to an administrative job. Could she do the office job for a month if necessary? Of course she could. Collecting intel would make the work interesting. That reminded her to pack the bugs and tracking devices she might get to plant on her targets.

What was she forgetting? Her special purse with the hidden pocket in the bottom for her Kel-Tec, a little backup gun she carried on assignment. Dallas tucked it into the suitcase she would check at the ticket counter. Reluctantly, she placed her Glock in the gun safe. Normally, she slept with it on the nightstand and set the motion sensor in the hallway before getting into bed. No one would ever surprise her in the middle of the night.

Time to call Stacie, her best friend, and let her know. Her *only* friend, Dallas corrected. The undercover assignments made it impossible to maintain long-term relationships of any kind, which was true for lots of field agents as well. Her shrink's voice popped into her head, telling her it was bullshit. Dallas groaned. She would have to call Dr. Harper too—her most difficult conversation. But it could wait until she was in San Diego.

While Stacie's phone rang, Dallas stood at the window and stared at Camelback Mountain in the distance. It was more like a hill—especially compared to Mt. Shasta where she'd been on her last assignment—but at least it was a break in the desert.

"Jamie. Good timing. I was just going to see if you wanted to grab a drink later."

"Sure, but I can't stay out long. I'm leaving for San Diego tomorrow."

"On assignment?" Her friend's voice fell. "You've only been back a month or so."

Why did she have to keeping justifying her work? "An agent is dead and more lives are at stake. This one is really important."

"If you're trying to make me feel better, you're taking the wrong approach."

Dallas laughed. "Don't worry. It's not dangerous for me. I'll be in an office."

Now Stacie laughed. "You won't last a week.

Dallas took no offense. "I can do anything."

"Except sit still. Have you told Sam?"

"Not yet. But don't worry, we're not serious, and I prepared him for it already."

A big sigh. "Okay, meet me at the Apollo at eight."

"See you soon."

In her galley kitchen, she opened a can of vegetable-beef soup and heated a bowl of it in the microwave. While she paced the apartment, listing pre-assignment details, her phone rang. Stacie calling back? She grabbed the device from her black leather shoulder bag and looked at the ID: *Roxy*

Stuck. Her mother. Her parents had never married because they collected more benefits as individuals—another source of shame.

Irritation and worry jammed her thoughts. Why was her mother calling? It had to be about money. Dallas let it ring. She had too much to do and needed to focus. She had walked, no run, away from the Queen Liar/manipulator and her worthless father at sixteen and never looked back. She sat at her desk and made a list for the next day: new driver's license, new burner phones, text Sam and break it off.

Her cell rang again, and she knew it was her mother without looking. When Roxy wanted something, she could be overwhelming. It was better to deal with her now than put up with fifteen calls. Dallas picked up. "Hey, Mom. What's going on?"

"Your dad's in the hospital." Her mother's pack-a-day voice choked up. "He's dying. You have to come home and see him."

Grief and anger squeezed her heart, but the grief quickly let go. The idiot had been trying to kill himself with drugs and alcohol for decades, so it was no surprise. "Why should I? He's never called me once since I left home, and he wasn't much of a father before that. I don't exist for him."

"He wants to see you. He regrets a lot of his choices and he wants your forgiveness."

Dying bastards always did. "Pat his hand for me and tell him I said goodbye. But I'm not coming. I have an important work assignment that can't be put off." Dallas hung up before her mother could argue. An FBI agent, a good man who'd dedicated his life to serving his country, was dead, most likely murdered. Investigating his death and the sabotage of medical devices was a far better use of her time than making a dying asshole feel better.

She ate her now-lukewarm soup and got moving again. Guilt followed her around the condo as she watered her cactus, closed the blinds, and set the AC down a notch in preparation to leave for weeks or months. *Damn him.* Her good vibe about flying to San Diego on assignment was slipping away. Dallas changed into workout clothes and jumped on the elliptical machine—the best way to clear her head and work off tension.

Forty minutes later, she was drenched in sweat and at peace with her decision. Unwilling to risk another confrontation, she texted Sam: *I have an out-of-town assignment and I'll be gone for a month or so and too busy to communicate. We might as well see other people.*

She hoped he would take it well. Sam was smart enough not to be clingy with her, unlike her last boyfriend, who'd gotten too serious too quickly and ruined a good thing. But once the sex lost its sizzle, she had to move on. When men got too attached and emotional with her, banging them became boring, more of a chore than a sport. She knew it was fucked up, but so far, Dr. Harper had failed to fix her.

Dallas showered, put on the one cocktail dress she hadn't packed, and went out to meet Stacie.

Chapter 4

Tuesday, July 8, 3:05 p.m.
Kiya spotted the stripper getting out of a car, stuck in a piece of Juicy Fruit, and braced for action. After the pretty woman in the phony cop uniform crossed the parking lot, Kiya climbed off her motorcycle, grabbed the prop from her saddle bag, and hurried toward the building. She carried a bouquet of black roses that had cost a small fortune and wore a shirt with a Flower Power logo above the pocket. She'd bought the uniform from a young deliveryman two days ago. Some of her assignments required months of preparation. Others, like this one, came together easily. But it was too soon to count this one as a done deal. The main challenge was still ahead.

Inside the glass doors, the stripper walked through a security checkpoint and showed her ID. "I'm with PartyParty. I have a birthday present for Sanjay Mallick. Your company ordered it."

Kiya waited just inside the door, hoping someone else would come through first. But DigiPro was a medtech company and didn't get much foot traffic.

The security guard crossed his arms. "What kind of present? Show me."

The stripper pulled open her easy-snap shirt and leaned forward. Kiya couldn't see the display, but she imagined the woman was wearing a sexy black bra that revealed plenty of cleavage. The guard grinned and waved her in. "Sanjay's in the lab on the left upstairs."

One hurdle down. Kiya had ordered the strip-o-gram as a distraction. She hoped the woman was good at her job. Touching the gold chain on her neck for luck, Kiya stepped forward.

"I'm Amy Johnson with Flower Power. I have a delivery for Sanjay Mallick too. He's having quite a birthday." She handed the security guy a phony driver's license and gave him a quick smile. She hated smiling. Her teeth were small, and it wasn't in her nature to be charming. But being a freelance contractor required it sometimes. She hoped the guy didn't call the floral company.

He looked at her uniform shirt and compared her face to the tiny photo on the license. What was he thinking? That she was sort of pretty, but her green eyes lacked warmth?

"Black roses? Is that a joke?" The guard, thirty-something with a bitter expression, pretended to do his job by asking questions.

"I believe so. The birthday boy is thirty today, so someone probably wants to remind him it's all downhill after this." She was about to hit that milestone herself.

"He's gonna like his other present better." The guard waved her in.

Hurdle number two. Kiya hustled toward the stairs, not wanting to wait for the elevator to return. The stripper was already on her way up to the research lab. The company was still small, with only nineteen employees, and most were scientists, computer geeks, or some freaky combination.

They were working on a password pill her client wanted. The larger company had the resources to speed up the development—or kill the project to keep it off the market. She didn't care which, as long as she got paid.

At the top of the stairs, the stripper waited in front of a solid door with a large window next to it. Kiya crossed the open space as a young man walked to the glass and sized up both visitors.

The door opened, and he grinned at the busty woman in the tight blue uniform. "Who are you here to arrest?"

"Sanjay Mallick. He's been a naughty boy."

The stripper was working it already. Kiya eased up behind her. "I've got something for him too."

The man barely glanced at her, then stepped back to let them both in. "Sanjay is back in the corner."

Kiya glanced in the direction he was pointing. A dark-haired man, skinny as a pencil, stood at a long metal counter, staring into a monitor. Sanjay had posted his birthday information in several social network sites, and the proximity of it had inspired her plan.

He was surrounded by gadgets, but the microscope was the only piece of lab equipment she recognized. All she needed was for him to step away from his workspace. She touched the stripper's arm. "Why don't you set up in the front? I'm sure all the guys will enjoy your birthday song." Four other men, all wearing white lab coats, had workspaces in the wide room.

"Thanks, but I know what I'm doing." The stripper set her boom box on the floor near the solid front wall, then sashayed back to Sanjay's corner. The researcher looked more scared than pleased. Kiya stood back. The less anyone looked at her the better. She wore fake glasses and pale makeup and had her hair pulled tight into a bun, but she was already taking a chance by doing this so openly.

"Sanjay Mallick, you're under arrest." The stripper winked and led the timid scientist to the open space in front. She grabbed a chair from another workspace and pushed him down into it. As the stripper "read him his rights," including some weird birthday stuff, the other workers moved into a semi-circle around the chair.

Roses in hand, Kiya walked boldly toward Sanjay's workspace, sizing up the area. First, the computer. As she set down the flowers, she slipped a tiny flash drive out of her pocket and into his laptop. The device was designed to automatically copy everything on the hard drive. While it sucked up files, Kiya looked around for the actual product. A small clear case near the back of the counter caught her eye. In it were three little pills, the cylindrical kind with thin, plastic-like coating. A glance over her shoulder reassured her that the men were still occupied with the stripper, who'd just yanked off her peel-away pants.

Kiya grabbed the case, shoved it into her shoulder bag, and spun back to the computer. Did she have all the files yet? She didn't care. What they really wanted was the little pill that, once activated by stomach acid, would emit an 18-bit EKG-like signal, which could be detected by a phone or computer, essentially turning the body into a password. Or at least that was how it was supposed to work. The idea seemed brilliant and pointless at the same time.

Too nervous to wait, she yanked the flash drive out and slipped it into her pants pocket. She strode toward the door.

An authoritative man came in, looking directly at her. "Who are you, and what were you doing back there?"

He'd seen her through the glass. "Floral delivery for the

birthday boy." She pointed at the roses on the back counter. "I dropped them off because the stripper was too hard to compete with."

But the man had already turned toward the raunchy music and gyrating semi-naked woman. Kiya slipped past him and out the door.

Later, she met her client in the back booth of a hole-in-the wall taco stand. The client wore huge dark glasses and a Panama hat that hid much of her face, but Kiya knew who she was and where she worked, even though she'd given her a phony name. They'd done business before. The woman set a small canvas briefcase on the floor under their table and pushed it toward her with her feet. Kiya smiled, sipped iced coffee, and asked if she'd seen the new production at the Civic Theater. A minute later, Kiya lifted the case into her lap and unzipped it halfway. Stacks of cash that should total twenty-five thousand. She would count the money later. Her client knew if she cheated her, Kiya would sabotage her company, because that's what the client paid her to do to her competitors.

Kiya pulled an envelope from her shoulder bag and set it on the table. Her client mentioned a coming storm, which in San Diego, didn't mean much, and Kiya offered an appropriately meaningless response. A moment later, the client slid her hand across the table, fingered the envelope to feel for its content, and eased it to her side. They chatted about the weather again, then the woman opened the envelope and peeked at the thumb drive and password pills.

A tight smile of relief. "Thanks. Walk with me for minute?"

The request surprised her. Another job already? "Sure." Kiya left a five on the table for the waitress, strapped the canvas case over her shoulder, and slipped out of the booth. Her client followed her outside. A breeze blew in from the ocean, keeping the hot air from being insufferable. Instinctively, Kiya headed to the end of the building and turned up the alley. The brick-walled space was empty.

The woman caught up to her and walked shoulder to shoulder. Keeping her voice low, she asked, "Do you ever do any strong arm work?"

A tingle played on the back of her neck. What the hell did her client have in mind? Did she even want to know? "Not usually. What do you need? A shakedown?" Her criminal-enterprise experience—and sociopathic nature—qualified her to do enforcer work, but she preferred not to interact closely with people. Even for money. After being sold into marriage at the age of seven and passed between old brothers like an opium pipe, she wanted as little close contact with men as possible.

"I need something more direct," the client said. "But if you're not interested, it would be foolish to tell you about it." Her mouth closed in a stern line.

The woman knew better than to give her any unnecessary information, because Kiya could—and would—use it to take her down if things ever got ugly between them. "Then we're done here. See you next time." Kiya turned and strode away.

"Wait."

She stopped. The urgency in her client's tone put Kiya at an advantage. Slowly, she turned back. "Yes?"

"I'll double what I just paid you. And no one gets hurt. I need access to a secure building, and it's easier if you have the guy with the password."

They wanted her to extract it? "I don't do torture." Kiya

shook her head and turned away.

"No, it's not like that. I need you to grab him, drug him, and bring him along."

"That's crazy. If he's drugged, how does he provide the password?"

"It's in his palm. So you can either cut off his hand or take him along."

A radio-frequency implant. Intriguing. "Why not use the password pill I just acquired for you?"

"It's not ready. I just like to see what my competitors are up to."

"Double?" The money enticed her as well. It would be enough to pay for the revenge she had in mind for the father who'd sold her two decades ago. "What's the target?"

"Three small implants. And if that goes well, I have another sabotage job for you soon."

The industry was keeping her busy. "I want half up front."

The client turned her head. "So you're in?"

"I'm in."

Chapter 5

Wednesday, July 9, 4:05 p.m.

Dallas pulled into the Palm View condos on Bayard Street, and a sense of belonging washed over her. She loved the pale stucco, arched windows, and blooming flower boxes. Stepping out of the rental car, she took a deep breath. The air was better here too, but she couldn't pinpoint the difference. Why did she stay in dry, ugly Phoenix? Stacie was there, but clinging to a location she hated for a childhood friend seemed, well, childish. She would have to talk to Dr. Harper about it.

She looked around the parking lot for River. The agent was supposed to meet her here. Maybe she was inside. Dallas headed upstairs to unit seven. She'd received the information that morning before catching her flight and had studied the TecLife founders' profiles on the plane. Background info for this assignment was less critical than her last, where she'd had to infiltrate a group whose members were inherently paranoid. Going to work for a business was less challenging and less fun. But if someone at the company had killed Agent Palmer to protect their activities, it would be no less dangerous.

On a brighter note, a gorgeous young man came out of a condo on the ground floor and jogged toward the parking lot.

Dressed only in shorts and lovely tanned skin, he spotted her moments later. Dallas wished she'd had a chance to freshen her makeup, which tended to disappear on flights.

He trotted over, showing perfect white teeth. Just under six feet and a little small for her taste. But his body was a sculpted work of art.

"Hello, sunshine." He nodded toward her luggage. "I hope you plan to stay awhile."

She gave him her most charming smile. "Long enough to get acquainted, I'm sure." She held out her hand. "J.C. Hunter. My friends call me Jace."

"Davis Longmore." He shook her hand, stroking her palm as he let go.

A player. Nice. She could use a little recreational sex, with no ulterior motive attached.

"I'm out for a run," he said. "What unit are you in? I'll stop by with a proper housing-warming gift later."

"Seven. Give me some time to unpack and freshen up."

"You look as fresh as it gets." He grinned. "See you later."

She waved, not wanting to open her mouth and drool.

Upstairs, she found the condo unlocked and River seated at a small breakfast table, working on her laptop. The agent stood, looking leaner than Dallas remembered. But the tall, forty-something woman still had a curveless body, with wide shoulders that her gray jacket couldn't hide. Dallas rolled her luggage inside and closed the door. "Hey, River. Good to see you."

"Likewise." She stood and offered her hand. "Thanks for coming. This case is important to me."

"You worked with Joe Palmer?"

"No, he took me in when I was an orphaned teenager."

That surprised her. "You grew up here in San Diego?"

"Yes. I stayed in touch with Joe and his wife, but this is only my second time back." River's eyes signaled pain.

Dallas decided it wasn't appropriate to ask her about it. They needed to get down to business. She spotted a Bunn brewer on the counter. "Is there any coffee?"

"Sorry, you'll have to shop. I just got the keys an hour ago. But you're close to the beach, and the view isn't bad."

"Sweet." She'd never lived anywhere near the beach—even on assignment. Dallas dropped her purse on the table and took a quick tour of the rental. "This must be costing the bureau some serious outlay."

"I know you work quickly, so I figured we could afford it."

"Thanks." The condo was furnished with the basics: an overstuffed, microfiber couch and chair, two paintings of the harbor, and a large area rug in bold turquoise and red. She probably wouldn't spend much time here, but she appreciated comfort and color. Dallas opened a kitchen cupboard and discovered a full compliment of dishware. "This place must be typically rented to vacationers."

"It's owned by snowbirds who are only here in the winter." River sat back down. "I felt lucky to find it. Saved us both a lot of setup."

Dallas grabbed a glass, filled it with water, and joined River at the table. "When and how do I make contact with TecLife?"

"Upload your résumé to their website today, and Jana Palmer, their human resource director, will set you up with an interview tomorrow."

"Will she be an inside ally for me?"

"Not really. She'll help you get hired, but beyond that, we won't involve her."

"Who am I interviewing with?" Male or female made a difference in how she would dress and prep for it.

"I'm not certain, but most likely it will be Max Grissom. He's reportedly very hands-on about hiring decisions."

Good. She would apply pheromones. They'd proved to be effective in winning quick trust and affection in her last infiltration. "Is he my main target? Or does Mrs. Palmer have a sense of which executive is behind the sabotage?"

"She overheard a suspicious conversation and thinks Max Grissom was the person talking. And Jana says Grissom is more aggressive and less ethical than Cheryl Decker."

That fit with what she'd learned. Decker had spent years working on a cure for a rare disease and never gave interviews for business articles. "What about Curtis Santera? I understand he has a significant financial stake in the company."

"You'll have to target all three until you find something tangible. They could all be involved." River reached for her briefcase. "We want to get ears inside their offices as quickly as possible. But we need something to justify a court order."

"What about accessing their computers and turning on the cameras?"

"We'll do that too, but we still need warrants. You'll have to eavesdrop and elicit gossip to get us started."

A tremor vibrated up her spine. She couldn't wait to get going. "How do you want me to contact you?"

"Whatever is safest for you at the time. I've still got the same Gmail accounts. Do you need a burner phone?"

"I'm covered. Where are you staying?"

"In an apartment not far from here, but our future contact needs to be more discreet."

Fine with her. She enjoyed furtive conversations in moving

cars and dropping evidence into pockets as she passed.

River stood. "I'd better get out of here before anyone sees us together."

"I'll be in touch daily."

"Good luck with your interview. If they don't hire you, we'll have to move to Plan B."

"Which is?"

"A sting. But we would need to start over with a new UC agent." River flashed a grim smile. "So nail this one please."

Dallas gave a mock salute. "Yes, ma'am."

After River left, she read through the files again, refreshing her knowledge of the TecLife executives. Max Grissom was a doctor who'd gone straight from med school to a biological company, then eventually founded his own medical device startup with cutting edge technology. But TecLife had branched out, and news reports speculated that it was developing drug-device combinations. Cheryl Decker had a much thinner file. After leaving Stanford with a masters in molecular biology, she'd gone to work for ProtoCell, then four years later, joined with Grissom to form TecLife. But there were no online profiles or news stories, and the only picture they had of her was fifteen years old. A mystery woman or just a dedicated scientist who shunned social exposure?

Dallas would soon find out.

Chapter 6

Wednesday, July 9, 6:25 p.m.

As the music stopped, Raul Cortez kissed the cheek of his partner, a lovely older woman he saw only in class. "I have to check my messages. Meet you back here in five minutes." He hurried to the chair where his jacket hung, not wanting to miss even a moment of instruction. Tonight, they were learning advanced steps for the samba.

He grabbed the phone and a wave of panic washed over him. He'd missed three messages—all from his supervisor, Sergeant Riggs. The first message told him everything: "Cortez. Team three has a homicide at an abandoned cannery on Sicard Street in the Barrio Logan area. Hawthorne is running the case, but he needs the whole team down there ASAP."

Another homicide to investigate. His already-thumping heart swelled with anticipation. He'd only been a detective for four months, but this was his dream job. Or, more honestly, a great backup plan. He knew he'd never be a professional ballroom dancer, but law-enforcement made him feel good about himself, and not at all like he was settling. And the promotion to detective had been a huge bonus. Cortez hurried over to his dance partner, who was downing a bottle of water. "I'm sorry, but I have to leave. I have a homicide." A rush of pride made him smile.

"Then go already. You're one of the good ones." She smiled and waved him off.

Outside, the pink sun shimmered near the horizon and heat rolled off the asphalt. But he could smell the ocean, so he never complained about San Diego's weather. In his car, he changed out of his tank top and pulled on a white, long-sleeved work shirt. The dark jacket could wait until he reached the crime scene, a twenty-minute drive. Once he was on the expressway, he called Sergeant Riggs but didn't get a response. He started to call Hawthorne, then changed his mind. The senior detective wouldn't want to be interrupted at the crime scene. He'd learned that on the last case. Working with him was a challenge, but also an opportunity to learn. Cortez vowed to not make a single mistake this time.

The GPS took him to an industrial area along the bay, east of Coronado Island. The abandoned cannery had probably processed tuna decades ago, before most of the industry had shifted to Japan. He was surprised the property hadn't been re-developed. Cortez pulled into the fenced lot, noting that only two squad cars and one detective sedan were on the scene. Detective Harris, another team member, hadn't shown up yet, and neither had the medical examiner. The fourth detective on their team had been pulled into a unit-wide serial killer investigation a month earlier, so he wouldn't be involved.

What was a dead body doing here? It must have been dumped. Cortez cringed, thinking the case could be difficult. He wanted a chance to prove he could help close homicides. Pulling on his suit jacket, he climbed from the car. A powerful scent of rust, seaweed, and decay hit his nostrils. Sometimes, he wished he didn't have a heightened sense of smell.

A uniformed officer stood in front of the long, low building. Cortez hurried over and showed the badge on his belt. "Detective Cortez." He felt his mother smiling every time he said it.

"The body's around back," the officer said, gesturing. "In the little room near the platform."

"Thanks." He trotted around the building, sweat forming on his brow as soon as he pulled on latex gloves. Twenty feet away, another uniformed officer talked to a young woman in jogging clothes who held a small dog on a leash. Behind them, a decrepit loading dock stuck out from the cannery. The jogger had probably found the body. But where? Cortez hurried over, nodded at the officer, and pulled a camera from his zippered briefcase. He stepped toward the decaying wood still holding up the building. A broken door led into a small room. Inside, a big man in a dark suit squatted next to a man's body. A dust-covered desk hugged up against the back wall and a chair stood in the middle of the old office. The smell of wet metal hung heavy in the air, and a reddish-brown stain coated the steel gray of the right front chair leg. Cortez snapped several photos, seeing the crime scene through the lens, as if it were a movie setting. This one was black-and-white, a noir piece with solemn investigators. All that was missing were the fedoras.

He moved to the other side of the corpse, waiting for Detective Hawthorne to acknowledge him. A glance at the victim's face sent a shock wave through his chest. James Avery! One of his favorite movie actors. Cortez dropped to his knees, and a strange sound escaped his throat. Hawthorne looked over, his expression grim.

"That's James Avery, the movie star," Cortez blurted.

Hawthorne glanced at the victim again. "Shit. No wonder he looked familiar."

The actor's aging but handsome face had been beaten, leaving it swollen and bruised, but still recognizable. "Why would someone do this?" Cortez tried to mask his distress. "How did he die?"

"Not sure. Other than the beating, I don't see any wounds. And those bruises don't look lethal."

Cortez stared at the man who'd been so daring and vibrant in his movies. He seemed so much smaller. Like any other guy on the street. James Avery wore dark pants, sandals, and a long-sleeved button-up shirt. Stains dotted the front where blood had dripped from his face. Cortez wanted to see his body and check for knife or bullet wounds, but he would have to wait for the forensics technician on his team. "I assume the jogger found the body."

The older detective shrugged. "She says her dog started barking, pulled away, and ran back here. She followed, then called it in. Not much to go on."

"We won't find a witness here either."

"Well, shit," Hawthorne muttered. "I really didn't need an impossible high-profile case. I just want to finish out this year, then collect my retirement."

"We can solve this," Cortez offered, sounding more confident than he felt. He'd only worked two homicides so far, one domestic and one gang-related, both with witnesses. No real detective work involved.

"A dumped body scenario?" Hawthorne scoffed. "You don't know what you're saying. But I like your naive enthusiasm."

Naive? Cortez's cheeks flushed. Just because he wasn't bitter and jaded... Plus, he saw the scene differently. "What if he wasn't dumped?"

Hawthorne scowled. "You mean the bruises? You think he met someone here and had an altercation?"

The scenario in Cortez's head was more sinister. "Or they brought him here and beat him."

"Maybe."

With a gloved hand, Cortez pushed back a cuff on the dead man's shirt, exposing his wrist. A livid red mark encircled his pale skin. "He was bound."

"Who the fuck would kidnap and beat an aging movie star?"

"He was only fifty-seven."

Hawthorne raised an overgrown eyebrow. "Why do you know that?"

Cortez flushed again. "I like his work. Especially the Jack Kramer series. I love those action flicks."

"They were decent, but he was too old for the last two."

Cortez disagreed but didn't argue. "He was a good guy and recently raised a lot of money for sick children."

"So how the hell did he end up here?"

Cortez wished he had a good answer. "Did you find a wallet or anything personal?" They needed a starting point.

"I haven't spotted a single piece of evidence, but let's look around." The older detective stood, so Cortez did too. Even with his rounded shoulders, Hawthorne's Ichabod-Crane body-type made Cortez feel short at five-seven. Next to his father and cousins, he was the tall one.

The abandoned office was only twelve-foot square and nearly empty, except for the decades-old, crumbled paper trash in the corners. A ten-minute search left them empty-handed.

Hawthorne scowled again. "Are you sure it's James

Avery? Movie stars often look different in real life, and this guy's been beaten."

They heard two more vehicles pull up outside. Probably, the medical examiner and the final member of their team, a crime scene specialist. Detective Harris had kids at home and couldn't respond as quickly. She made up for it later by taking on the grunt work.

Cortez knelt down and quickly unbuttoned Avery's shirt.

"What are you doing?"

"Checking for a tattoo." He pushed the fabric aside, exposing the victim's shoulder and a black-and-red Chinese symbol. "It's definitely James Avery. He mentioned his ink in an interview with *Entertainment Weekly*."

"Get away from the body and clear the area." The ME, a sturdy older woman, stepped into the room, followed by a younger man. Both wore white coveralls and carried forensic toolkits.

The two detectives stepped back, and the floor made a loud creaking sound. Cortez glanced down. With a loud crack, the wooden slats split open. He jumped toward the side wall, hoping to land on a support joist.

Hawthorne let out a shriek, followed by a crashing thud. A string of curses came next. Cortez turned.

His partner had fallen through the busted boards, with only his chest and head visible. "Call an ambulance! I think I broke my fucking leg."

Cortez reached for his cell phone. As he called dispatch, he had a flash of excitement. What if he got to take the book on this case? He wouldn't give up until he found James Avery's killer and brought justice to one of the finest actors Hollywood had ever known.

Chapter 7

Thursday, July 10, 8:30 a.m.

Dressed in a tight black skirt and cream-colored silk blouse, Dallas pulled her newly dyed hair into a messy bun at the back of her neck. She'd cut it for her last assignment, and it hadn't grown much past her shoulders yet, but she was glad to be rid of the mousey brown. She wanted to darken it permanently to a burgundy brown but hated the idea of blond roots that would need to be colored every three weeks. For this assignment, she was glad to be light-haired. Nobody at TecLife would suspect a strawberry-blond secretary of spying.

She dabbed pheromones behind her ears and on her wrists, then tossed the bottle into her purse, in case she had more than one interview and needed to reapply. They were most effective for intimate encounters, but she needed to use a full arsenal to ensure the company hired her. Mrs. Palmer had called an hour after she uploaded her résumé and asked Dallas to be at TecLife at ten this morning to meet with Max Grissom. Davis, the cute neighbor, hadn't shown up, and she'd gone to bed early and disappointed.

Out of habit, she slipped her fingers into the outside pocket to check for her cloth. The square inch of fleece was all that remained of a security blanket she'd had since she was a toddler. As a child, she'd carried the blanket in her backpack everywhere—to the home of whoever she would stay with next, to school everyday, and to all the activities her aunt had enrolled her in. She'd kept it into college, but hid it better and sniffed it less. Dr. Harper had finally convinced her to cut the unwashed blanket in half and toss a chunk. Eventually, she'd done it again. And again. The small scrap was all she had left.

Dallas started to rehearse answers to mock questions, and a case of nerves made her get up and pace. She wasn't worried about the interview. It was just another acting job that might require some improvisation. What concerned her was the possibility of not getting hired, of failing the bureau and being sent home. Interviews were completely subjective. If she reminded the CEO of some girl in high school who had rejected him, he might subconsciously choose someone else. Fortunately, Mrs. Palmer had sabotaged two other applicants already, so the TecLife executives should be eager to hire the first qualified person they talked to.

She checked her purse for essentials such as lip-gloss and a burner phone, but left her weapon under the mattress, waiting to see what security was like at the company. If they had metal detectors, she might not be able to take her gun to work with her. Being without it made her uncomfortable, but at least she would be in a public place.

Downstairs, she climbed in the rental car and said "TecLife" into the GPS on her phone. She couldn't imagine finding her way around new cities without it. After her interview, she planned to come home and change, then head to the beach just to make sure she put her toes in the ocean while she was here. Once she dug into her assignment, she might be on task until the case was resolved.

TecLife sat at the end of a short cul-de-sac in the midway between the bays. A tall brick-and-glass building occupied the front of the property with two single-story industrial buildings set back from the road. She guessed them to be the headquarters, flanked by a lab and a manufacturing plant. Dallas parked in the visitor's spot up front and strode to the building. A security camera mounted above the glass doors informed her they were probably locked, but she tried them anyway. When they didn't open, she stepped back and smiled at the glass eye. At least there was no metal detector, so she'd be able to bring her weapon if she got hired. It would be tucked into her special handbag, along with a burner phone, plastic evidence bags, and some zip-tie handcuffs. Just in case she caught someone in the act.

A twenty-something man came to the door and spoke into the intercom. "State your name and business."

"J.C. Hunter. I have an interview at ten with Mr. Grissom for the administrative position."

"Show me your ID please." Dallas dug out her new driver's license and held it up to the glass. She'd had to upload a photo with her résumé as part of the security, so the company was obviously a little paranoid. But if they were conducting sabotage or stealing proprietary secrets, then they probably worried their competitors were too.

The doors clicked and slid open.

"Welcome to TecLife." He stepped aside and gestured for her to enter. "I'm Adrian, the front desk host."

Aka, receptionist. "Nice to meet you."

"Have a seat in our lobby and someone will be with you in a minute. Would you like something to drink?"

"No thanks."

The room was narrow and tall, with a fifteen-foot ceiling and black low-slung couches lining the walls. A giant flat-screen filled one side, rotating with scientific images, most of a molecular nature. The company's name was displayed on the opposite wall, spelled out in oversized chrome lettering. *Egotists,* she thought. Filled with the importance of their work. She wondered what the company culture was like for employees. From here, the building seemed silent. Even Adrian, the receptionist, had disappeared behind a brick wall.

But she didn't feel alone. Someone was watching her. Dallas looked around for cameras but didn't see anything overt. After a ten-minute wait, she heard footsteps coming down stairs, and a moment later, a woman entered the lobby. Late-thirties and bone-thin, she had flawless pale skin that nearly blended into her white shirt. Close-cropped auburn hair and dark-blue eyes that didn't smile.

"I'm Cheryl Decker. We had a last-minute change, so I'll be conducting the interview."

Damn. The pheromones were probably wasted, and this audition would be more challenging. Dallas stood and shook her hand. "J.C. Hunter. It's a pleasure to meet you."

"This way, please."

She followed her to a door at the end of a short hallway. Decker spoke over her shoulder as she opened the door. "I don't trust elevators, so I hope you don't mind taking the stairs."

"It's fine." Odd that a scientist didn't trust technology. Or maybe it was just a personal phobia.

Cheryl Decker moved quickly for someone who displayed little muscle tone and looked like she'd never set foot outside. Dallas hoped the executive was confident enough to hire a younger, more attractive woman—or that she was gay.

Two flights up, they stepped into another hallway and headed for an office at the end. Decker hadn't spoken since they left the first floor, and Dallas was worried. They entered an outer office, with no one at the desk, then Decker unlocked the inner door. *Not good.* The woman kept her office locked whenever she went out. Snooping, or even planting a bug, would be challenging.

Her corner office was huge, but messy, and it looked more like a lab than an executive suite. The windows were covered with dark drapes that blocked out the bright sun.

"Have a seat, and we'll get right to this." Decker gestured but stayed clear of her desk.

The guest chairs were the only surfaces not covered with papers. Dallas sat, her mind working madly to find a way to win this woman over. Why wasn't Max Grissom interviewing the person who would be his assistant?

"We've had a change of plan since we posted the job." Decker sat next to her, without a notepad or list of questions. "My assistant asked to take the opening with Mr. Grissom, and we all agreed that would be for the best. So the open position is now as my assistant. Can you work for a woman?"

Oh great. She was difficult to work for. "Of course. As long as a boss is competent and respectful, gender is irrelevant."

"Define respectful." She didn't smile.

"I just mean no verbal abuse. I'm pretty thick-skinned about everything else."

"Will you work late if needed?"

"Of course. I don't have kids or social obligations."

"Good. Your résumé has all the qualifications, so the decision is personal. I need someone who won't run out of here at five if we're in the middle of something."

"I'm task-oriented, so I never quit halfway."

"I see you worked for MediGuard. I'm curious about what's in their pipeline."

A test. "That was a few years ago, but I'm not comfortable revealing anything they consider proprietary."

Decker nodded. "Then you understand that everything you learn here must be kept strictly confidential."

"Of course. This is a very competitive business."

A flicker in her eyes. "What are your ambitions?"

"I'm taking business classes in the evening, and I'd like to run a consulting firm some day."

Decker cocked her head. "Why?"

"I want to get paid for telling people things they already know or should know."

The executive laughed. "I like you, J.C." Decker suddenly leaned in. "What do you know about microbial research?"

Not enough, Dallas realized. If it was Decker's passion, this might be the critical question. She smiled. "Intestinal microbes have tremendous potential to cure diseases, and I'm not squeamish about the idea, if that's what you're asking."

Cheryl Decker pushed out of her chair, as if she just remembered something. She grabbed a notebook from her desk and began thumbing through it. Glancing over her shoulder, she said, "I don't allow social media during work hours. Are you on Facebook?"

"No. I'm a private person." Fortunately, the undercover team hadn't created any media accounts for her background. And now she wouldn't either.

"Our dress code is pretty flexible, but no cleavage and no hooker outfits."

Dallas wanted to laugh. "I respect that. Who needs

unwanted sexual attention at work?" She was glad she'd left her blouse fully buttoned.

"I'm in the middle of an important project that needs immediate assistance. Can you start tomorrow?"

"I'd love to."

"Then go see HR for the paperwork and a security pass."

Chapter 8

Thursday, July 10, 9:15 a.m.

The hospital room door was open, so Cortez stepped in. Sergeant Riggs stood next to a bed where Detective Hawthorne lay with his leg in a cast. The sergeant turned. "Come in, Cortez. This is good timing."

A ripple of apprehension caught in Cortez's throat. The sergeant usually supervised from his desk. Was the boss taking over the case? "Yes, sir." He moved toward the two. Politeness required him to ask Hawthorne how he was doing, but everything he came up with sounded stupid, so he simply nodded.

Riggs turned to him. "Hawthorne and I were discussing the Avery case. With him being injured and you so inexperienced, I think we should turn it over to the next team in the rotation."

No! "I'd really like to keep it, sir. I think I can be an asset."

"Sorry, but this one will get a lot of media attention, and we need to solve it quickly." Riggs—with arms like an orangutan—slapped his shoulder. "Please turn over any notes or photos to the lieutenant and he'll reassign it."

"But Mr. Avery's wife hasn't been contacted yet," Cortez argued, surprising himself. "I finally found their information, and I'd like to be the one to tell her."

The sergeant blinked in surprise. "Why?"

"Because I respect James Avery's career. I think his wife will be more receptive to someone who's a fan."

Hawthorne spoke up. "Let him. In fact, I want to keep the case. I can run it from a wheelchair with Cortez and Harris doing the legwork. I can't afford to take any time off."

"I don't know." Riggs rubbed his dark, shaved head.

Cortez had to fight for this one. "Avery and his wife are private people, and their contact information isn't public. But the widow's name is Veronica Scappini. She's a part-time model, and I contacted the agency and acquired her phone number and address." He hoped he'd demonstrated his resourcefulness.

Riggs didn't look impressed. "A gimp and a newbie? We'll see how you do."

"Thank you, sir."

"Keep me updated, because I'll be taking the calls from the press and the fans." The sergeant turned to leave. "Better get to work."

Cortez pulled up a chair and took out his notepad. "What's next after I talk to the wife? Phone and bank records?"

"Yes, but I'll make those calls. You need to do the legwork and find out where the victim was yesterday and who saw him." Hawthorne sat up, grimacing. "What did the medical examiner say after I left in the ambulance?"

"Avery died between eight and ten last night." Cortez tried to remember the blood-pattern terminology, but couldn't come up with it. "Blood had pooled on his side, so the ME thinks he died right there on the floor. The autopsy is tomorrow." Cortez hadn't decided whether he would attend. The report would be the same either way.

"Ask them to send us everything, including photos, as soon as it's done. I'll have uniforms question people in the crime scene area, but I'm not optimistic about a witness."

"I'll track the victim's timetable."

"Harris will read through the paperwork as soon as we have the phone and credit card statements."

Cortez thought it was unfair to give all the boring stuff to Harris, but he wanted to question witnesses, so he didn't say anything. Harris would have to fight her own battles. He stood, eager to get going. "I'll go talk to Veronica Scappini now."

"Remember, she's a suspect, no matter how pretty she is." Hawthorne reached for his call button. "Go easy and learn what you can, but be skeptical of everything she says."

"Copy that." Cortez couldn't wait to tell his mother about his assignment. What if his name and picture ended up in the newspaper after he arrested the murderer? Maybe Risa Rispoli, the reporter he liked, would finally go out with him.

In his car, he called the medical examiner's office and asked to speak to one of the pathologists. After a long wait, a woman's voice came on the line. "This is Dr. Dean."

Cortez introduced himself. "I'm investigating James Avery's death. He was brought in today. I know the staff is busy, but considering Mr. Avery's status, I hope you'll prioritize his blood work. The media will be calling every day until we give them some information."

A pause. "Who exactly is James Avery?"

How could she not know? "He's a movie star. You know the Jack Kramer series?"

"I don't watch many movies. But I'll do what I can to move his toxicology along."

"Thank you. Please send the report and the photos to me

and Detective Hawthorne as soon as you have them." He gave her their email addresses. "Please treat Mr. Avery's corpse as respectfully as possible."

"We always do."

James Avery's house in La Jolla surprised him. The single-level home sprawled across a hill near the ocean with a three-car garage on a lower level in front. But its modesty seemed unusual for a movie star. Then Cortez remembered that James Avery had a home in Hollywood as well. And Avery wasn't exactly an A-list movie star anymore. He should have been, but the cruel industry tossed people aside if they started to go gray or put on weight. Avery had chosen not to dye his hair or starve himself the way some actors did. Cortez respected that.

He parked behind the red Miata in the driveway, wondering who drove it and if another vehicle was in the garage. The summer sun beat down on his head, but he was used to it. The task ahead was what made him sweat.

Before he reached the ornate double doors, a woman flew out of the house, her beautiful face stricken with panic. "Are you here about James? Was he in an accident?" Her loose white clothes didn't hide her long, lean body and full breasts.

Stunning! And so much younger than her husband. Avery had been a lucky man. Well, until he was killed. "I'm Detective Cortez, SDPD." He held out his hand.

She ignored it. "Tell me. Is James in the hospital? I haven't been able to find out anything."

He shook his head. "I'm sorry. Can we go inside?"

Her mouth opened in shock and her hand flew to cover it. "No!"

Oh dear. What should he do now?

Veronica's knees buckled and she doubled over as if in pain.

Cortez regretted volunteering to do this. "Let me help you into the house." He reached for her elbow.

She slapped at his hand, sobbing now. "No! Just go away! I don't want to hear this."

He would wait it out. Cortez took a deep breath and counted slowly to twenty, while the widow cried with her face in her hands. A car on the street slowed down to gawk.

"Miss Scappini? Let's go inside and get you comfortable. We have things to talk about." Cortez put his arm around her and led her toward the door. She didn't object.

Inside, he guided her toward a pale sofa in a sunny corner. The windows were draped in a gauzy material that softened the white room. A very different interior than his small house, which he'd painted in rich colors.

He sat on the coffee table, afraid to dirty the furniture. "I'm sorry, but James Avery is dead. You're his wife, Veronica Scappini, correct?"

She nodded, her head still down. "Tell me what happened."

"We found his body in an abandoned cannery south of downtown. "

"What?" She stopped crying and looked up, her forehead crinkled.

"He was probably murdered there sometime last night."

"That makes no sense. Why would he be in an abandoned factory?" She gulped in air.

"We think someone took him there and roughed him up. Do you know what they could have wanted?"

"No." She pushed off the couch. "Where's my purse? I

need to take something."

Cortez followed her through the house while she searched, marveling at how beige and white everything was. She found her bag in the kitchen and gulped a tablet from a pill bottle. A second later, she grabbed a partial bottle of red wine from the granite counter and downed three long gulps, splashing some on her white blouse.

Unfazed, she set down the bottle, reached for a paper towel, and wiped her mouth. "Sorry, I was starting to hyperventilate."

Startled by her reaction, Cortez wondered how he would handle the death of his mother or sister. "If you're feeling better, I'd like to ask some questions."

"I'm feeling a little numb, but not better. Let's get this over with." She plopped down at the small breakfast table, her bony hands gripped tightly together.

Cortez took out his notepad and stuck a piece of cinnamon gum in his mouth to keep his throat from going dry. "When did you last see your husband?"

"Yesterday morning when he went out to play golf."

"What was his mood?"

"He seemed fine. Maybe preoccupied. He hadn't made a movie in a while, so he was a little depressed."

Cortez realized he would never see another Jack Kramer movie. "Was James taking medication? Or seeing a therapist?"

"No."

"Was there anyone new in his life? Anyone pressuring him?"

"I don't think so." The widow fought to keep from sobbing. "He did see his lawyer last week, but I don't know what it was about."

Cortez would find out. The next question was delicate

and he hated to ask. "Do you know about his will? About who would benefit from his death?"

A flash of anger in her eyes. "I signed a pre-nup, so I didn't marry him for his money. But his son and I will inherit his estate. What's left of it."

"Do you have a copy of his will?"

"You'll have to ask his lawyer."

He asked for the lawyer's name and contact information, then continued with questions about Avery's immediate family—his son, parents, and siblings, hoping to contact them all. Sometimes wives were the last to know when a man was in trouble. "Had anything unusual happened in James' life recently?" Her mention of depression made him think the chain of events leading to the murder may have started a while ago.

"He was hit with a paternity lawsuit. A woman named Alicia Freison claimed he was the father of her three-year-old son."

Cortez made notes. Avery's beating and death could have been about blackmail or extortion. Someone probably wanted his money. "I'd like to see her legal papers. She could be a person of interest."

Veronica stood, her voice bitter. "The lawsuit was bullshit. She's probably one of those DNA grabbers who stalk celebrities."

"What do you mean?"

"They follow movie stars and famous athletes around, waiting for a chance to snatch a strand of hair or a drop of saliva." The widow made an angry grabbing gesture. "Then they file a paternity claim or blackmail the celebrity into keeping the claim quiet."

Vile. Such a person might kidnap and kill a movie star too.

"I need everything you know about this woman and her lawsuit." He couldn't wait to tell Hawthorne he already had a lead.

Chapter 9

Friday, July 11, 8:40 a.m.
Dallas flashed her ID badge and hurried through the TecLife doors before they locked again. First-day jitters made her clutch at her shoulder bag. She had to be professional at this administrative gig—so she could keep the job long enough to gather incriminating intel. No pressure. She stopped at the reception area and spoke with Adrian. "Jace Hunter again. Cheryl Decker said you'd get me set up with an email account."

"I will. Welcome." He held out his hand. "Write down how you want your first and last name to read, then I'll add *at teclife dot com,* and you'll be good to go in an hour."

She jotted down *JaceHunter* on a sticky note. "Anything else I need to know?"

"Ms. Decker likes her coffee really hot. We have an espresso machine in the break room, but you'll need to nuke it before you take it back to her."

Coffee fetching? *Whatever.* Dallas smiled. Between both paychecks, she'd be the highest paid barista on the planet. Waiting tables in college had taught her that there was value in serving others. And had given her opportunities to charm strangers with elaborately fabricated background stories.

"Did your boss tell you about the morning staff meetings?"

"Not yet."

"First floor atrium at nine-fifteen sharp."

"See you there." She was eager to meet everyone and size them up. The weak links—who she could extract information from—were easy to pick out. One of the three top executives was most likely the mastermind, and she had to narrow it down to focus on a target for her probe. Catching the perp in an act of setting up a sabotage would be the ultimate reward. More likely, she'd have to cobble together emails, bank statements, and photos to create enough evidence for a conviction or plea deal.

Dallas took the elevator to the third floor and strode down the hall. The click of her heels was an unexpected but happy sound. In the Phoenix bureau, she wore pants and sensible shoes like everyone else. It felt good to wear a skirt and show some leg. She stepped into Cheryl Decker's front office without knocking, dropped her bag on the assistant's desk, and glanced around. A small window next to the door opened into the hallway, but otherwise the room was suffocating and dreary. She'd have to bring in a plant or maybe fresh flowers every day.

Decker opened the door between their offices and stuck in her head. "Would you bring me some coffee from the break room? The good stuff. Then we have an employee meeting. After that, I'll get you started on some data entry I need done." Decker started to walk away, then turned back. "Impress me today."

Hardass. "I will." Coffee fetching and data entry. Oh boy. Good to see her college education and sniper training paying off. But she would enjoy the challenge, at least for a while. If she had to do the same thing every day for the rest of her life, she'd put her Glock to her head. Some people thrived on predictability. She wasn't one of them.

The employees gathered in the atrium outside the break room. The space had tables on both sides of a glass wall, with the patio being accessible through a locked door. She would have to remember to keep her badge with her if she ever stepped outside. Only one person approached and introduced himself.

"Max Grissom, CEO. Thanks for joining us." He was short, and because she wore heels, his eyes stared directly into her chest. He caught himself and looked up again. "I hope you find our gathering inspirational." His face was pleasant, with a deep worry wrinkle on his forehead and a patch of dark pigment along one jawline.

She would have to fake an interest in him to get close enough to access his texts and emails. "I'm excited to be here."

He touched her arm, then trotted to the glass wall that everyone was facing. Most of the employees were women between the ages of thirty and fifty, dressed in gray or black A-line skirts and jackets. Not one was smiling. Sales and marketing, she guessed. Two men in short-sleeved cotton shirts stood in the back, commenting in voices too low to understand.

She stepped toward them. "What's this about?"

The guy next to her let out a little laugh. "You'll see. I'm Eric. You must be Cheryl's new assistant."

"Yes. Jace Hunter."

He shook her hand and introduced his pal, Nikola. She committed their names and faces to memory.

"Good luck with Cheryl," Eric leaned over and whispered. "She can be demanding. And you might as well know that

Max Grissom will hit on you right away. Just tell him no. He won't fire you."

"Thanks for the head's up."

A moment later, the CEO's voiced boomed, "Good morning! Let's get physical!"

A loud version of *Eye of the Tiger* blasted into the room. Grissom began a series of stretches and jumps, and the employees joined in.

What the hell? Was it mandatory? Dallas glanced at the other women in skirts and heels. They were participating, so she did too. The sales reps had to be making a damn good commission, or the job market was even worse than she'd heard. Cheryl Decker, in the front row, wore black pants and a white pullover shirt. Smart woman, but maybe she was the only one who could get away with wearing casual clothes. Her background file indicated that she didn't socialize or meet with clients.

After the physical routine, Grissom announced the week's sales numbers—which everyone cheered. Then he burst into a pep talk, urging a better performance, stopping intermittently and calling, "Give me a 'hell yeah'!"

The employees raised their hands and gave it their best. Dallas was too stunned to do much but watch, wide-eyed. Was this typical in the medical device industry, or was Grissom an ambitious wingnut? She decided to focus her probe on him first, and she'd probably have to get cozy with his administrative assistant to gain access to his files. Thank goodness this wasn't her real job. Even her love of acting couldn't get her to embrace the drink-the-Kool-Aid crap.

The cheerleading was abruptly over, and the employees quickly dispersed. Eric paused to caress her shoulder and say, "Let's have lunch today, and I'll give you survival pointers."

An opportunity to pump him for information. "Thanks. I think I'll need them." She gave him a look of mock distress, followed by a smile. "Unless my boss has other plans for me, I'll meet you in the lobby at noon."

In the hallway, Decker grabbed her elbow. "Walk upstairs with me and we'll get started."

On the climb, her boss laid out her training philosophy. "I'll show you how to open the software I use and sort the data I've collected, but I'm not going to explain how our server works or where to find everything." Decker looked back to check her expression, then continued, "Your one reference that I could reach said you were smart and competent, so I assume you'll figure it out. The product I'm working on will be a blockbuster, so I can't waste time on anything else."

"That sounds exciting. What is it?"

Decker stopped on the landing and locked eyes with her. "This is strictly confidential, and I'm only telling you because you'll see it once you start working with the data. It's called Slimbiotic, and it's a device that you swallow. Once it reaches the intestines, the case dissolves and releases special microbiota that begin to change the patient's metabolism and response to inflammation. The molecular chemistry is more complex than that, but no one will care. The product is incredibly effective and safe, and every overweight person in the developed world will want it."

The holy grail of pharmaceutical research? "What a breakthrough." Dallas wanted to know more. "What exactly are special microbiota?"

"You don't want to know."

"I really do."

"They're living organisms that originally came from the

intestines of healthy, naturally slim people. But they've been produced in large quantities through recombinant processes."

"You mean like a fecal transplant?"

Decker scowled and shook her head. "We never use that term. Our product is an advanced, patient-friendly form of that medical procedure."

Bacteria. Slimbiotic was the intestinal transfer of healthy bacteria without surgery. The concept was brilliant. But it also meant TecLife could have produced the bacteria that killed Agent Palmer. Was Decker, or maybe Santera, a killer, or had it been accidental? The product could be more dangerous than anyone realized.

"What are you thinking?" her boss demanded. "Are you bothered by it? We know we have a public relations challenge, but most people won't even question the device if it works."

"I think it's brilliant. And by calling it Slimbiotic, people will think it's like the good stuff in yogurt."

"Exactly."

"How did you get interested in this line of research?"

Decker paused, a flash of something in her eyes. *Pain?* "We've known for ages that antibiotics help fatten farm animals, so it seemed logical that certain gut bacteria kept us from getting fat and that killing them led to weight gain. Following that line of thinking, I hypothesized that overweight people don't have enough of the right microbiota."

Could it be that simple?

"Obesity is more complex than that," Decker continued, "And for some people, food is an addiction, but many scientists and doctors have come to believe that gut bacteria is the primary determination of our overall health."

"Where is it in development?"

"We've completed Phase Three trials and submitted to the FDA, but they want more data." She pushed through the door into the hall and kept talking. "We did the clinicals in Costa Rica to help keep the device confidential. Our competitors would love to get their hands on this one. So you must never talk about it outside these walls."

Yet TecLife was the company suspected of sabotage. Was there more going on? Was the whole industry cutthroat? "Is the research being done here in one of the other buildings?"

"Mostly."

"You must be excited."

"You have no idea how personal this is for me." Her eyes misted. "Eight long years, but we're almost there."

They reached their offices, stepped in, and closed the door. Dallas lobbed her first probe. "Isn't ProtoCell about to launch something similar?"

Decker's eyes hardened again. "No. Their product releases peptides and requires a doctor to implant it. I'm sure it'll work, but the SlimPro is more invasive, more expensive, and insurance companies might not even pay for it."

A full-throttled competition. Jana Palmer could be right about TecLife starting the fire in ProtoCell's warehouse. Even though a different product had been destroyed, a financial setback could slow down research. She couldn't wait to hear what River would discover about the competitors. She herself couldn't risk visiting their businesses and blowing her cover. "It's interesting that both companies are developing devices to treat obesity."

"There are good reasons for that." Decker gestured at the computer. "Let's get started."

Dallas spent the next few hours pasting codes into search

fields and creating new files with the results. Boring. The monotony of it would have driven her insane without taking occasional peeks into other files on the server. But she had to be careful until she knew whether her computer activities were monitored. The patient files also made her think about her father in the hospital. How sick was he really? Her mother tended to exaggerate. But if he was really dying . . .

Decker breezed into the outer office. "I'm running over to the R&D building to check on something. Take a lunch break while I'm gone." Her boss kept moving.

Yes, ma'am.

Dallas closed the program, grabbed her purse, and headed out. In the hall, she ran into another young woman coming out of Grissom's office. "Hey, I'm Jace Hunter, Ms. Decker's new assistant."

"I'm Holly Jaseria." She didn't smile or offer her hand.

"You're Mr. Grissom's assistant?"

"I am now." The heavyset woman sounded unhappy.

"I heard you wanted the open position."

"Only to keep my job. Cheryl would have fired me soon."

More intrigue. "But why?"

"I can't tell you." She glanced up and down Dallas' body. "I'm sure you'll do fine. Just don't gain any weight." Holly stepped on the elevator, hit the down button, and the doors started to move.

"What do you mean?"

A wailing fire alarm drowned out Dallas' voice, and the elevator closed. The noise made it hard to think, but instinctively she headed for the stairs, not wanting to wait for the elevator to return. Inside the stairwell, shielded from the ear-splitting racket, her brain kicked in and she turned around. With everyone out of the building, this was a perfect opportunity for spying. Dallas trotted back upstairs, trying to calculate the odds that there really was a fire. Not likely. Unless she took into account the fire in ProtoCell's warehouse, the intense competition, and the possibility that the other company was getting even.

Even if this was a case of revenge arson, she still had a few minutes. Dallas hurried back to her office and tried the interior door leading into Decker's space. Locked. She had picks in her purse and was pretty good with them, but maybe this was a better opportunity to snoop around Grissom's office. His intensity at the meeting flagged him as aggressive and a more-likely saboteur. And this might be her only chance to sneak into his office during the day, certain that he wasn't there. With Decker, she would have a chance every time her boss left her office.

Dallas rolled up some tissue and stuffed it into her ears, then hurried next door. The alarm was still deafening in the empty hallway, but she tried to tune it out. The door to Grissom's exterior office stood wide open. She stepped in, closed it, and glanced around. The same size and shape as her little space and no cameras that she could spot. Most employers, except banks, didn't spy on their crew. She tried the interior doorknob and it turned easily. *Yes!*

Inside, the drapes were open and the lights on. Grissom had left in a hurry. His computer monitor was dark but blinked an invitation. She glanced around, noting that, unlike Decker's, his office was clean and organized. It was also bigger, with a private bathroom and closet. She sat at the desk and tapped the keyboard. The monitor lit up, and she looked for icons, indicating open programs or files.

She clicked one, and a Word document opened. A correspondence, addressed to someone at the FDA, on company letterhead. Dallas scanned the text. It mentioned clinical trials and a product called HealthPatch. She noted the details to add to her file later, then opened his email program. If Grissom was smart, he wasn't using his company email to correspond with a criminal-for-hire, but she checked anyway, skimming through batches and folders, looking for anything personal.

After a minute, she looked up at the doorway out of habit. Through the outer office, she saw the exterior door opening. *Shit!* Dallas bolted out of the chair. Should she hide or try to bullshit her way out of this? She ran for the bathroom, hoping it would give her time to come up with a plausible story. She swung the door behind her but didn't let it completely close. She might get lucky. Maybe Grissom had just come back to grab something and would leave right away.

Adrenaline pumped in her veins, and the roar of the fire alarm made it worse. She took deep breaths but couldn't get her pulse to slow. She stayed next to the cracked-open door and watched.

A man with a beard and a baseball cap strode into the room. Maybe thirty, dressed in jeans and a dark T-shirt, and wearing a backpack. He headed straight for Grissom's computer, plugged in a thumb drive and started downloading files. *Holy shit! A data thief.* Had the intruder triggered the fire alarm? ProtoCell, with its competing product, came immediately to mind. What had she gotten herself into the middle of? Dallas reached for her cell phone, clicked the zoom on the camera, and took pictures through the crack. They wouldn't be great, but she had to document the activity if she could.

She checked the time on her cell, wondering how long he

would stay. The noise was maddening and she covered her ears. While the thumb drive was in the machine, the intruder searched drawers but didn't seem to find anything he was interested in. The alarm shut off, but the wait still seemed to take forever. The intruder finally yanked out the drive and left. Dallas glanced at her cell again. The whole thing had taken nine minutes.

Follow him or try to get some intel while she could? She was running out of time. The fire department had probably arrived and would clear out the building. Dallas bolted out of the office. Down the hall, the elevator door was closing. She sprinted to the stairwell. He had to exit the building on the ground floor, didn't he?

She pounded down the stairs, regretting the damn heels. She'd be lucky not to twist an ankle. On the first floor landing, she pushed out the door and ran into a fireman.

"Excuse me." She stepped around him and bolted toward the lobby. The intruder wasn't in the hall ahead of her, and she didn't see him in the foyer a moment later either. Had he exited already? Through the glass front doors, she noticed employees milling around the grassy area while firefighters dragged a hose off their truck. No one who resembled the intruder was in sight.

Dallas sprinted down the opposite hall toward the break room and atrium. Behind her, the fireman called, "Hey, you need to get out!"

She turned into the atrium and caught sight of the thief scaling over the cement-patio wall outside. *Hell!* She could climb over the damn wall even in a skirt, but could she catch him? And how would that activity look to her boss and co-workers? She couldn't risk blowing her cover.

A firm hand grabbed her shoulder. "Miss, you have to

leave the building now."

"I know. I thought I saw someone running this way and it worried me." Dallas smiled and let him rush her out the front door. Her co-workers stared and whispered comments to each other. Hopefully, they thought she was just a newbie who hadn't been able to find her way out. If anyone asked, she would tell them she'd been stuck in the bathroom with a personal emergency. She'd originally planned to simply stay inside. This little public display was embarrassing and possibly detrimental to her operation. Still, the event had been educational, and she had to report to River.

The big question was: Should she tell Grissom what she'd witnessed? The risk in reporting the incident was to make herself look suspicious for not leaving the building during a fire alarm. But telling Grissom could earn the CEO's trust and affection, which could be leveraged into information.

After they were allowed back into the building, she headed straight for Grissom's office. His assistant looked surprised to see her. "Do you need help?"

"I need to see Mr. Grissom."

"He's with Cheryl Decker right now, and they're not very happy. I would come back some other time."

The voices on the other side of the wall grew loud for a moment, then softened. Dallas hesitated. Giving bad news at a bad time could backfire. But it was good that Decker was in there too, so she didn't find out later and feel betrayed. The longer Dallas waited, the worse it looked for her. "This is important. I have to see him now." She stepped to the inner door and knocked loudly.

After a pause, Grissom jerked open the door. "I said no interruptions." His face softened when he realized she wasn't his assistant. "Jace, can this wait?"

"I don't think so. I saw something during the fire alarm that you need to know about."

His body stiffened. "Come in." His eyes probed her with a worried look. "Should Cheryl stay?"

Did he mistrust his partner? Or want to hide information from her? "Yes, I think so." Dallas smiled at her boss, who looked distressed.

"Have a seat."

They all perched on the edge of their chairs, the tension palpable. Dallas launched in. "When the alarm went off, I headed down the stairs, then decided to go back for my purse." She gave a sheepish look. "I know I shouldn't have, but my keys and my credit card..." She trailed off purposefully, because it was natural, and glanced back and forth between the two. She was an expert storyteller. "Then when I was in my office, I started having horrible painful cramps." She cast her eyes down. "I couldn't function for a minute. When I went out in the hall again, I saw someone go into Mr. Grissom's office. It clearly wasn't you, and it concerned me."

"Who was it?" Grissom's voice was tight.

"I haven't met everyone yet, but I don't think it was an employee. He wore jeans, a baseball cap, and had a beard." She focused on Grissom again. "It seemed wrong for him to be there, so I stepped into your outer office to see what he was doing. I think he copied files from your computer." She wouldn't mention chasing after him unless someone brought it up.

Decker cut in. "Give us more description."

"About five-eight, I think, and lean. I couldn't see his hair or eyes, so I didn't get a good look at him. Plus, the alarm was ringing, so I was a little rattled." She made her face look apologetic.

"Please don't tell anyone else about this. I don't want the employees to worry." Grissom stood, his mouth a tight line. "Let me walk you out."

In the hall, he stood close and squeezed both her shoulders. "Thank you for telling us. I'm so grateful, I'd like to buy you a drink after work. Dinner if you have time. Strictly professional."

Yeah, right. That wasn't what she'd heard, but it was an opportunity to gather intel. "The drink sounds nice."

"Perfect. Let's meet across the street at Saber's at five-thirty. Now, you'll have to excuse me. I have things to take care of."

"Of course." Dallas walked away, pleased with the opportunity to get Grissom drunk and probe him. Maybe steal his cell phone. She was grateful they hadn't questioned her role in the incident. Nor had they seemed surprised by the espionage. This was an intense industry, and the idea that Palmer had been killed to silence him seemed more likely than ever. She would have to be careful.

Chapter 10

Friday, July 11, 5:26 a.m.

River woke and turned to look out her window, expecting to see her lush backyard and overgrown vegetable garden. Instead, an adobe wall filled her view. *Oh right.* She was sleeping in a rented apartment in San Diego, working a corporate-sabotage investigation, with an undercover agent depending on her for backup. How had she let herself get sucked into this? She was supposed to be in Eugene, Oregon, handling low-profile cases and adjusting to her new life.

Ache seeped into her chest, and she forced herself to get up. But it wasn't the ranch-style house or the Eugene bureau she missed. Jared, the man who'd come to remodel her house and ended up as her roommate, was all she could think about in her free time. River felt at peace knowing he was there, watering the corn and resurfacing the kitchen cabinets, but she missed the smell of his morning coffee and bacon. She missed laughing with him over the often-silly local news. So far, they were only friends and roommates, but she wanted more. He'd stirred up a long-repressed sexuality that both excited and terrified her. Jared had no idea she'd been a man for most of her life, and River had no idea how to tell him.

She padded into the kitchen and heated water to make

tea. If she were at home, she would practice yoga, then go out for a brisk walk, but she had too much to do for the BioTech case, as they'd named it.

River opened her laptop and wrote an email to Jared, but didn't send it. She made a cup of tea and took it out on the balcony to watch the sunrise. She loved being outside this early without a jacket. A childhood memory of sneaking out of the house in the middle of the night made her smile. She'd been so innocent then. Before she realized she had the wrong body. Before the FBI invaded their home and dug up the dead women in the basement. River let it go. Thinking about her father, the serial killer, was self-destructive. She laughed at herself. Better to pine for a man she would probably never be intimate with.

A faint sound caught her attention. Her phone? River hurried inside to check. Law enforcement never had the luxury of ignoring a call. Her work cell showed a missed call from a local number. She listened to the message: "Special Agent Richard King. The BioTech task force is meeting this morning at nine, and you need to be there. The CDC has some concerns about Palmer's blood and tissue samples."

The Centers for Disease Control? What the hell had Joe Palmer died of? Wide awake now, River kicked up her speed. She modified her email to Jared to make it less sentimental, hit Send, and headed for the shower. Afterward, she dressed in dark slacks and a jacket, the same basic clothes she'd worn all her years as Carl River. Only now, she was thirty pounds lighter and would sometimes wear burgundy or brown instead of black. She ate a bagel, tucked her Glock into her shoulder harness, and headed east.

The conference room in the San Diego bureau was three

times the size of the one in Eugene and had a nice view from the fourth floor. Neither made her glad to be there. Gratitude for Joe and Jana Palmer, who'd saved her life and given her purpose, was all that made her take a seat, surrounded by stiff-shouldered men who didn't look happy to see her. Agent King, at the end of the table, nodded as she entered. No one else greeted her. Was it because she was an out-of-town agent with more experience, or did they know about her gender transformation and disapprove? The change was part of her file, if anyone with clearance wanted to look at her background.

I am secure in who I am and do not need their approval.

Next to King sat the only other woman at the table. Middle-aged with a skunk-like streak in her hair, she wore a dark-green dress with no jacket. A scientist from the CDC, River speculated. An introduction a moment later proved her correct.

"This is Ms. McDowell from the Centers for Disease Control," King said. "She'll present first, so she can leave before we get into confidential details."

The woman stood. "This case came to our attention when the San Diego County Medical Examiner's office sent us blood and tissue samples from Joe Palmer's autopsy." She paused, as if for respect. "The ME noticed a wound on the corpse's hand that resembled a MRSA infection, so he decided to be precautious and send us samples. The tissue revealed the presence of a previously unidentified bacterium."

McDowell drew in a nervous breath and continued. "The microbe is closely related to Methicillin-resistant Staphylococcus aureus, but appears to have mutated. The good news is that it's not particularly contagious—yet. The bad news is that, like MRSA, it can be deadly to anyone with a compromised immune system or any other body-weakening conditions. We believe the bacterium, which we've labeled SA-13, may have killed Mr. Palmer, who was already suffering from an upper respiratory infection."

"Are you worried about an outbreak?" River had to ask. Her own body wasn't exactly healthy after the operations and hormones she'd been through.

The CDC official nodded, a vigorous gesture. "It could mutate again and become highly contagious. Everyone working on this case needs to be very careful."

River remembered the device Jana had found in her husband's pocket. "What about the PulseTat I turned into the ME's office? Did you test it?"

"What's a PulseTat?"

"It's a medical patch—a little sticky film that transmits data. Joe Palmer had one in his pocket, and I took it to the ME's office to test."

McDowell's eyes went wide with discomfort. "I don't believe that came to our lab. Please check with the county and have them send it over."

River hoped it hadn't been misplaced. "Mrs. Palmer told me the PulseTat had to be pulled from the market a few months ago because it started causing skin infections. I think you should look into those infections and compare them to Joe Palmer's tissue."

"What's the company?" McDowell picked up a pen.

"DigiPro. It's owned by ProtoCell."

"We'll investigate, but bacteria doesn't live long on inorganic surfaces."

That failed to be reassuring. "What are the symptoms of the infection? In case one of us gets exposed."

"We're not sure because we've only had one case, and

he's dead. But fever is a classic symptom. Or if an area of your skin becomes red, swollen, or painful, get to a doctor, get some antibiotics, then call us." The CDC woman gave a grim smile. "But until it becomes contagious, don't worry about being quarantined."

Small comfort.

"Any other questions?"

River had one more. "Do you think it's more likely that Palmer's exposure to the bacteria was purposeful or accidental?"

McDowell looked startled. "Are you asking if someone could have killed him by deliberate contamination?"

"That's what we all want to know."

"I suppose it's possible, but also unlikely. A perpetrator wouldn't know how the bacteria would react in a particular individual, other than that they would be sick for a while." She stopped and reconsidered. "Unless the killer was a scientist and had already tested antibiotics against the pathogen."

Agent King spoke up. "What is the most likely source of the infection?"

"Probably a food product." McDowell started to gather her papers. "We're tracking everything Mr. Palmer ate in the last week of his life, and we expect to find the source in a restaurant or a public gym."

A new level of tension filled the room. Widespread bacterial infections could result in dozens of deaths.

The CDC speaker turned to Agent King. "If there are no more questions, I'll excuse myself."

No one spoke, so she scooped up her briefcase and left the room.

King glanced around. "We're still checking into Palmer's

death. But we'll let the CDC conduct its investigation first."
His eyes landed on River. "You should continue your probe
into TecLife's activities. But if Palmer wasn't murdered, and
your undercover agent doesn't come up with intel in a few
weeks, I'll have to shut it down. UC operations are a drain on
resources."

Bullshit. The bureau was only paying for two apartments
and rental cars, and it didn't lack for funds.

"Do you have anything to report?" King asked.

"Our undercover agent started work today at TecLife, so
she's already inside." River knew it wasn't much, but she'd
been busy setting everything up, including finding the rentals
and flying home to Eugene to pack for a longer stay. "There's
also the PulseTat I mentioned. It's still in development, so I
have to wonder how Palmer got his hands on one. Has
anyone gone to DigiPro to ask questions?" The rest of the
task force was supposed to be investigating Joe's death.

"I did." Agent Kohl straightened in his chair. "The director
said Palmer had been there, but that he hadn't given him any
product samples."

"Did you ask about corporate sabotage of the PulseTat
product?"

Kohl checked his notes. "He said they only produced one
batch that caused a problem and had to be recalled. He thinks
their security is fine and that it was human error."

River didn't buy it. Joe Palmer had died from a mutated
bacteria, and a competitor's product had caused a skin
infection. Something was going on. But why would a director
cover up an attack on his company? Unless his corporate
boss had started the product war. River decided to visit
ProtoCell, even though it technically wasn't within her scope
of the investigation. Something nefarious was going on, and if

the CDC was concerned, the potential for collateral damage was huge.

After a quick lunch from a burrito vendor, River drove southeast and parked in front of ProtoCell's headquarters. Double the size of TecLife's office, the building was gray brick and utilitarian. The warehouse where the fire had destroyed the stockpile of their migraine device—and killed a security guard—was a half-mile away. She'd requested the report from the fire marshal, but it hadn't come through yet. A second call to Jonas Brickman, the CEO, had gone unreturned. Why did he think it was acceptable to ignore the FBI?

River crossed the parking lot, wishing she didn't have to wear socks. She could handle most temperatures as long as her feet were comfortable. Inside the building, an icy blast greeted her in the vestibule. A security guard stood in front of the interior doors and asked to see her ID. She pulled her badge from her jacket pocket and held it out. "I'm here to see Jonas Brickman."

"Top floor. Check in with the receptionist, please." He held open the door.

Good. Brickman was in the building. She moved inside and strode toward the elevator. The receptionist called out, but River waved and kept going. After two unreturned calls, she didn't intend to give Brickman any warning. The interior lobby seemed dark and uninviting, but she could hear the hum of phone conversations from an open space down the hall.

River exited on the top floor and instinctively turned right, toward the ocean side. Brickman's name was on the door at the end. She knocked once and stepped in. A middle-aged woman on a cell phone sat behind a desk in the outer office, and two men in suits were near the inner door, as if finishing up a conversation. She recognized the older man as Rick Kimball, who'd been mayor when she left San Diego to train at Quantico. What was he doing here? Both men turned, Kimball's voice cutting off mid-sentence.

She held out her badge toward the other man, who had an overweight linebacker's body, topped by an aging model's face. "Sorry to interrupt, but you're hard to reach, Mr. Brickman."

The ex-mayor gave his companion a sideways glance. "I'll be in touch." Kimball left without acknowledging her.

"Your timing couldn't be worse." Brickman crossed his arms. "I'm trying to garner political support for my candidacy. Now he's wondering what the hell this is about."

He was running for mayor? "I'm sure you'll be able to explain. Can we sit down?"

"I really don't have time right now. Please make an appointment." He gestured toward his assistant, an older woman who pretended not to be there.

"You're not curious about why I'm here?"

He sighed and gestured for her to enter his office. "It's about the fire again, right? I talked to the fire marshal at the time, and I talked to an FBI agent about three weeks ago. There's nothing left to say. It was just a fire." He sounded surprisingly defensive.

"What was the cause?"

"Faulty wiring in an exhaust fan." He plopped down and unbuttoned his jacket, letting his belly hang out.

"Did you ever suspect one of your competitors?"

A pause.

The words *Of course* cut through the space between them, and River heard them, even though they hadn't been spoken.

Sometimes when people were distressed and about to lie, she could hear strong, simple thoughts. She'd never told anyone. Other agents wouldn't understand, and it rarely affected how she did her job.

"No," Brickman lied. "The medical device business is very ethical, very regulated." He straightened the cuffs on his sleeves and didn't look at her.

Why wouldn't he admit he thought his company had been sabotaged? Was he protecting someone? Or plotting revenge? "When did you talk to Agent Palmer?"

"As I said, about three weeks ago. We met at the warehouse, and it was a waste of time."

The time and location matched Joe's notes, so he was telling the truth about that.

"Have you had any unexpected bacterial outbreaks in your labs or processing plants?"

His dark eyes narrowed. "No, but your question concerns me. Why do you ask?"

"DigiPro had to recall its skin-tattoo product because of infections. Did you know about it?"

"Yes, I pay attention to our subsidiaries. But it wasn't an outbreak, and they did everything right to correct the problem."

"What do you think of your competitor, TecLife?"

"They're very secretive about their pipeline."

"Do you know the executives?"

He made a funny sound in his throat. "One of its founders used to work for me. She's brilliant, but paranoid, and far too focused on her research to engage in corporate sabotage. I don't know much about her new partner."

Interesting phrase. "Was Cheryl Decker once your partner?" River gave the word an intimate emphasis.

"Long ago." He pushed to his feet. "I have another meeting to attend, and you have to stop bothering me." Brickman walked out, so eager to get away from her that he was willing to leave her sitting in his office, free to look around.

But not for long. His assistant rushed into the room. "I'm sorry, but he said to call security if you don't leave."

River had wasted enough time. She left the office and called Jana Palmer on the way out. Joe's widow was probably eager for an update, and River wished she had something more to report.

Her best hope was that the real answers would be uncovered at TecLife by Dallas—who would employ more creative methods.

Chapter 11

Friday, July 11, 5:35 p.m.

Grissom was late, but Dallas knew he would show up. She'd been warned by two co-workers that he would hit on her, and the way he'd touched her earlier was overtly sexual. But the gossip said that once she told him no, he'd move on and act like it never happened. Her looks had been one of the only things that saved her from being a total outcast in school. Garage-sale clothes that smelled like cigarettes, no one showing up for parent-teacher conferences, and her own unwillingness to compromise—all had made other kids whisper behind her back. But she'd snagged the lead in school concerts and plays, and the same girls who gossiped about her to others, were secretly drawn to her and the rumors of her unconventional home life. The boys had simply liked to stare.

Seated in a booth along the side, Dallas watched as groups of people in business casual clothes filed in. She recognized several TecLife employees, but suspected most of the crowd might be. The company's office, lab, and manufacturing buildings were all close by at the end of the cul-de-sac, and the area didn't host any other large offices, just a mishmash of small businesses. So this was TecLife's hangout. She wanted to meet Curtis Santera, the head of R&D, and probe his brain, but she didn't see him in the crowd.

She remembered the pheromones in her purse and discreetly dabbed some on. Not that she had any intention of hooking up with Grissom. He was not her type and also was married. She wasn't a home wrecker, not even for a case she was working—unless it would prevent a massive terrorist attack or something equally devastating. But the more Grissom wanted her sexually, the more likely he would answer whatever questions she threw at him. Maybe even get careless.

The CEO hurried in a few minutes later and apologized for being late. "I had a last-minute important phone call." He slid into the booth across from her.

"I understand. You're a busy man doing important work." Sometimes her own bullshit was hard to take.

"I like to think so." He gave her a teasing smile. "We are about to launch a revolutionary product. It will change millions of lives."

"Do you mean the data I'm working on for Ms. Decker?"

"Yes, but we shouldn't talk about it. This biologic has so much potential, our competitors would kill for it."

Interesting choice of words. "Is that what the thief took today?" She infused her tone with concern. "Has the product been compromised?"

"Everything will be fine." He patted her hand.

A cocktail waitress stopped at the table. "What are you drinking?"

The heat walking over had put her in a mood for something icy. "Margarita, please."

"Make that two." Grissom handed the server his credit card, then turned back to Dallas. "How do you like the job so far?" He laughed. "Not counting the fire alarm and the data breach."

"It's interesting, and everyone seems friendly."

"We hope you stay. We offer a year-end bonus to keep our employees from jumping ship."

Another interesting phrase. "Do you mean going to work for a competitor?"

"Startups are always trying to poach our researchers, and our competitors try to steal our top sales people."

The server brought their drinks, and Dallas said, "Bring us another round in a moment please." She raised her glass to Grissom for a clink. "To a long work relationship."

"Hear, hear." He took a sip.

Dallas downed hers. "It's Friday. Try to keep up, man," she joked.

Grissom smiled and took a long pull. "I like you."

She returned his grin. "We're just getting started."

A sales rep stopped by their booth and chatted for a moment. When he left, Dallas asked, "Who do you consider your main competitor?"

"ProtoCell. The prick had a mole in our company who stole the data for our new migraine product. That's why we've kept the Slimbiotic clinicals out of the country and out of the media."

Had ProtoCell started the corporate war? "That's sneaky. How did you find out?"

"I probably shouldn't tell you."

"But this spying stuff is interesting. I didn't know companies did that."

"No one talked about it at MediGuard?"

"Not really. So how did you catch the mole?" She said the phrase with a silly ominous tone to lighten her question.

"He was foolish enough to use his company email once to report to Brickman, or Prickman, as we call him. The system flagged it. We have it set to watch for key words. And now, unexpected data downloads."

She would have to be careful. "Good to know. I'll have to confine my sexting to my phone and not use the work computer." She winked at him.

Grissom flushed. "We don't care about office relationships. Just don't share our data." He winked back.

The timing of the server's arrival with their second round was a welcome relief. Dallas took a sip of the margarita and felt the head-rush-squeeze of drinking on an empty stomach. *Oh hell.* She could normally drink like a sailor and still be functional. But she'd missed lunch because of the alarm/spying episode. It was time to get Grissom up and away from his phone so she could peruse his recent messages.

"Excuse me for a minute." She went to the ladies room, vomited up her last drink, and called River with her burner phone.

She picked up right way. "Everything okay?"

"Yes. I need you to call Max Grissom in about three minutes. Say some gibberish like a wrong number and hang up. Call me about ten minutes later, so I have an excuse to break away."

"You got it."

A minute after she returned to the booth, Grissom's phone rang. He excused himself, pulled it from his pocket, and answered. A look of surprise, followed by irritation. "You must have the wrong number."

Dallas reached for the plastic menu stand and knocked his drink into his lap.

Startled, he dropped his phone on the table and cursed.

"Oh no! I'm so sorry." Dallas grabbed for the only other thing on the table, a wet cocktail napkin. "You need a towel. Or maybe some of the thick paper towels from the bathroom."

Scowling and wet, he scooted to the edge of the booth.

Leave the phone, Dallas mentally pleaded. "I'll buy you another drink," she promised, hoping to distract him.

"Good plan." He strode toward the hall.

Dallas looked around, then slid his phone over, and began scrolling through his contact list. She glanced up occasionally to ensure he still had his back to her.

Three people named Grissom were at the top of his list, followed by Cheryl Decker, Curtis Santera, and three other people coded blue as TecLife employees. Dallas kept scrolling, looking for a number with no name association that also had a history of several calls. Nothing popped, so she clicked over to texts. Grissom, in his late forties, either wasn't much of a texter, or he was diligent about deleting them. There was a series of exchanges with Emma Grissom—his daughter, she assumed—about a softball tournament and whether she could stay the weekend with a friend. Dallas scrolled through, annoyed by the time waste. Then bingo. Below those, an unnamed person had texted him Wednesday with a brief message: *Meet me at our usual spot at 8. Bring cash.*

Suspicious. But lacking substance. Dallas snapped a photo of the message with her own phone, then slid Grissom's back into place on the table. None too soon. He was headed her way.

When he sat down, he gave her a forgiving smile. "Should we get out of here? Have some dinner in a quiet little place?"

She didn't expect to learn much more and wasn't in a mood for fighting him off. "I'm sorry. I'm meeting a friend for dinner soon. Some other time?"

Her phone rang and she glanced at the number. It was River. Dallas picked up. "Hey, Nicole. Don't worry, I'm on my way." She thanked Grissom for the drinks and scooted out.

She hurried back to the TecLife parking lot and sent the image of Grissom's cryptic message to River, along with the phone number. With any luck, the bureau could trace it. Maybe they would put a tail on Grissom too and check out who he was meeting with cash.

Chapter 12

Friday, July 11, 4:40 p.m.
Kiya rode north along the coast, loving the sensuous combination of bright sun, blue ocean, and high speed. If she had to die, this was how she wanted to go, pushing her motorcycle to its limits. But she had stopped wanting to die years ago. Coming to America—even if she'd had to enslave herself financially to another man to get here—had been the first step toward living a real life, as a full human being. As fully as she could, anyway. She would never have real friends or a life partner, or even empathize with other people, but she could feel joy now. And this was bliss. High doses of endorphins always juiced her creative thoughts, and on a recent ride, she'd figured out how she would approach her target. Today, the adrenaline would carry her through the project—kidnapping Dominic Prill, a lab researcher for ProtoCell.

At home in her hillside apartment, Kiya attached a tip to the end of her nose, added cheekbone padding, and applied a heavy coat of makeup. She dressed in layers, pulled on a short blond wig, and filled a tote bag with glasses, scarves, and hats. After a job, she could duck out of sight for twenty seconds and transform herself into an entirely different person. A pocketed money belt went around her waist to hold keys, cash, and lock picks. She tucked a knife into a sheath and felt ready. She owned a Luger but rarely carried it. Too bulky and too noisy to use in most circumstances. In Southern Uzbekistan, the men were quick to draw their automatic rifles, and she didn't want to be anything like them.

When it was dark, she headed out on foot toward a shopping mall a mile away. She planned to borrow a car to get across town. She could have pulled off the kidnap-for-theft without a vehicle, but she liked to keep her skills sharp. The man who'd rescued her from hell—as a child wife/servant/punching bag—had a big heart for abused kids, but he wasn't an angel. Quite the opposite. He'd run a criminal enterprise, dealing mostly in stolen goods, extortion, and bank fraud. Martel had brought her to San Diego, taken her in, and put her to work stealing cars at the age of thirteen. He'd gone to prison thirteen years later, and she'd left the organization to become a freelancer. Kiya still had acquaintances she could call on if she needed backup, but she preferred to work alone. Prison was not on her agenda. Revenue, revenge and retirement were her focus.

Behind a movie theater, she spotted an older Buick, then used a Slim Jim to unlock it. A quick check under the passenger seat produced a purse with a set of keys. Nice. She could have hot-wired the car, but keys were much simpler and people left them lying around with complete carelessness. The research building she was headed to this evening was a different story. The security was tight, unless you were an employee. Finding a workaround would have taken too much time and required a second person. Her method was cruder, but efficient.

Kiya slipped behind the wheel and drove off. Her next stop—WorkFitLife, a gym located a mile from the ProtoCell R&D building. She'd been tracking Dominic Prill for days, and he was at the fitness center every evening from eight to ten. He also stopped, filled his water bottle on the way out, and drank half as he walked to his car. She would be there tonight to intercept that ritual.

Kiya parked the stolen car two blocks away and walked to the gym. The counter person didn't look happy to see her ten minutes before closing. She nodded at him. "Don't worry. Just waiting for a friend." A hint of her Uzbek accent still came through, but most people didn't notice. She pulled a cell phone from her bag and leaned against the wall next to the drinking faucet. Just a bored girlfriend, waiting for her muscle-pumping guy. But between keying in text messages, she was watching the door to the men's locker room down the hall.

A few minutes later, Dominic came out. At five-nine, he was slightly taller than her, but small-boned and narrow-shouldered. He spent his time on the elliptical machine rather than the weights, so she would be able to overpower him even without chemical help. She sent the first text: *Your girlfriend is with another guy right now at the Bayside Tavern.*

After a count of ten, she sent the next message: *Her tongue is down his throat. You should call her.* Kiya typed in a third and had it ready to go.

She watched Dominic walk up the hall, but he showed no sign of getting her texts. Kiya turned toward the wall and called the front desk. She heard the young man behind her answer the phone.

"There's a huge mess in the woman's bathroom. You need to get in here." She hung up and slipped her phone in her pocket before turning back. The desk clerk swore under his breath, rounded the counter, and charged down the opposite hall. Now it was just her and Dominic. Three feet away, his phone beeped in his shirt pocket. He stopped, pulled it out with his free hand, and read the text. His face crumbled in confusion and disbelief. He shook his head and stepped up to the drinking faucet. Kiya gave him a distracted smile, then looked back at her tablet.

The phone in Dominic's hand beeped again. He set his water bottle on the back edge of the chrome faucet and checked his message. "What the fuck?" He turned away from her and made a call.

The scenario was working better than expected. With a thin sleeve over her hand, Kiya grabbed the half-empty metal bottle, slid open the tab, and dropped in a roofie. She closed it, set it back down, and eased toward the door. The safest move was to step outside and be gone when he turned around. But she was curious to see if his girlfriend would answer, and if so, how long they would fight on the phone before he picked up his water bottle and headed out.

The silence told her the girlfriend wasn't answering. Kiya slipped out and strode toward the end of the building. She rounded the corner and leaned one shoulder against the wall. Just someone killing time. If Dominic behaved according to pattern, he would pass by her in a moment, sucking down his water as he crossed the parking lot to his Honda Civic. After a workout, the roofie would act quickly, and he would be staggering by the time he reached his car.

It didn't go quite according to plan. Halfway across the nearly empty lot, his phone rang. Dominic stopped, tucked his water bottle under his arm, and answered his phone.

"Tricia, where are you?" He sounded a little drunk.

Not good. The last thing she needed was a freaked out girlfriend calling the police. Kiya rushed toward him, her rubber-soled shoes making no sound. He turned just as she got there. She casually reached for his phone and hung up.

"What are you doing?" He blinked rapidly, like a man fighting exhaustion.

"You look like you're going to pass out." She moved toward him. "Can I help you to your car?"

"I do feel weird." He touched his head.

"Maybe you're dehydrated. Drink some water."

Dominic dropped his phone and downed the rest of the bottle, liquid dribbling off his chin. Kiya slipped on latex gloves, grabbed his phone, and shut it off. She put the cell into her bag, then steered the drugged man to his car. His phone might come in handy later. Tech people kept a lot of information in their cell cards.

"Where are your keys?" The parking lot was empty, but she kept her voice low. "I'll drive you home."

He rolled his head and patted his gym bag. The keys were in an outside pocket. Some people were too easy. As a tech guy who worked with proprietary information potentially worth billions, Dominic Prill should have known better. Kiya helped him into the passenger's side, where he promptly slumped over. She climbed behind the wheel, drove out of the parking lot, and headed for a storage locker about a mile from her apartment. She kept the unit under a phony name and used it to hold equipment she didn't want her neighbors to see her carrying in and out. On the drive, Dominic mumbled a few times but stayed slumped over.

As she passed the security camera on the gate, she

averted her face out of habit. In the dark walkway, she hustled to her locker, grabbed the wheelchair, and took it back to the car. Her hostage hadn't moved. She'd used the chair several times to gain access to a building. People had trouble saying no to the disabled, or ignored them completely. The wheelchair would come in handy this evening. Hauling Dominic's unconscious body into the R&D building would be cumbersome, but cutting off his hand would have been too messy.

The ProtoCell R&D building sat behind and to the left of the administrative office and had its own security gate. Lights glowed on the inside, but they were always on at night. She'd done enough surveillance to know. Kiya parked on the empty street and dug through Dominic's gym bag, looking for his badge. It wasn't there. *Dashat!* But he had to have it. He always worked late, stopped for Japanese takeout, then went to the gym. She searched the car and finally found it in a pocket under his seat. A five-minute setback.

She drove up to the entrance. With her head back against the seat to avoid the camera, she slipped the badge under the scanner, and the gate opened. A car in the parking lot unnerved her. Was someone in the building? That might complicate things. She pulled her knife out of its sheath and shoved it in her pocket, just to be ready. This job was worth too much money to turn back, and her client wanted it done now. The little SlimPro device she was assigned to steal had to be worth millions in potential sales. Maybe she would negotiate for a bigger cut.

Time to get it done. Kiya climbed out, grabbed the wheelchair, and brought it around to the passenger's side. Getting Dominic into the chair would be the most challenging part of the evening. She reached in and slapped his face. He sat up and mumbled something that sounded like "I'm not late."

"You're home. Get out of the car and into the chair." Even some cooperation would help. If he woke up too much, she had a benzo handy to stick under his tongue. Kiya pulled his legs out and got him turned and ready to go. She grabbed his arms near the top. "Come on. Stand up." She pulled hard and he gave a weak assist. A moment later, she had him buckled into the wheelchair. His head lolled to the side with eyes closed.

Kiya pushed him up to the door, flashed his badge again, and maneuvered inside. Unfortunately, his badge wouldn't get her into the product vault. Only a few employees had access to the high-value, pre-launch prototypes, and they needed the code. Her client apparently knew ProtoCell's inner workings. The development on the SlimPro was done, and the company was gearing up to launch it worldwide. To Kiya, it seemed late in the game to steal it, but her client wanted to reverse-engineer the device and discover its secrets.

The good news was that Dominic liked to test his own inventions and wore a tiny chip in his hand that acted as a password and allowed him access to the lab. Kiya suspected her client had a spy on ProtoCell's staff who fed her information. This was a cutthroat business, and she'd done some reconnaissance work for ProtoCell earlier that day. Why should she be loyal to either one? She was in this for the money. But until recently, she hadn't realized how valuable a weight-loss product could be. If it was effective and affordable, it could reach a billion consumers globally.

She glanced around, noting the interior had high ceilings,

but the only windows were horizontal and at the top of the walls, like in a dental office. There was plenty of space and light, but no view of the outside. Did the company mean to keep their employees on task or to prevent others from seeing inside? Kiya pushed the wheelchair down the central hall, watching for cameras, while making left turns and listening for the employee whose car was in the parking lot. She wasn't worried about being recognized if caught on video, but she was concerned about triggering an alarm. Some companies used sophisticated software that detected unusual movements or patterns in their buildings at night.

When they reached Dominic's work area, he rallied and tried to resist. But the tech guy couldn't get his buckle undone. He finally managed to say, "You can't do this." Or that's how she interpreted his drugged speech. Kiya was tempted to give him the benzo to shut him up but wanted to wait until she had what she came for. She might still need more information.

She parked him next to the door and studied the security device. It had a scanning eye, as well as a keypad for a code. She hoped it only needed one or the other. Kiya grabbed his hand and waved it in front of the little red eye. Dominic let out a squawk, so she didn't hear a click. But she tried the handle and the door opened. They rolled into the top-secret lab space. Glancing around, she found the product vault in a corner. *Almost there.* She pushed past worktables covered with components and stopped in front of the heavy metal door. The security pad had a rounded vertical slot. *Dashat!* Her client hadn't mentioned that the final breach required a fingerprint. She could produce Dominic's, but which one? If she guessed wrong, would the device lock her out?

She snapped to get his attention. "Which finger?"

His index digit twitched involuntarily. Good enough. She grabbed his hand again, slid his finger into the slot, and heard the lock click open. *Yes!* She was in.

The first drawer she opened was filled with SlimPros. Kiya grabbed three, per instructions, so it wouldn't be obvious that some were gone. It was possible Dominic wouldn't remember much of the evening. The roofie-benzo combination could do that. He might also choose not to report the theft because it could get him fired. She tucked the one-inch implants into the wide belt under her clothes and rolled Dominic to his computer, which she recognized by the nearby photo of him and his girlfriend.

The password chip in his hand allowed her access, and she spent ten minutes downloading files to a thumb drive. Her client wanted both the data and the product, but had been clear that grabbing the prototype was the priority. While Kiya waited for the last file to transfer, she stuck the dissolvable benzo under Dominic's tongue. Now all she had to do was get out of the building, drive him back to the gym, and call it a night.

She pocketed the little USB and rolled the wheelchair out of the research area. In the hall, a voice called out, "What are you doing?"

Chapter 13

An older woman in sweatpants approached, her wrinkled face curious but not fearful. The dust rag she held indicated she was there to clean the building. Kiya scrambled to come up with something plausible. "I'm helping Dominic. He hurt himself at the gym and needed to come here to pick up his cell phone." Which she still had in her pocket.

The woman gave her a skewed stare of skepticism. "He looks passed out. Are you his girlfriend? You're not supposed to be in here."

"I know. We're leaving. He just needed his phone." Kiya started forward. Thank Allah she looked young enough to be Dominic's girlfriend.

The cleaning lady's hands were on her hips now. "I have to report this."

"Please don't. He could get fired." Kiya reached for Dominic's pocket, hoping to find a wallet. "We're supposed to get married. He can't afford to lose his job." The wallet was thin, but he had a couple of fifties. Kiya shoved the cash at the woman.

She frowned, hesitating, then reached for it.

Were the cameras catching this? "We'll get out of here." Pushing the wheelchair, she trotted down the hall. If the cleaning lady called the police, Kiya would be long gone before they arrived. But if the woman reported the incident to her boss, the ProtoCell executives would know about the theft. And her client had been adamant that they not find out. This could hurt her chances of negotiating a bigger payment.

* * *

Cheryl Decker woke to the sound of her daughter's sobs. She threw back the sheet and glanced at the clock. She'd only been in bed for an hour. Exhausted, she trudged into the center of her house. The sobs came from the kitchen. No surprise. Her nine-year-old girl sat on the floor in front of the locked refrigerator. She had a roll of paper towels in her lap and had eaten a chunk off the end.

Not again. "Amber, sweetie." Cheryl knelt down and hugged the poor girl, who couldn't help herself. The Prader-Willi Syndrome gave her a ravenous appetite she couldn't control. "We've talked about this. It's better to wake me up and let me get you some real food."

Amber looked up, eager. "What can I eat?"

"We have some leftover fruit salad. I'll get the key. Do not move." She kept the key hidden, changing the location every couple of days. Her daughter never stopped looking. Cheryl had tried keeping the key in a locket around her neck, but Amber had woken her too many times trying to get to it. Neither of them ever got enough sleep.

Cheryl retrieved the key from a hidden pocket in the clothes hamper and returned to the kitchen. Amber had stopped crying and was now seated at the table with a bowl and a fork. "I'm sorry, Mom, but I couldn't sleep. My belly hurts."

It crushed her to witness her daughter's psychological

pain. Even worse, she hated herself for keeping all the food locked up. But she had no choice. With free access, Amber would eat nonstop and quickly become morbidly obese. Her child's life was difficult enough without more teasing from other kids. Cheryl had tried keeping only small amounts of food locked up, but grocery shopping daily had worn her down. Her time was better spent finding a cure for the heinous disease.

The product she'd just submitted to the FDA—after nearly a decade in development—had turned out to be an excellent weight-loss treatment for adults, but it hadn't helped Amber's genetic disorder-driven appetite. A devastating personal blow, but the profit would fund a lifetime of research. She would never give up. Treating Amber with unapproved therapies was illegal and could land Cheryl in serious trouble, but what else could she do? The house was leased, she had money in several bank accounts, and she was prepared to leave the country on short notice if necessary.

Cheryl dished up fruit salad for both of them, giving Amber most of it, then sat down at the table. "There's a new medicine we can try, if you're up for it." Assuming K, her freelance agent, came through tonight.

Amber looked wary. "What do you mean?"

"It's an implant, so I'll have to make a tiny incision in your abdomen." That was the only downside to ProtoCell's soon-to-launch device.

"Will it hurt?"

"No, we'll numb the area first. I'm optimistic that it will help you." She gave her a special smile. "It's one of my best projects."

The SlimPro was based on her glucagon-peptide research

via a slow-release implant. A decade earlier, Brickman, the bastard, had dumped her, stolen her idea, then fired her. She'd recently learned he was weeks away from launching the product and had decided to sabotage his first, small batch to force a recall and setback. Which is why she needed K to steal a few from their lab before she contaminated the test run. That way her daughter would have a few that weren't tainted. Each device would last six months or so, and during the next year, Cheryl could reverse engineer the device to see what Brickman had used to encapsulate it. Cheryl desperately wanted the SlimPro to fail because Brickman didn't deserve the profit. Even more, she wanted the SlimPro to work—because it would validate her peptide idea and possibly change Amber's life.

Because Prader-Willi was so rare and profitless, no pharma companies were working on a cure. The one clinical-trial drug Amber had tried a few years back—which had failed to get approved—had been developed by a parent, like her, whose child had the disease.

Amber had wolfed down her snack and looked at her with pleading eyes.

"No, sweetie. Get a drink of water and go back to bed. I'll make you a big breakfast."

"I don't want the implant. I just want to eat!" Amber slammed her bowl into the sink, cursed like a sailor, and stalked off.

Cheryl bit the inside of her cheek to keep from yelling. As much as she loved her daughter, she often hated living with her. Again, Cheryl considered her options. Institutions wouldn't take her, and Amber's father didn't know about her. The girl was better off without him. The *black forest* thought crept in again. Amber might be better off dead than living with her condition. The girl's IQ was far below average, her facial features were unusual, she lacked muscle tone, and suffered from insomnia. Her daughter would probably never live on her own. The thought terrified Cheryl. Was it too late for mercy?

A moment later Amber came into the kitchen and hugged her. "I love you. Thank you for making medicine for me."

Cheryl blinked back tears. "I love you too."

Her daughter went back to bed. Watching her pudgy body shuffle away was bittersweet for Cheryl. After growing up with a father who'd been obsessive about her own weight, followed by years of research into weight-loss products, the universe had given her a child with Prader-Willi Syndrome. A bitter slap in the face. Yet, Amber's condition had recharged her drive to pursue the world's most important—and potentially rewarding—research. Too bad her grandfather had been a jerk, who'd become ashamed of Amber and had avoided seeing the girl. Cheryl would never forgive him.

Her cell phone beeped and she went to find it. A text from an unknown number. The message was simple: *I have the devices.*

Thank goodness. Her freelancer had been successful. Cheryl texted back: *Meet me at the Cantina in twenty minutes.*

She threw on clothes from earlier and pulled fifty thousand from the safe under her bedroom floorboards. Half for the job K had just completed and the rest as a down payment for the sabotage she needed next. She'd borrowed the money, plus more, from one of TecLife's investors and hoped it was the last personal loan she would need before Slimbiotic hit the market and sold well enough to pay it all back. Max Grissom, her founding partner at TecLife, didn't know about the spying or sabotage. He thought great research and optimism would take them to the top. Cheryl knew better. The business was full of people who would do anything for money, recognition, or both. She was done playing by the rules. Amber's life depended on her success.

She stuffed the cash into two zippered pillowcases, then put those into an old backpack, hoping it would be less likely to attract a mugger's attention than a briefcase would. Next she tucked her Smith & Wesson into her waistband under her shirt. She wasn't going far and she lived in a nice neighborhood, but still, her heart pounded with anxiety. This was the most she'd ever paid the woman she knew only as K. And bad things happened to people every day. That was why she'd stopped reading and watching the news. It only escalated her natural paranoia and made her reach for her own medication too often.

Cheryl looked in on her daughter, double-checked all the windows and locks, then hurried out into the humid darkness. She almost never left Amber alone, but the girl was sleeping and this was an important exception. Cheryl needed to get the SlimPro now so she could begin analyzing it first thing tomorrow. The product was set to launch next week, and she planned to hire K to sabotage it as well. If SlimPro hit the market with success before her product, Slimbiotic, would always be second and possibly have a fraction of the sales—even though it was less invasive. Doctors were creatures of habit like everyone else. Once they started prescribing something or using a technique that worked, they were reluctant to try something else. Especially one that would be hard to explain to patients without making them squeamish. But with the right marketing message and branding, they could get around public perception.

Hurrying down the block, Cheryl reminded herself that

Amber's cure was the most important issue. The millions in debt she'd accrued, both personally and professionally, while pursuing the research was a close second. Crushing Brickman's product—which he'd stolen from her—and setting him back a few million was a sweet incentive too. She had an idea for how to sabotage the first batch of devices, but it was risky and she didn't know if K could pull it off.

Inside the dark tavern, she found a small booth away from the bar counter and TV. She hated television, especially the news, and limited her internet use to research only. As a result, her world had become closed off, but it was the only way she could focus. The meds she took for paranoia could only do so much. She controlled it best by limiting what she exposed herself to.

Sitting in the bar, so close to home, made her nervous. Her previous meetings with K had been more clandestine, but with Amber home alone, Cheryl didn't have time to travel. And K already knew who she was. The woman was resourceful and had let her know that she not only knew who Cheryl was and where she lived, but that she "understood her motive." Which she'd interpreted to mean that K knew about Amber. Cheryl hated the thought, but backing out wouldn't change the past or accomplish her goals. K might try to blackmail her someday, but she was prepared for that. She always had a backup plan, and K wasn't someone who would be missed. If things got sticky, Cheryl would head for Saul's ranch near the border. Her long-time friend, and sometimes lover, would help her get into Mexico if she ever needed to run.

K strolled in moments later, wearing a blond wig and a long black skirt. Cheryl didn't know it was her until she'd bought a beer at the counter and headed her way. The woman was a master of disguises and a capable thief and arsonist. Cheryl wondered who her other clients were and what she did for them.

"Mind if I sit here?" she asked.

As if anyone was paying attention to them. But Cheryl respected her careful approach.

K sat down across from her. "I had a great evening. How are you?"

A tremor of excitement. Did that mean she'd acquired the SlimPro files too? Cheryl pulled out the little notepad she always carried and wrote: *Did you get the research?* She slid the note across the table. The bar was noisy, so even if K was recording their conversation, it wouldn't be worth much. Still, Cheryl tried to be as cautious as possible. This woman was a criminal.

K nodded and held out her hand, a closed fist. She rotated her wrist and opened her fingers. In her palm lay three implants, each about an inch long and cased in a dissolvable polymer-sucrose blend. An electric charge ran up the back of Cheryl's neck. The culmination of her insight into peptides' role in appetite. She couldn't wait to see how well the device worked. How frustrating that she would never get credit. She reached for the implants.

K yanked her hand back and closed it into a fist again. "You first."

Cheryl slid one of the cases out of the backpack and pushed it across the floor with her feet. K casually pulled it into her lap and examined the cash. After a moment of small talk, K slipped the implants into a napkin and discreetly slid it across the table. Cheryl scooped it up, checking with her fingers for all three devices, then stuffed the napkin into her pants pocket. Too excited to bother with paper and pen,

Cheryl leaned forward and whispered, "Where's the thumb drive?"

The woman's expression was deadpan. "That will cost extra."

No! The bitch. Cheryl wanted to scream. She bit her lip, then grabbed a notepad and scribbled: *That wasn't our deal. I don't have enough cash.*

K shrugged. "So get it. Same amount." She scooted to the edge of the booth seat.

Another twenty-five grand? She could feel her pulse pounding in her ears, but she fought for control. Maybe she didn't need the data. But she did need K for one more job. "Wait."

K turned back. "I'm listening."

Cheryl grabbed the notepad and wrote: *I have another project. Let's take a walk and discuss.*

K nodded and slipped out of the booth. Cheryl tore up the paper with their exchange and stuffed it in her other pocket. She paid for her drink and left the tavern. K waited in front of the closed business next door. Cheryl walked past her, heading in the direction of her home. K called out, asking for a cigarette she didn't really want, then quickly caught up and matched her stride.

"What's the job?"

Cheryl kept her voice low. "Sabotage the SlimPro units in the factory before they ship. I have a contaminating agent you can add to the peptide solution."

"What is it?"

"A bacteria that will cause minor infections."

"What's the timeline?"

"It needs to be done this weekend. The first scale-up batch starts Monday." Her informant inside ProtoCell had given her the update that morning.

"That will cost you another fifty, with half up front. But I have to check out the location and security and see if it's doable."

They walked past a young couple waiting for a cab and were quiet for a moment.

"I may be able to get some of the information you need. And I have the first payment with me."

"What's the address?"

Cheryl relayed the location and slipped her the cash.

"I'll be in touch." K handed her the thumb drive, then abruptly turned and darted across the street.

Cheryl hurried home, racking her brain for where she could borrow more cash, so she didn't have to touch her emergency supply. Her father would probably give it to her—he'd gotten more generous with age—but she hadn't spoken to him in six years. Not since he'd been ashamed to be seen with Amber as a toddler—before they'd diagnosed the disease that explained her bizarre behavior. Cheryl couldn't bring herself to ask him for a favor now.

Chapter 14

Friday, July 11, 6:35 p.m.

Dallas grabbed Thai takeout on the way to the condo. She was eager to check in with River but didn't want to drive and talk on the phone until she was more confident about getting around San Diego. Her hometown of Phoenix was laid out in a massive grid, so driving there required little skill or attention. At home, she called River on the BioTech burner phone, eating bites of fresh summer roll while she waited for her to pick up. Dallas was about to click off when River answered. "Hey, how was work?" They didn't use personal names, even on their case phones.

"Splendid. If you like data entry." Dallas washed down her food with a long slug of cold beer. "Did you get the text image I sent?"

"The number's not registered, which makes the message suspect."

"Is it enough for a subpoena of Grissom's phone records?"

"No, but in combination with something else, it could be."

"There's more. We had a fire alarm during lunch break."

"That's odd."

"It's stranger than you think. While everyone was out of the building, I stepped into Max Grissom's office. But before I could dig into anything, someone came into the outer office."

Talking about it recharged her energy, so Dallas got up to pace. "I ducked into the bathroom as a cover story, then watched to see if he would grab something and go. But it wasn't Grissom. Some guy downloaded files from his computer to a flash drive, then left."

"Good glory. A competitor spying on TecLife?"

"It had to be. I followed the guy, but he went out a side door and scaled a patio wall. Then a fireman forced me to exit."

"Describe the unsub."

"Five eight, slim build, maybe one-fifty or less. He had a beard, but it could have been fake. He wore jeans, a baseball cap, and loose black pullover. I took a picture on my cell phone from the bathroom, but it's probably worthless. I sent it right before I called."

"Maybe the facial recognition software will pick him out."

"Unless he's not in the databases. This was a dirty, white-collar crime. He could be from the competition." Dallas sat and took another pull of beer. "We should look at a roster of ProtoCell employees. Maybe they know TecLife is engaged in corporate warfare, so they're striking back."

"Good idea. If they have nothing to hide, they should open up their files."

"Don't count on it. The public isn't very trusting of us watchdogs anymore."

"I can be very charming."

Dallas heard the smile in her voice. "Indeed you can." River had kept an eco-terrorist from killing his shrink. Which reminded Dallas that she needed to talk to Dr. Harper.

"Did you find out anything else?"

"Mostly background details. For example, Max Grissom is a rally-the-troops kind of CEO who hits on all the women, and Cheryl Decker is a no-nonsense workaholic. But she's developing a top-secret weight-loss product that she says will be a blockbuster and that her competitors would love to get their hands on."

River made a skeptical sound. "I'm surprised she told you on your first day."

"She had me sorting data and wanted to express how confidential the information was."

"But today's unsub stole files from Grissom's computer?"

"Yes. But they're likely networked, and Decker locks her door every time she leaves her office."

"Do you have a feel for which is more likely the mastermind?"

"Grissom is more competitive, and that text asking him to bring cash is compelling."

River added, "If you locate their IP addresses, I can get a tech guy to activate their computer cameras. Then we can overhear phone conversations."

"I'll prioritize it." Dallas snuck a small bite of summer roll. "Do you have anything new for me?"

"The CDC was at our task force meeting for Joe Palmer. The ME had sent over tissue samples, and they say Palmer was exposed to a new bacteria, similar to a staph infection." River paused, and when she continued, her voice was throaty. "The bacteria probably killed Joe, and if it came from one of the med-tech companies, then we need to be cautious. You especially, if you access the lab."

"I'll wear gloves and a face mask." Dallas knew it probably wouldn't be possible, but she didn't want River to worry. "Decker's product is bacteria-based."

"If you can get a sample, we could compare it to Palmer's tissue."

"I'll do what I can." Dallas wasn't optimistic, but she knew how important this was to River. "I'll check in soon."

They hung up, and Dallas finished her dinner while watching the news on her laptop. From the bedroom, she heard her personal phone ringing in its case. Damn, she'd forgotten to turn it off. Might as well see who was calling. She hoped it wasn't Sam, or worse, her mother again.

But it was her mother. She let the call go to voicemail, then stared at the phone, trying to decide if she should listen to the message. This would be about her dad, and she didn't want that responsibility right now. Her work was more important. She walked out to the patio to clear her mind, but moments later turned back inside. Her mother's message was brief but typically manipulative: "Your dad is dying. If you don't come see him, you'll regret it."

A white-hot rage burned in her chest. How dare her parents demand anything of her? She'd always been an afterthought to their addictions and self-indulgence. Except for two brief phases of sobriety. They'd had a good year when she was four. Dallas remembered trips to the park and her dad pushing her in a swing. Then after a short stint in jail, her father had been sober for a couple of months when she was thirteen. He'd apologized for past behavior and even come to one of her school plays. A mixed bag—joy that he'd come and embarrassment about his crappy clothes and unshaved face.

A groan escaped her, and Dallas shook it off. She went to her laptop, clicked open Skype, and called her shrink, not really expecting the older woman to respond. Why should she? It was after hours and the start of a weekend. But Dr. Harper's wrinkled face came into view in the little box. Her brow was puckered, and Dallas couldn't tell if she was worried or cranky.

"Are you okay, Jamie?"

Only her family, her best friend, and her shrink called her Jamie. Even her boyfriends called her Dallas because that's how she introduced herself. "Yes and no. I'm sorry about bothering you in the evening."

"I'm glad you reached out. But I only have a few minutes. I have tickets to a concert." A pause, then quickly. "Unless you're in crisis."

Not a chance. "I'm fine. I just wanted to run something by you."

"What is it?"

"My dad is sick, maybe dying, and my mom wants me to fly home and see him. But I'm involved in an undercover assignment, and I don't want to go."

"I thought you'd forgiven your parents."

"I never said that. And even if I did, it doesn't mean I owe them anything."

Dr. Harper spoke with a gentle tone. "This isn't about your father. It's about you. If going home will make you unhappy, then don't. But if not going will have a long-term negative effect, meaning guilt and regret, then suck it up and get it over with."

Right to the heart of it. That's why she kept having sessions with this woman. "But what if I don't know how not going will make me feel? I'd like to think I don't really care."

"And yet, you're talking to me about it. And you hate talking to me." The shrink smiled, looking every day of her seventy-some years. "You must feel somewhat guilty about not going."

"My mother's making me feel guilty."

"She has no control over your feelings."

So easy to say. "Okay, you win. I'll fly out this weekend while I have some time, give the old man his peace of mind, and come right back."

"Probably a good choice. Where are you, by the way?"

"San Diego. It's pretty here. I love the ocean."

"Did you break up with Sam before you left?"

"Not exactly. But I told him he was free to date someone else."

"How is the sex? Were you getting bored with him already?"

The question no longer bothered her. It was why she'd started counseling with Dr. Harper in the first place. "It was still fine, but that's because Sam isn't clingy."

"I guess we'll see what happens when he starts talking about a commitment."

Dallas started to mention that she might look up an old boyfriend while she was home, then changed her mind. Dr. Harper had plans. "Thanks for your time. I'll let you go. Have fun at the concert."

"What are you not telling me?"

Dallas waved and closed Skype. They could talk about it afterward, when she had something to report. Time to get online, buy a last-minute ticket to Flagstaff, and notify River. Being gone from her target location, even for forty-eight hours, felt wrong. But there wasn't much she could do for the assignment this weekend, and it was still early in her investigation—so nothing was likely to happen while she was gone.

Chapter 15

Saturday, July 12, 7:45 a.m.

Cortez woke to the sound of soft grunting. A wet tongue licked his hand, and he opened his eyes. Grumpy, his aging pot-bellied pig, nudged him. Cortez sat up and scratched the pig's head. The little guy was always hungry. "Okay, already. It's the weekend. Can't a guy sleep in?"

He trudged to the kitchen, put last night's leftover macaroni and cheese in his pet's bowl, then started a pot of coffee. His phone rang before he'd taken his first sip. A glance at the caller ID: *Detective Hawthorne.* Maybe it was a break in the case. "Good morning, sir. How's your leg?"

"The same pain in the ass it was yesterday. And just call me Thorn like everyone else. Okay? We're working this case together."

Partners. Cortez beamed, glad Hawthorne couldn't see him. "Do you have something new for me?"

"A patrol officer spotted Avery's Mercedes on a dead-end street about a mile from where we found the body. Just at the edge of National City." Hawthorne read off the address. "I need you to check it out and have the vehicle towed to the processing building."

"I'll go right now."

"Did you establish a timetable or get anything unusual from the widow?"

"Sorry, but no." Frustration surfaced again. "I called the top fifteen people in Avery's cell phone, and no one saw him Tuesday after he left his house. I questioned his wife and his brother in person, and neither has any idea who would want him dead."

"What about the Freison woman who filed the paternity suit? Did you find her yet?"

He felt downright incompetent. "I've called three times and stopped by the only address on file for her. I called her lawyer too, but he didn't answer and didn't return my call. I'll try again today."

"Let's put out a BOLO if she doesn't turn up."

"What about Avery's bank records and credit cards?" Cortez asked, shifting the focus.

"Harris didn't find anything unusual." A voice in the background sounded like a nurse asking Hawthorne to get up. After a moment, he said, "You'd better hope the Hollywood reporters have another story or scandal to latch onto soon. If they keep calling the department, Riggs will pass this case to another team."

Cortez doubted that, but he said, "I'll work through the weekend. There has to be a lead somewhere."

"Keep checking in."

"Copy that." Cortez felt a burst of energy. He hung up and vowed again to find his icon's killer. He regretted telling his mother he would do yard work for her that afternoon. He texted her and said he had to work instead. She read his texts, but never responded. His mother had adopted the parts of technology that worked for her—such as free TV on the internet—but ignored the rest. Plus her mix of English and

Spanish didn't work well for written communication.

Cortez usually made huevos rancheros on Saturdays, but now he didn't have time. He threw a burrito in the microwave, got dressed, and put Grumpy outside. The pig could come and go through his little pet door, but Cortez always encouraged him to get out in the morning while it was still cool.

If the silver Mercedes Benz S had been left closer to Division, it would have been stolen, stripped of its license plate, and sold for a fraction of its value. Instead, it sat on a dead-end side street, mostly out of view of the main road. Cortez parked behind the black-and-white squad car and wondered what the patrol cop had been doing in the area. As he approached the car, the officer climbed out and strode up to him. A pretty woman about his age.

His throat tightened. "I'm Detective Cortez. I'm working James Avery's homicide."

"Officer Adie Silva." Petite and curvy with big brown eyes, she held out her hand.

Adie for Adelena? Her warm touch sent a charge up his arm.

"Avery's death is a shame. He was a fine actor and a good man."

She was a fan too. "I agree. I've seen every one of his films."

Officer Silva gave him a crooked smile. "He hasn't made a movie in a while, but I still love him."

He wouldn't let himself think of her as *Adie* while they were working. Torn between continuing their conversation and his responsibility to Avery, Cortez finally stepped toward the Mercedes. "Have you searched the vehicle?"

"Just a quick visual. Then I ran the plates, recognized the victim's name, and called it in. I knew he'd been killed around here somewhere."

"About a mile from here, at an old cannery."

"How did he die?" She stayed close, making his body hum.

"They did the autopsy yesterday, and the cause of death is still unknown. Avery was beaten, but the blows didn't kill him. I'm waiting for a toxicology report." Cortez hadn't attended the post, but instead, spent the day talking to Avery's family members and friends. None of which had been helpful.

As he took a series of photos to document the location and condition of the vehicle, Officer Silva commented, "I can't imagine why someone would kill him and dump his car."

"I think he was driven out here, then assaulted." Such a sad ending for a classy movie star. "I'd better search the car. A tow truck will be here soon to haul it to the processing bay." Cortez pulled on gloves and examined the two front door handles. They'd been wiped clean, but left unlocked. He opened the passenger's side door and pulled the paperwork out of the glovebox. He thumbed through it and found only registration and insurance stuff. Nothing suspicious. He bagged the documents as evidence, knowing they would sit in a locker for decades, taking up space, and no one would ever look at them again. A quick glance inside the car revealed it was pristine, what he would have expected from Avery, but little help to him.

"I'll search the back," Officer Silva offered, "but I don't see anything."

"Maybe the technicians will pick up a print." He wasn't optimistic.

After a few minutes of searching, he found a receipt for

ProLabs, dated Tuesday, July 8th. The day Avery died. Was the lab the last place he'd been?

"What did you find?" Silva asked.

"A receipt for lab work on the day he was killed." Closer inspection revealed the nature of the visit: DNA analysis. It was probably connected to the paternity suit. Would the lab be closed until Monday? He was eager to question the staff and look at the video surveillance, if they had any. Cortez bagged the receipt as evidence and headed to the back of the Mercedes, which was flawless—no scratches or dings. The trunk was locked.

"I have a crowbar in my cruiser, if you want to bust it open." Silva's expression was neutral, but her eyes sparked.

Should he? It seemed unnecessarily destructive. "I think I'll let the technicians handle it." He grinned. "If I thought there was a body in there, I'd be all over it."

"Your call."

Cortez wanted to check with the lab and get going. Yet he was enjoying Adie Silva's company. "Excuse me for a moment." After locating the number on the receipt, he called and listened to a canned voice message indicating they weren't open on weekends.

He turned to Silva. "I have to question a suspect this morning. Will you stay with the car until the tow truck arrives?"

"Sure."

He glanced at her hands. No wedding ring. Was it smart to date another cop? His mother would like that Adie was at least part Hispanic, but that didn't matter. *No,* he decided, she was too pretty and would never go out with him. He would just make her uncomfortable and force her to come up with a reason to turn him down.

"Would you like to get coffee later to discuss the case?" she asked.

His heart skipped a beat. She was asking him. He tried to sound casual. "That sounds good." He handed her a business card. Should he ask for hers? No, he didn't want to press his luck. "Which division do you work out of?"

"Mid-City."

"I'll see you later."

Her smile made his day.

Feeling optimistic, he drove toward Alicia Freison's apartment, about five miles south on the edge of Chula Vista. The woman didn't seem to have a place of employment, but a surprise Saturday morning visit seemed like the ideal time to catch her at home.

Two tenants chatting on the sidewalk made the complex seem less abandoned this time, but the new graffiti gave it a slum look. How had someone from this world crossed paths with James Avery? It seemed unlikely—unless she was an opportunistic grubber. Cortez approached the end unit on the ground floor and heard a TV. *Yes!* She was home. He knocked, prepared to be assertive.

A disheveled woman in her late twenties yanked open the door. "I told you I—." She stopped mid-sentence, her mouth open. "Who are you?"

"Detective Cortez, SDPD." He started to show his badge, but she pushed the door closed.

Cortez stepped forward and caught it with his knee. A painful save. "We have to talk."

"Not without my lawyer." Her eyes were defiant, but her lip trembled.

"Tell him to meet you at the department because that's

119

where you'll be." He pulled out his handcuffs. "Or we can talk here."

"About what?"

"James Avery."

A defeated look. "Oh christ." She stepped back to let him in. "I saw the news about his death, but I don't know anything."

Cortez entered the dark space that reeked of fried food. "Why didn't you return my calls?" A little boy watched from the couch.

"Because there's nothing to say."

Dishes, canned food, and unopened mail covered the kitchen table, and every sitting place in the small unit was stacked with laundry. It was no way to raise a child. Being poor was no excuse for being messy. Or so his mother always said. "When did you last see James Avery?"

Freison laughed, a bitter outburst. "About four years ago, when we screwed in the bathroom at a party."

He didn't believe any of it. "You filed a paternity suit recently. You must have seen Mr. Avery at some point."

"No. My lawyer handled it."

"Why file the lawsuit now?"

She gestured with both hands, inviting him to look around. "Why should his son grow up this way? John deserves more."

It didn't explain the delay. "Did you tell Mr. Avery about his son at the time of his birth?"

"I had a boyfriend. We were trying to make it work." She became aware of her appearance and pulled her hair back into a ponytail. It didn't do anything for her stained pajamas.

Cortez wondered how Avery's death would affect the lawsuit. "Will you drop your case now?"

"Why should I? John will inherit a good chunk of money."

"If you can prove paternity."

"His DNA is a match. Just look at him."

Cortez glanced over at the child again. The boy had the same sandy hair and wide forehead as the actor, but it didn't prove anything. "Where were you last Tuesday night between eight and ten p.m.?"

A worried expression crept onto her face as she thought about what he was asking. "Oh yeah, I was at my sister's for dinner."

If Freison had killed the actor, she probably hadn't done it by herself. "Did you hire someone to assault Mr. Avery? Were you trying to extract money from him?"

She blinked a few times, then scowled. "Are you serious? Why would I do that? I have a solid paternity suit that's worth a million bucks."

Good point. "Maybe Mr. Avery threatened you. His wife says you're a DNA hustler. That you stalked him until you managed to snatch a strand of his hair. Then you filed suit, hoping for a quick settlement to keep it out of the press."

"That's a lie." Freison moved toward the fridge, not looking at him. "I've answered your questions. Now leave me alone." She pulled out a milk carton and gulped some down.

Unsanitary. Cortez didn't know what else to ask. He didn't trust the woman, but she hardly had a reason to commit murder. "Give me your sister's name and contact information, so I can confirm your alibi."

Freison rolled her eyes, but wrote the information on his notepad. "Maybe James' wife killed him to get his money. Or because she was tired of his screwing around. She seems pretty cold to me."

Startled, he asked, "You've met Veronica?"

121

"No, but I saw an interview with her a while back. She seemed upset that he hadn't been offered any good movie roles recently. I think she was worried about money."

Wasn't everybody? "I may have more questions. Don't ignore my calls and don't leave town." He'd always wanted to say that.

She rolled her eyes again and gave a smart-ass wave. The lack of respect offended him, but he was slowly coming to accept that police officers weren't seen as heroes anymore. Cortez let himself out, then waited in his car for a few minutes to see if Freison would leave the apartment. If she did, she might be headed to warn the thug who'd helped her assault Avery.

Chapter 16

Saturday, July 12, 1:07 p.m.

The sight of Flagstaff below the plane's window triggered a flood of emotions: first, nostalgia for the beauty of the trees and the quaintness of the architecture, followed by a fear of becoming stuck there again. Rippling under the surface was a fading bitterness that her childhood in this mountain town had been disappointing at best. This was her first visit in years. She often thought about making the drive from Phoenix to see her aunt, but never did. Fortunately, Lynn made occasional trips to the city, so they had dinner and drinks at least once a year. Ten minutes later, she walked off the plane into a blue-sky day and gulped in cool, fresh air. Flagstaff in July was about perfect. But she was here to witness a death, and her mood darkened in spite of the scenery.

All of her dread washed away when her aunt wrapped her arms around her and murmured, "I've missed you."

Dallas had called Lynn to pick her up because her aunt was dependable, and she didn't want to commit to seeing her mother. Just because her dad was dying didn't mean she had to pretend everything was okay with Mom. They had both been lousy, neglectful parents, but she blamed her mother more. It was sexist and unfair, but that was the cultural expectation. Mothers were supposed to give a shit.

"You look great," she said, meaning it. Lynn took excellent care of herself, and Dallas hoped to look as good as she did at fifty.

"Hah. But thanks. How have you been?"

"Excellent. I love my job."

Her aunt didn't ask about her love life. That would come later, after they'd had a few drinks. "How about you? What are you writing now?"

"A futuristic paranormal romance."

They both laughed. Her aunt's strange fiction was popular, and her success had inspired Dallas to dream big. "Have I thanked you recently for everything you did for me? All the acting lessons and day camps and tutors. I know it cost you a fortune."

Aunt Lynn winked. "You're a great investment."

"You spent time just hanging out with me too. It changed my life."

Another quick hug. "Hey, I'm not the one dying."

"Thank goodness." They walked toward the exit of the tiny airport. "So how is Dad? Have you seen him?"

"He's moments from death. I think he's just hanging on until he sees you."

Dread filled her stomach like wet cement. The last thing she wanted was an emotional outpouring from him. It was too fucking late. A childhood memory pushed to the surface, demanding to be examined. She'd been ten, and her dad had taken her to the park. At first he'd hung out with her, pushing her on the swing and watching her use the slide. Then a friend had shown up, and they'd sat off to the side drinking and talking. She'd overheard her father say, "Jamie's a smart little cookie. Maybe too smart." A rush of joy at the unexpected compliment. Her father rarely praised anyone. Later, he'd gotten into a fight with his friend and someone had called the police. Her dad had gone to jail and the day had been ruined, but he couldn't take back his words.

She and her aunt stepped outside, and Dallas inhaled another deep breath of pine-scented air. She would drink her way through the obligatory hospital visit, hook up with an old boyfriend if she could find him, then get the hell out.

They ran into her mother in the hospital elevator. Roxie gave her an obligatory hug, smelling of cigarettes and unwashed hair. Some things never changed. Her mother's cheeks were hollow, and she looked as if she'd aged twenty years. "You get prettier as you get older," she complained. "It's just not fair." Her mother gave a tight smile, a lifetime habit of concealing bad teeth. That was what was different. Her upper teeth were all gone. Why didn't she wear dentures? It made Dallas sad and angry at the same time.

She forced herself to smile back. "How have you been?" A stupid, pointless question, but what else should she say?

"Not good. Your dad is dying and hasn't worked in months. If not for my dear sister, I would have been evicted already." Roxie patted Lynn's arm but didn't look at her.

The elevator door opened, and they all stepped off. Time to look at death.

"Jamie, darlin', you made it." Her father had always been lean and muscular, but now he was so gaunt he looked surreal. The white hospital blanket seemed to dwarf him as he struggled to raise the bed, and the yellowish tone of his skin told her what she had failed to ask—because she instinctively knew. His liver was failing.

She patted his hand, not wanting to touch him. "I didn't know you were sick until just a few days ago. I'm sorry to hear it."

"My liver just suddenly gave out." He let out a little laugh-snort. "We all knew it could happen." He grabbed her hand and held it. "Thank you for coming. It would have been my own damn fault if you had decided not to." His voice was whispery and weak.

Dallas didn't have any words for him. His frailty softened her anger, but he was almost a stranger. All she felt was discomfort and the need to escape.

"How have you been? Tell me about your life in Phoenix."

Dallas pulled a chair over to his bed. Her aunt and mother had stayed in the waiting room, and she was on her own. "My life is good and I love my job. It's important work and I get to travel."

"You always did like to be on the move."

She held her tongue. No point in blaming him now. "I may relocate to another bureau. Every time I go on assignment, I realize how much nicer other cities are compared to Phoenix."

"Phoenix is hell."

Now what? She'd already run out of things she was willing to talk about.

After a long silence, he said, "I'm sorry I was a crappy father. And I'm so relieved you turned out okay."

"Me too." Dallas knew she could have easily become a single mother or an addict. Or gone to jail. "You know I'm seeing a shrink?" Why had she said that? She didn't tell anyone.

"I'm not surprised. I hope you find some happiness." His eyes watered, and he squeezed her hand again.

"I'm very happy. The shrink is just someone to talk things over with."

Another moment of quiet.

"Do you forgive me?" he asked.

It wasn't yes or no. Forgiveness took time. "I'm trying."

"I've made my peace with God. And now with you. I can let go."

An unexpected sadness overwhelmed her. She couldn't bear the thought of watching him close his eyes and then simply be gone. She pushed out of her chair and impulsively kissed his cheek. "Bye, Dad." Dallas bolted from the room.

Later, she had dinner with her aunt and mother in a restaurant near the hospital. She enjoyed Lynn, who was educated, soft spoken, and humorous. But her mother was her typical self—uninformed, self-involved, and often embarrassing. Dallas sat with them for an hour after the meal, then announced she had an errand to run.

"I can take you," Aunt Lynn offered, getting up.

"Thanks, but that's not necessary. I'll get a cab." She gave Lynn enough cash to cover everyone's meals.

"Will I see you before you leave tomorrow?" Her mother seemed genuinely concerned.

"Probably not." She gave Roxie a quick hug and hurried from the restaurant. Lynn had her overnight bag, so she would see her again at some point.

Dallas skipped the cab and walked a mile to Lucky's, a tavern owned by the Mayfield family. She'd dated Cameron Mayfield her senior year in high school, then broke off with him to attend Arizona State. They'd both been crushed, but she had been desperate to get out of Flagstaff and pursue an education. Being back here made it hard to breathe. A drink or two was her first order of business. Then maybe a little dancing. And if Cameron was available, she would indulge in an overdue sexual romp. If she was still attracted to him.

The crowd at the bar surprised her. But it was Saturday night, and Flagstaff had grown in the last decade. Old Man Mayfield was behind the counter and that surprised her too. He used to work at the mill, while his wife ran the tavern. Dallas edged her way up to the counter, squeezing in between two middle-aged men, both watching TVs in opposite directions.

"Shot of Cuervo Gold and a microbrew if you have something decent."

"Jamie Dallas?" Mr. Mayfield beamed. "What are you doing in town?" A second later his expression sagged. "Oh, right. I heard your dad was in the hospital."

"He's dying." She pulled out her wallet, wanting to change the subject. "Is Cameron still around?"

"Actually, he's back in town. He moved to Sedona, but split with his girlfriend and came home a few months ago." Bob Mayfield poured her a shot. "Cameron would probably like to see you. Why don't you call him?"

"I might." She downed the tequila without salt or lime. "Now I need the beer."

He set a bottle of Jack-Booted Thug on the counter, and she handed him a twenty. "How's business?"

"Good. It was rough for a while in the recession, but we survived."

"By home, do you mean Cameron is living with you? Or just that he's back in Flagstaff?" An important detail. She couldn't hook up with anyone who lived with his parents.

"He's got his own place." Mr. Mayfield smiled. "And his own business. He's doing great." The proud father handed her a card. "Excuse me for a moment." He turned to a cocktail waitress who was trying to get his attention.

Dallas glanced at the card and smiled. *Lumberman Brewing Co.* So Cameron had become a brewer. Or an entrepreneur who'd bought a business. In high school, he'd wanted to be a musician—like half the boys she'd known. She glanced at the brand on her bottle. It was from his company. Dallas tasted the beer. Dark and pungent, just the way she liked it. She punched Cameron's number into her phone and sent a text: *It's Jamie. Join me for a drink at Lucky's? I'm only here until morning.*

She had another shot, nursed her beer, then hit the dance floor when the band started. Country-rock wasn't her favorite, but if it had a beat, she could enjoy it. Cameron showed up twenty minutes later and silently pulled her in for a long, gripping hug. He didn't speak until he let her go. "I can't believe you're here. And that you contacted me." He was still built like a basketball player, but more muscular now. His brow and jawline had become more pronounced, but his sweet silvery-blue eyes hadn't changed.

"It surprises me a little too."

"You're more beautiful than ever." He led her off the dance floor, not giving her a chance to respond. He knew she preferred not to focus on her looks.

Cameron passed the tables, heading for the front. "We're getting out of here," he said, holding open the door.

"Good. This place is too noisy. Where are we headed?"

"My place?"

She didn't want to rush this. What they had was too important. "Yes, but let's take a walk and get caught up first."

Chapter 17

Sunday, July 13, 10:35 a.m.

River took her omelet and laptop out to the patio to read the local news online and enjoy the seaside air before the day heated up. The main story about a politician sentenced to prison made her think of her father, who was serving life in San Quentin, about a five-hour drive away. She hadn't seen Gabriel Barstow since she was a teenager and had no desire to. But this was the first time she'd been anywhere near the prison, and something deep in her brain was telling her to go visit, that this might be her last chance. What did it matter? She owed him nothing and didn't have anything to say. She had questions, but didn't want to hear the answers. His death would mean little to her or anyone else—except the families of his victims, who might sleep better.

She would make the right decision when the time came. *Because every decision was correct in the moment.* The mantra gave her a sense of peace. She took a bite of egg and clicked to a new page. A breaking headline caught her eye: *Researcher Found Dead in Home.* River scanned the two-paragraph story. A thirty-two-year-old man had died of a gunshot wound to the head. The weapon belonged to him, and the police thought it was probably a suicide. Near the end, the article mentioned that he'd been employed by ProtoCell.

Adrenaline shot up her spine. The company targeted by TecLife now had another dead employee. It couldn't be coincidence. Had the saboteur stepped up the attack? But why a scientist? Maybe the victim was a key researcher, whose death would be a setback to ProtoCell. The data theft Dallas had reported Friday came to mind. Were they connected? Was his death a payback?

River grabbed her phone to call Dallas, then remembered she'd flown to Flagstaff for the weekend to see her dying father. Now River wondered if hearing that had triggered a subconscious impulse to see her own father. She let it go and called the task force leader, relieved when he picked up.

"Agent King. It's River. Did you see the *Tribune's* website this morning?"

"I read the front page and the sports section. Why?"

"A ProtoCell scientist died last night, killed by a shot to the head with his own gun."

A quick intake of breath. "That's the company TecLife seems to be targeting? The one with the warehouse fire?"

"Yes. We need to meet with the police department and take charge of this supposed suicide case. The victim's name is Michael Pence."

"I'll make the calls and set it up for this afternoon. The sooner we investigate, the better. The same unsub or group may have killed Palmer and could be escalating their crusade."

"That's my concern as well."

"Notify Dallas. Her probe is more dangerous than any of us realized."

River thought so too. "Maybe we should pull her out. The

external intel is mounting, so we might not need her in there."

A pause. "We don't have anything solid yet to pin a search warrant on. Let's give her a couple more days."

River knew Dallas would want to stay in, so she let it go. "I'll keep a tighter watch and stay close by." That would mean sitting in her car or a nearby cafe while Dallas was inside TecLife, but that was the job.

By three that afternoon, King had called in the task force, including a detective from the San Diego PD. They met in the conference room at the bureau, and Agent Kohl showed up in slacks and a pullover, as if he'd just left the golf course.

King introduced Detective Ricci and thanked him for being there. "We appreciate the department's cooperation in handing over the case files. Will you summarize what you have so far?"

The detective nodded and stood. "Excuse me if I seem a little rough. We got called out at two a.m., and I haven't slept since." Ricci was in his late forties, with saggy cheeks and a faint stubble on his chin. "Michael Pence's wife came home from a night of dancing with her friends and found her husband dead on the couch. He'd been shot in the head with a Glock that is registered to him. The gun was still partially in his hand, and he had powder residue, indicating suicide. And there was an empty bottle of rum nearby. His wife—"

Ricci sat down to check his notes. "Tabatha Pence says her husband was prone to depression, but that he'd never talked about suicide." Ricci looked around at the group, his expression weary. "If it was murder, it was well staged."

"What about his phone and timeline?" River asked. "Did he get any calls? What had he been doing that evening?"

Ricci pointed at a box on the table. "His cell phone is in

there, but you'll see that he didn't get any calls or texts that evening. He'd been playing poker at home with friends earlier. His wife says it was a monthly Saturday night thing for both of them."

River cut in. "Had he been drinking?" Alcohol and guns were a deadly mix.

"Yes, he drank with his poker friends."

"Was he right- or left-handed, and was the gun in the correct hand?" A mistake an amateur might make.

"He's right handed, and the gun and residue were in his right hand."

Was she wrong about her suspicions? "What was Pence working on for ProtoCell?"

"I don't know that."

It could be important to a competitor. "Have you talked to his co-workers?"

"Not yet, just his wife and parents, who live in the area. They're all stunned to hear he committed suicide, but so far, we don't have any evidence to indicate anything else." Ricci gave a small shrug. "You're right about the alcohol. Sometimes people are self-destructive when they're drunk. And if he was depressed..."

River had another thought. "Did any neighbors hear the gunshot? Do we have a time?"

"One neighbor heard something around eleven-thirty, but can't swear it was a gun."

Agent Kohl spoke up. "Was he taking medication?"

"No, but he'd taken anti-depressants in the past, then gone off them four months earlier."

"Any flesh wounds?" River asked. She was curious to know if the mystery bacteria would show up.

Ricci seemed surprised. "Not that I'm aware of, but the

autopsy may reveal more, particularly about the bullet wound."

"Is it scheduled?"

"I haven't heard." Impatience crept into his tone. "I'd like to turn over my notes and photos and go home. You can call me if you have follow-up questions."

Agent King took possession of the file and shook Ricci's hand. After he left, River asked, "Can we have someone attend the autopsy? We need to know if SA-13 is present and to make sure the medical examiner sends blood and tissue samples to the CDC."

Kohl gave her a look. "Why can't you do it?"

"I have to stay close to Dallas. Two people connected to ProtoCell are now dead, and King and I are both worried about her."

"Three if you count the warehouse security guy," King added.

"If the connection is ProtoCell, maybe we're investigating the wrong company," Kohl suggested.

He had a point. And it reminded her of their update. "It's worth considering. On Friday, an alarm went off at TecLife, and Dallas saw someone download files from Max Grissom's computer."

King turned to stare. "You think the thief was someone from ProtoCell?"

"Very likely." River mentally reviewed the report Dallas had sent late Friday night and summarized it for the group. "The two companies are developing competing weight-loss products that could be worth billions on the market. ProtoCell plans to launch soon, but TecLife's product is waiting on approval. TecLife may have started the corporate war when it set ProtoCell's factory on fire, but it looks like their competitor fought back by sending in a thief to steal data."

Agent King's eyes widened. "You think the products are worth billions?"

"Dallas got the information straight from Cheryl Decker, one of the executives."

Kohl shook his head. "So which company killed Palmer?"

"TecLife has the most to lose," River said. "And they're the company Palmer was investigating." She remembered her conversation with Jonas Brickman. "This whole scenario is odd. I questioned ProtoCell's CEO, and he played down the fire and denied it was sabotage. But I think he lied."

"Why?" King asked. "To discourage us from looking too closely at either company?"

"Possibly. If he was planning to send a thief into TecLife, I probably made him uncomfortable with my questions."

Kohl finally warmed to the discussion. "Did Dallas get a look at the thief? Maybe the suicide victim is the one who stole the files, and the TecLife saboteur went there to get them back."

"Let's compare." River opened her laptop, plugged it into the big monitor, and clicked open the image Dallas had sent. "She took this photo, and I had it enlarged and brightened. Dallas says he's about five-eight and one-fifty. We both think the beard is fake."

King thumbed through the file Detective Ricci had turned over and pulled out a couple of photos. After a moment, he said, "Michael Pence is closer to six feet and one-eighty."

Not surprised, River looked over his shoulder at the corpse's image. "It wouldn't make sense for them to send a scientist. Most employees wouldn't have the nerve or the skill to carry out such a blatant theft. Maybe ProtoCell hired someone, or sent a security person."

River had a disturbing thought. "Maybe the TecLife saboteur killed Pence just to cause a setback for ProtoCell's research." She shuddered. "We need to question the neighbors in case someone witnessed a late-night visitor."

A silence while they processed the complexities.

Finally, River looked at Kohl. "Do you have anything new on Palmer's case?"

Kohl hesitated. "He might not have been murdered. He could have accidentally come into contact with the bacteria, which infected the wound on his hand. Then it led to his death because he had a weakened immune system."

River accepted the possibility. "And Michael Pence could have had personal problems, got drunk, and committed suicide. But we still have corporate sabotage and theft going on, with billions in profit at stake."

"We need a search warrant," King said. "Let's start tailing these people after hours and see if they lead us anywhere." He looked at River. "You take Max Grissom, and Dallas can follow Cheryl Decker. I'll watch Jonas Brickman." He turned to Agent Kohl. "You watch the director of DigiPro. Let's not forget that the subsidiary produced the patch Palmer had in his pocket."

River thought they needed more. "I'll sign a probable-cause affidavit and see if a judge will let us put ears in Decker's office."

King stood, signaling the meeting was over. "I'll try to get another agent on the case. This corporate war is escalating, and I get the feeling it could come to a head soon."

Chapter 18

Sunday, July 13, 8:40 p.m.

As Dallas walked into the San Diego airport, both her cell phones started beeping, indicating a bunch of texts had come in. A rush of panic washed over her tired body. River was trying to contact her, but who else? Had her dad died? She stopped, leaned against a wall, and checked her personal phone. A text from Cameron: *I miss you already. I was serious last night. I'm moving to Phoenix as soon as I can sell the business.*

Sweet, but scary. They'd had several rounds of crazy-intense sex, but what had been just as good was the laughter. She'd forgotten how attentive and funny he was. Or maybe he'd become that person in the decade since high school. But either way, it had been a terrific night, and she'd been thinking about him since she left Flagstaff.

The second text was from him as well: *Don't worry. I'm not asking for a commitment. I just want to be a part of your life.*

A nice thought. But not practical.

She dug out the BioTech phone, and River had messaged her twice as well: *We have a development. Call me as soon as you get in.* Followed by: *Let's meet in person at Charlie's Cafe.*

It's close to both of us. Text when you arrive. I can be there in 5.

What the hell had gone down? She'd only been gone for thirty-four hours over the weekend. Now she felt guilty about going to Flagstaff, but she didn't regret it.

Dallas looked for the cafe on her way to the condo, not wanting to go back out again. Unless she had to do field work. If that was the case, she'd suck down some coffee and slap herself awake. She'd done back-to-back all nighters before.

Charlie's was tucked into a little corner mall not far from the beach boardwalk where she'd gone running Friday night. The window sign said it served comfort food from both sides of the border. Inside, the place was colorful and aromatic, but nearly empty. Dallas sat in a booth away from the window, and the server trotted over, no menu in hand. "We close at ten."

"I just want coffee. Black, please." An older couple still occupied another booth, so the cafe couldn't lock up anyway.

While she waited for River, Dallas reread Cameron's texts. If any other guy had said he loved her the way Cameron had last night, she would have dropped him as fast as she could hit Send. But it was Cameron, her first real boyfriend, and they'd already said the dreaded "I love you" long ago. Those feelings had always been part of her.

But now she realized it had been a mistake to hook up with him. She didn't want a relationship that would make her feel guilty for leaving town to take undercover assignments. Now they would both hurt when she walked away. She might as well blame her father for this predicament too. The thought made her laugh.

"You look happy." River walked up and scooted into the booth.

"I just had a funny thought." Dallas slipped her phone into her pocket. "What's the development?"

"Let's get a drink first." River signaled the server, then glanced back at Dallas. "Don't worry. It's nothing you could have prevented by being here. We're not even sure what it means."

That failed to reassure her. "Am I doing fieldwork tonight?"

"No, but it's coming."

When the server came over, River ordered a glass of wine. Dallas sent back her coffee and asked for a bottle of beer. The server barely contained her irritation.

"How was your trip?" River asked.

"About what I expected. It made my dad happy...whether he deserved it or not."

River nodded, then looked away. "My father's in prison. And you're the only person in the bureau I've said that to. Except the agent I interviewed with to get the job."

River had her attention. "His crime?"

"Serial killer."

"No shit?" Dallas shook her head. "Okay, you win. I'm done being ashamed and frustrated with my loser-addict parents."

River laughed, and Dallas realized this would not be her first glass of wine.

"There's more." The other agent leaned forward and said softly, "I used to be Carl River."

Dallas stared, speechless. River had a pleasant face and stocky body that could have gone either way, but Dallas would have never known. She wanted to say the right thing. "Congratulations for having the courage to be who you are. Especially in the bureau. That must have been rough."

"I took some grief from a few assholes, then I transferred to a new office for a fresh start." River finally met her eyes again.

That explained the special agent's move to Eugene. "I'm glad you told me. I appreciate your trust." Dallas wanted to ask more questions but didn't.

"When this assignment is over, I'll probably never see you again. And who are you going to tell?"

They both laughed.

After the server brought their drinks, River told her a scientist at ProtoCell was dead, possibly a suicide. Dallas assumed the worst. "Someone killed him. The weight-loss market is worth billions, and both TecLife executives are intense in their own way." An ugly thought came to mind. "I told both Grissom and Decker about the intruder downloading files. What if they knew who it was and went after him?" *Damn.* She hadn't considered that might endanger his life.

"There's no match. The dead man is taller." River lowered her voice. "If they killed him, it was probably to hinder their competitor's research."

"Who knew this industry was so ruthless?"

"It's still all speculation. We need you to get something solid. And fast. This corporate war is escalating."

Dallas took a long pull of cold beer. "What did you mean about field work?"

"It's time to start tailing Decker for a few hours after work and see where she goes. I'll be on Grissom."

"I need to access their texts and emails. I have a hacker friend—"

River cut her off. "Don't tell me. One of us has to play by the book."

"Three people are dead. Fuck the rules."

"Please be careful," River said, the wine softening her voice. "I'll be near the TecLife building during the day, so if you need backup, I can be there in a few minutes."

A few minutes could be too late, Dallas knew. But in most of her undercover roles, she was typically even more alone. "I can bullshit my way out of anything."

River gave her a half smile. "Maybe you should stay late tomorrow and visit the lab. We're looking for a bacteria related to MRSA."

That was the key to getting a warrant. As an employee, she could take a legal sample. "I should have gone into the lab this weekend instead of placating my father."

"You made the right decision." River held up her glass for sincerity. "You've only worked there a single day. But our timetable is compressing now, and we need something tangible."

"I'll get it tomorrow."

"Oh, and I just remembered something I learned from Jonas Brickman, the CEO of ProtoCell." River finished her wine, then continued. "We knew Cheryl Decker had worked for him years ago, but I think they were lovers too. So this feud between the companies could be personal."

As if a billion dollars wasn't enough motivation. "We can't assume Decker is the mastermind. I still haven't met Curtis Santera, the head of R&D. He has so much stock in the company that he might benefit the most from the new product launch."

"We have some busy days coming up. Let's get out of here."

Dallas was already devising ways to get a look at Decker's phone. But how would she find the right bacteria sample in the lab and smuggle it out?

At home, she changed into shorts, tucked a pepper-spray canister into her pocket, and headed out for another run on the beach. The sound of the ocean was intense and soothing at the same time, and she couldn't get enough of it. She jogged six blocks to the boardwalk and headed south. Some of the restaurants were still open, but the tourist shops selling T-shirts and sunglasses were closed. Every couple of blocks, music spilled out of a bar, and people of all ages strolled the path, enjoying the evening air as it finally cooled down. After she passed the pier, she went another half mile on the paved boardwalk, then headed down to the beach to run back in the sand. The scent and sound of the ocean were intoxicating. If she ever decided to transfer out of Phoenix, San Diego would go on her list.

Chapter 19

Sunday, July 13, 7:15 p.m.

Kiya finished a crossword puzzle, surprised at how hard it still was. But her command of extended English was getting better all the time. She made a cup of espresso, then meditated while she waited for the caffeine to kick in. The meditation had replaced the morning prayers she could no longer say. She would rather chant to nobody than pray to a god that didn't care. When it was finally time, she called her contact in southern Uzbekistan.

He greeted her by her old family name, using a formal tone. Warlords could be polite to your face, then stab you to death a moment later.

"I have the money," Kiya said, cutting to the chase. "Is everything ready?"

"Except the final transaction. Do you still plan to bring the cash in person?"

"It seems wise." She didn't trust him to follow through with sending her father to prison unless she was present.

Abdul was silent for a moment, making her nervous. Finally he said, "I know you said you didn't want to hear about the rest of your family, but I have to inform you. You have a younger sister."

No! She especially didn't want to hear this. Kiya's throat closed and she couldn't speak.

Abdul continued. "She's eight now, and will soon be married to Farid Asa Samidi, a friend—"

Kiya cut him off. "I know who Farid is. But I don't want to know about the girl. I have a new life."

"Then why are you willing to spend so much money to take revenge on your father?"

"Because the bastard deserves it. Once he loses his freedom, I'll finally have mine."

"But your sister will still be a slave to a cruel old man. You could buy—"

"Silence!" Kiya had to block out the images. "I'll get a flight out this week and see you by Friday." She hung up before he could respond. The young girl was not her responsibility. Her father could keep siring children for another twenty years—unless she sent him to prison. She would use the money for revenge. It was the wisest decision.

Kiya dressed in dark pants and a reversible T-shirt; black on the outside but yellow if she turned it inside out. Her backpack was ready to go, except for the vial of bacteria her client had supplied. She wrapped the contaminant in a thick washcloth and zipped it into an outer pocket. This would be her last job for TecLife, for the whole medical device industry. Product sabotage made her uncomfortable. In the future, she would stick to data theft, financial manipulation, and character assassination. And someday, she'd walk away from the freelance life and retire in Greece or Southern Italy, so she could paint landscapes in pretty colors and feel at peace.

Twenty minutes later, she parked on a side street near the ProtoCell factory and climbed off her motorcycle. She would have preferred to wait until it was fully dark, but the night watchman took a smoke break at eight-thirty, and she needed to be in place before he stepped out of the building. Her reconnaissance over the past few days had required her to sit for hours, watching the building, in addition to accessing the blueprints online. But she'd learned patience and stillness at a young age and could channel her mind into a long pause while focusing on a single thing, such as the factory's back door.

Cloaked in a bandanna and sunglasses, she hurried around the block, then scaled the chain link fence behind the factory. She ran to the first outbuilding and hid behind it, not visible from the street or the factory. The structure lacked windows except for the front office and a second story corner office, but it might have cameras in the back. She didn't think so, but caution had kept her from getting caught for fifteen years. That, plus creativity and agility—and maybe a little luck. Another quick sprint and she reached the housing for the backup generators that jutted out from the rear wall. Kiya ducked in between the two small structures and wedged herself flat against the building. From there, she couldn't see the back door, but she would hear it open and smell the cigarette. The watchman wouldn't see her approaching until it was too late.

After ten minutes, she checked her cell phone: 8:03. Was he coming? She pulled on gloves and chewed a piece of gum while she waited, always careful to take the wrapper with her.

Two minutes passed. The door hinges squeaked. Kiya pulled off the bandana and replaced it with a nylon facemask. She dumped chloroform on the bandanna, then raced around the structure. The guard, an older man with hunched shoulders, dropped his cigarette in surprise. She rushed him, shoving the bandanna against his nose and mouth before he could call out or reach for his gun. Pressing hard, she pushed him back against the door, holding firm until his eyes rolled and his body sagged. She caught him under his arms and propped him in a sitting position against the wall by the door. He didn't look quite natural, but it was better than leaving him prone. She would be in and out in seven minutes, before he recovered consciousness. Kiya grabbed his employee badge and entered the factory.

Once inside, she sprinted for the production area to her left, passing a series of swinging doors with upper windows. The rooms contained equipment that looked like giant kitchen bowls and mixers. Decker had said to target the hopper, where the peptides were mixed with fillers, right before entering the capsulation area. Through the window of the fourth door, Kiya spotted the machine and pushed inside. She strode to the side of the V-shaped machine and found the black valve that opened, just as Decker had described. Kiya slipped off her pack, pulled out the vial, and unscrewed the lid. Holding her breath, she tipped the little glass container and dumped a large blob of the thick cloudy substance. She quickly screwed the cap back on, noticing that she'd dumped nearly all of the contents instead of the tablespoon she'd been instructed. *Oh well.* Decker had said the contaminant would only make people sick and feverish and that only a small batch would be made in the first run.

Kiya wrapped the vial in the washcloth again, shoved it back into the zippered pocket, and ran from the room. The guard could wake from the chloroform at any moment, and she wanted to be outside the building when that happened. Tomorrow, she would collect the second half of her payment and move on with her life.

Chapter 20

Monday, July 14, 8:45 a.m.

Cortez waited in his car for ProLabs to open, optimistic this lead would break open the case. He hoped Hawthorne would give him some of the credit. If he did, when someone wrote James Avery's biography, the murder investigation would be the finale chapter, and Cortez might be mentioned. He loved the idea that he would be forever connected with the late, great actor. Sipping his latte, he added to his list of questions.

At nine sharp, he entered the single-story building, located on a large corner lot off Skyline Drive, east of where they'd found the car and the body. The interior was bright and monotone, with minimal decor or seating. The woman behind the counter looked up and greeted him. She was young and pretty, and Cortez felt tongue-tied already. He smiled, showed his badge, and cleared his throat. "Detective Cortez, SDPD. I'm investigating a homicide, and I need to talk to everyone who was on staff last Tuesday."

Her mouth opened in a started O-shape, then clamped shut.

"Were you here on July eighth?"

"Yes, but I have no idea what you're talking about."

"James Avery had his blood drawn that day. What time

was he here?"

She blinked and stammered, "Umm, I'll have to look."

While she found the appointment, a client came in. Cortez turned and showed his badge. "Will you wait outside for a moment?"

The young man started to ask a question, then changed his mind and stepped back out.

The receptionist said, "James Avery's appointment was at four-thirty, the last one of the day."

Was that significant? "Do you remember him? He's fifty-seven with gray at his temples, but otherwise looks much younger. In fact, he's a famous actor."

She blinked again. "He is? I've never heard of him."

Cortez held back a sigh. "But do you remember the client?"

"Yes. He seemed nice." The receptionist looked at her monitor. "He was here for a DNA analysis."

"What time did he leave?"

She shrugged. "We don't document that."

"Did you see him leave? Did he talk to anyone in the parking lot?"

"I don't remember."

"This is important," Cortez implored. "He was killed later that evening, and I need to know what happened after he left here."

"I'm sorry. But I don't remember seeing him leave." She seemed a little defensive now. "I could have been in the bathroom or talking to a client on the phone and didn't look up. We're a busy lab."

"I understand." He took down her name, then asked to talk to the person who'd drawn Avery's blood.

She glanced through her digital records. "That was April Carson. She's setting up for our first client." The receptionist glanced at the door. "Can I bring him into the lobby to wait now?"

"After you take me to see April."

The phlebotomist was a woman of few words, who kept filling her supply drawers as he asked questions. In the end, she added nothing to his understanding of Avery's last actions. From there, he asked to see the manager. She led him to a corner office and introduced him to Jim Gao, who looked thirty, except for his clipped gray hair.

"How can I help you?" The manager, who wasn't any taller than him, shook his hand.

"James Avery was murdered about five hours after he left his appointment here last Tuesday. And no one saw him during that time. The two events may not be connected, but I need to investigate every possibility." *Or he might lose this case to another team and fail his cultural icon.* "Did you meet Mr. Avery?"

The manager looked puzzled. "No, I don't see clients. But I did read about his death, and I can assure you, all we did was take his blood and send it back to the lab."

"I'd like to see the results."

"The report won't be completed until later this week."

"Where were you Tuesday night between eight and ten?" He had to ask.

Gao pulled back, as if offended. "At home with my wife and children."

Strike two. He would check out the alibi, but his frustration mounted, mostly with himself. He had to look at his list of questions. "Who owns this business, and are they connected to James Avery?"

"We belong to an investment group called BioMed Holdings. I don't know the names of the investors or who they're connected to."

"What other businesses are owned by the group?"

"ProMed Manufacturing and ProtoCell Devices. They're both located on this campus, but they face other streets."

The names meant nothing to him, and he was probably wasting his time. But Cortez decided he would check into Avery's finances and see if the actor had any association with the companies. Or maybe Detective Harris already had that information. "Do you have security cameras in the building?"

"No, but we have one just outside the front door."

"Please send me the video from that afternoon, between say, four and six."

"We close at five and everyone leaves by five-thirty."

"Then that will cover it." He handed the manager a business card. "Here's my email. If the file is too large to send, put it on a drive and I'll come pick it up."

Back in his car, Cortez tried to figure out what other leads he could explore. He had already talked to Avery's family, and his wife's alibi had held up. His son, who was the same age as his widow, lived north in Oceanside. Cortez had called, but maybe he should drive up there and question him in person. Julian Avery stood to collect half of his father's inheritance, always a motive for murder.

His phone rang, startling him. A number he didn't recognize. "Detective Cortez."

"This is Maria Gomez with the San Diego County Medical examiner's office. I have a preliminary toxicology report for James Avery. Should I email it to you?"

"Please." He gave her his contact information. "But I'm not in my office. Can you summarize it for me?"

"Sure. It was a little unusual."

"How so?"

"His blood had a significant level of phenobarbital and trace amounts of sodium thiopental."

"Is that first one a sedative?"

"Yes, the drugs are what caused his death. The ME has ruled it a homicide."

Surprised, Cortez processed the information. Avery had been bound and beaten, then injected with enough sedative to kill him. "What is the other drug you mentioned?"

"That was what was unusual. Sodium thiopental used to be the first drug administered in lethal injections for death-row inmates, so it's hard to access. But it's also sometimes used by psychiatrists to treat patients with phobias."

He didn't understand. "Why would a kidnapper or killer use it?"

She thought for a moment. "Some people call it a truth serum because the drug interferes with complex brain activity and makes it difficult for the person to lie."

A shock wave rippled through his body. Had Avery been drugged and beaten to gain information? What could he possibly have known that a criminal would want?

Chapter 21

Monday, July 14, 7:50 a.m.

Feeling apprehensive, Dallas walked into TecLife. She hadn't slept well after her session with River, and she felt pressured to nail down viable intel ASAP. But first she had to check with Jana Palmer to see if employees had after-hours access to the building and what the security was like if they did. So far she'd avoided any personal contact with her, not wanting to risk Agent Palmer's widow if things went south.

Dallas took the elevator up to her office, sneezed six times while she adjusted to the air conditioning, then settled in to explore files on the server. A moment later, Cheryl Decker stepped through their adjoining door. "Good morning. Ready for the spirit meeting?" Her face seemed pinched, and a new worry line creased her brow.

Dallas started to joke that her boss looked like she needed more than spirit, then remembered that Decker could be a murderer and her stress well earned. So she kept it simple. "Sure." She tucked her purse into her desk drawer, locked it, then pocketed the key. Her own lying and spying had made her distrustful of nearly everyone. She walked with Decker to the stairs. "How was your weekend?"

"Busy. Once we get Slimbiotic launched, I'm taking a long vacation."

"When is the launch scheduled?"

"That depends on the FDA. We're still waiting for marketing approval."

Once they entered the atrium downstairs, Decker moved to the front of the employee group already gathered. Max Grissom came in late and didn't seem like his chipper self either. He rushed through the stretches, jumps, and cheerleading—thank god—then made a somber announcement. "Due to a security breach on Friday, we're making changes to our system. No after-hours access will be allowed unless you get pre-approved from me or Cheryl."

Well, hell. Dallas kicked herself for taking the weekend off. Around her, a few employees groaned.

"I'm sorry," Grissom said. "I appreciate your dedication to working extra hours. We just want to know in advance who'll be in the building." He paused. "We're also installing a fingerprint activated security door, so everyone will have to get processed. We'll start tomorrow. Let's go kick ass."

Half the employees responded with the expected *Hell, yeah!* but the rest muttered to themselves as they fled the room.

Dallas hurried out and caught up to Eric, head of sales. "Hey, sorry about Friday. The alarm went off, and I got a little rattled and forgot we were supposed to have lunch."

"No worries. Should we try again today?"

"I'd like that." She walked with him toward the lobby.

"The new security protocols seem like overkill to me," he said. "I think something serious happened on Friday to spook the partners."

"Like what?" They stopped in front of the elevator behind a group of employees.

"We'll talk about it at lunch."

Dallas touched his arm. "I'm taking the stairs. See you at

noon." She could tell by his body posture that he was attracted to her, and she was glad she'd put the bottle of pheromones in her bag again. They would come in handy. If he was a lunch-hour drinker, she might pry some useful intel out of the encounter.

Upstairs, Decker waited by her desk. "I heard from the FDA this morning." Her jaw was locked so tight it affected her speech. "They still want more information. We have it, but we have to pull the data out of the patient files and present it in the way they want."

"This is slowing down your launch plans, isn't it?" Dallas scrunched up her face to show sympathy.

"Yes." Decker crossed her arms. "I need you to get started right away."

"I'm sorry about the setback." She took a seat. "Does it hurt the company's finances?"

"This isn't about money," Decker snapped. "It's about human lives. People who are miserable and dying and desperate for help."

Her passion was unexpected. "Show me what I need to do."

Decker explained the process, then watched while Dallas extracted the first batch of clinical information.

"Well done," she said. "But don't hesitate to ask questions." Decker started toward her office, then turned back. "I'm sorry I snapped at you. This research is personal for me in several ways. I can't afford to fail."

"I'll do everything I can to help you." Dallas wished she could mean it. Decker obviously believed she was doing life-saving work, and if she were, Dallas wanted her to succeed. But how far was the scientist willing to cross the line to reach her goals?

Dallas worked for an hour on the project, so she could report actual progress and not get fired before she accomplished her mission. As best she could tell, the data for Slimbiotic was surprisingly good. The clinical trial patients had lost an average of eight percent of their body weight. No wonder ProtoCell had sent someone to steal data. But what had they actually downloaded? To replicate the drug-device combo, they would need R&D files, not clinical trial information. But maybe that's what they'd taken. The other company would still have to alter the molecule and the device enough to not violate patent protection. And if TecLife's product was that good, why was it sabotaging other companies? Unless it was out of cash to continue development and needed a drastic boost in sales.

Dallas took screen captures of the trial outcome statements and downloaded them to a thumb drive. But the information wouldn't help them get a warrant. She spent twenty minutes scanning through file names in both Grissom and Decker's folders, but didn't see anything that looked personal. They probably kept their personal files on their hard drives instead of the server. After a few failed attempts to access Decker's email, she went back to sorting data. She needed more personal information about Decker, such as a pet name or favorite hobby. But the FBI background search had produced very little.

At noon, Eric met her in the lobby, and they walked across the street to Saber's. By the time they arrived, Dallas was sweating and grateful for the air conditioning. They sat at a table near the window and ordered Cobb salads.

"If it was Friday, I'd have a beer." Eric looked longingly at the table of drinkers next to them.

"So let's call it Friday." Dallas turned to the food server, who'd started to walk away. "And two bottles of Pliny the Elder."

When she was gone, Dallas got right to business. "So what happened Friday to get Grissom's panties in a bunch?" As if she didn't know.

"The rumor is that someone broke in and stole some of Decker's research data."

So it was Decker's. "You mean like a competitor?"

"Probably. But ProtoCell is our main pipeline competition, and their weight-loss device is well ahead of ours." He rubbed his head. "So why would they steal the data?"

Good question. "Maybe ProtoCell's product has problems."

"It's about to launch, so it was probably another company. Or maybe a disgruntled ex-employee."

The server brought their beers, and Dallas raised her bottle to Eric. "To Fridays."

He laughed, clicked drinks with her, and took a long pull.

There was so much she wanted to know, but she couldn't turn this into an interrogation. "How did you end up in sales at TecLife?"

"That's a loaded question, but here's the sad, short version. I washed out of med school and took the best paying job I could find with the education I'd acquired."

"Do you like it? Or just tolerate it? Those pep rallies are hard to take."

He laughed. "You'll get numb to them. At least they don't frisk us every day when we leave."

What? "Why would they do that?"

"Some tech companies do it so their lab employees don't take home samples."

She realized she should have known that—for someone

who'd supposedly worked in the industry. "Does everyone in the company know about Slimbiotic? Decker acts like it's top secret."

"Some people do. But no one outside TecLife is supposed to know. They even conducted the clinical trials in Costa Rica to keep it away from the doctors who also do clinical trials for other companies."

The server brought their salads, and they ate quietly for a few minutes. But Dallas was on task and needed more. "Do you know why Decker's research is so personal to her? She kind of went off on me about it this morning."

Eric leaned in. "She has a daughter with Prader-Willi Syndrome. I overheard her talking to a specialist once. But no one else knows. Except maybe Max."

That was the personal connection. "What is Prader-Willi?"

"Insatiable appetite. People who can't stop eating. There is no cure, so they end up morbidly obese with all kinds of problems."

"That's sad." It also explained a lot about Decker. "How old is her daughter?"

"I think Amber is nine."

Yes! That would be her next password guess.

Eric reached out and squeezed her hand. "What about you? Do you have a boyfriend?"

"Not really. I like being single."

"You date, don't you?"

"Hell yeah," she said, mocking the morning cheer. "I like men. I just don't want a partner yet."

"We should go out sometime."

"Maybe this weekend." Dallas pushed her salad aside and finished her beer. "I should get back. Decker is under pressure from the FDA, and I'm trying to find the data she needs."

Eric dismissed the idea with a flick of his hand. "Decker is always under her own pressure. Don't let her push you."

"This is my first week, so I'll try to be Miss Industrious. After that"—Dallas gave an impish shrug—"We'll see."

They paid the check, each asking for their own receipt, and headed out into the intense July sun. Dallas was mentally moving on to her next plan. She needed to get her hands on Decker's phone and ensure that her boss would be occupied long enough for her to search it. Maybe even access Decker's email if she could get the scientist out of her office. Dallas had an idea but it required a little finesse. But now that she had the daughter's name, she could probably figure out Decker's password and peruse the files from her own desk.

"What about Friday night? Dinner and dancing?" Eric broke into her thoughts.

"Would love to. Unless Decker wants me to work late. Even then, we could always make it a late evening." He wasn't her type—cute but soft and too metrosexual—but it didn't matter. If Eric thought he might get laid, he could be manipulated. And she needed an ally in this crazy company.

They parted ways in the lobby, and Dallas headed for the stairs again. At her desk, she opened the data files she was supposed to be working on, then logged out of her own email. She found the internal email center, keyed in Decker's address, and tried *Amber* as a password. No luck. She tried *Amber9*, then *AmberDecker*, followed by *AmberDecker9*. A strikeout. She wished she knew the kid's birthday. Or her father's last name, if it was different. Dallas keyed in *AmDeck9* on a whim, and an email dialogue box opened. *She was in!*

The main inbox had only a dozen emails, all from the previous two days, but the saved folders contained thousands of messages. The labels had names such as FDA and San Carlos Clinic, and none looked personal. Dallas scanned the dozen in the inbox and spotted one from AmberGrace. She opened it and learned that Decker had missed a parent-teacher conference the week before and her daughter wasn't happy about it. Three of the other emails were a conversation with the FDA, and two were from Curtis Santera. Before she could access one, the door between their offices flew open, and Decker stepped in.

"I can't seem to access my email. Will you contact Pete, the tech guy?" Decker gestured impatiently. "I need the problem corrected immediately."

"Sure." Dallas logged out of Decker's account. Would the IT person know she'd accessed it? "I was having a problem with mine earlier, so I restarted my computer and that fixed it."

"I'll try it, but send Pete an email anyway. He needs to know we're having issues." Decker stepped toward her with a sealed manila envelope. "When you're done, take this over to Curtis Santera in the R&D building. His office is near the front, but he's probably in the lab. I'm about an hour behind schedule and don't have time."

"Happy to. I haven't seen the lab yet."

"Don't bother taking a tour while you're there. We need to finish this project and send the files to the FDA by tomorrow."

"All right." Dallas reached for the envelope, noticing a small lump in the middle. A product sample? A thumb drive? "I'll send a quick email, then scoot over and back."

"Thanks." Decker pivoted, rushed into her office, and closed the door.

Dallas didn't bother to send the email, not wanting to

alert the tech guy, and instead fingered the envelope. Could she open it, check the contents, and reseal it? Not without the proper tools, which she didn't have at the moment. She checked the pocket in her purse and still had the handcuffs and evidence bags. *The item in the envelope probably wasn't important,* she told herself—unless it was a proprietary product stolen from ProtoCell.

She headed downstairs and out the back of the building. A sidewalk led to the nearby R&D building. The factory was farther back and had its own entrance on a side street, but she could see a covered walkway between the two back buildings. A young man passed her going toward the offices and smiled. An employee she would probably never meet—if she succeeded at her mission.

The air was stagnant and humid, so she hurried across the open space and flashed her ID at the camera on the drab building. Inside, she blinked in adjustment to the indoor light. The small foyer had no windows and no reception area, just a chair and table by the door. Dallas ventured into a circular open area with doors on both sides. A narrow hall lay straight ahead. At the end of the darkened space, loud voices caught her attention. She moved quietly and stood outside an open door. The space led into a rectangular room filled with stainless steel appliances, microscopes, and cluttered workbenches.

A dark-toned man with a delicate mustache shouted at a younger man in thick glasses. From his profile on LinkedIn, she recognized the shouter as Curtis Santera.

"We don't have time to repeat every damn test. You have to be more careful!"

"I'm sorry. I didn't know the test bacteria was still stored in there with the microbiota." The lab worker gestured with both hands, his voice distressed. "We haven't used it in a recombinant process recently."

Bacteria. She needed a sample for the CDC.

"It's clearly labeled." Santera squeezed his forehead, as if to calm himself. "Cheryl will be distressed. The FDA has already set us back by asking for more information." His voice softened and he seemed to be talking to himself now.

"What do you want me to do?"

"Start over, work late, and don't screw up again."

The younger man walked away. Dallas watched him head toward a stainless steel vault with three big drawers. He opened the bottom one. Was that where she would find the right sample? The CDC had labeled it SA-13, but she had no idea what this company called it. She stepped into the room.

"Who are you?" Santera snapped.

"Jace Hunter. Cheryl Decker's new assistant. She asked me to bring this to you."

He snatched the envelope out of her hand, tore it open, and extracted a small container. Santera noticed she was still standing there, so he paused and waved her away. "You can leave."

Dallas nodded and turned, pausing in the hallway.

Behind her, Santera said, "SlimPros. Where the hell did Cheryl get these?"

Chapter 22

Monday, July 14, 10:35 a.m.

Jonas Brickman was sick of hearing about his weight, but he worked to keep his anger in check. This potential supporter was too important to alienate. "Do you really think voters care? I've been active in city politics for a decade, plus I'm a generous philanthropist. Shouldn't that be all that matters?" He'd been seeding his career shift for years.

"It should. But it's not. Your weight sends a message." Don Tavakole—fifty-eight and not exactly slim—shifted in the chair across from him, clearly uncomfortable. The millionaire and political activist had come to Jonas' office to talk about the mayoral campaign, but Tavakole was still in a negative mode. "People will make assumptions that you're lazy or unhealthy. Even if it's not a conscious thing. Even if they say they like you in political polls. At the voting booth, they'll abandon you. I'm sorry. But unless you start losing weight, my group can't support your campaign."

There it was. The PAC was withdrawing the money they'd promised. A hot rage filled his chest, and he wanted to punch Tavakole's ugly pinched face. Everything he'd been building for years was being snatched away. He would never be governor if he didn't get elected as mayor first. "I can lose the weight. I'd planned to anyway." He scrambled to form a convincing plan. "My company is ready to launch a revolutionary weight-loss product. It's called SlimPro, and I can be one of the first patients to get one implanted."

"I don't think there's enough time. The election is three months away."

"It's plenty of time. In fact, this is a great public relations opportunity." Liking the idea, Jonas leaned forward in his leather chair. "I'll issue a public challenge for people to join me in a city-wide weight-loss program. Then I'll do a series of interviews and talk about the challenges of losing weight. I think people will relate to it."

Tavakole was silent for a moment. "I don't know. It sounds like a great promotional idea for your product, but I don't think it will help your political campaign. It shows weakness."

Jonas' hands clenched into fists. *Weak?* He wanted to punch the prick in the mouth and show him some brute strength. But he forced himself to sound calm. "People love rooting for the underdog—as long as he wins in the end. And I intend to win." Rage, fear, and excitement drummed in his veins and he had to stand up. "I can lose three or four pounds a week for three months. By election day, I'll be transformed and voters will be won over." Jonas could see himself in front of City Hall, talking to reporters after the election, looking slim and healthy like he used to. He could do this.

"You have a lot of faith in your product." Tavakole's mouth turned up. "If it's that good, you'll end up so rich you won't need my money."

Jonas forced himself to smile back. "In time." SlimPro would be a moneymaker, for sure. But it didn't work for everybody. No drug did. Most medications only helped half, or fewer, of the people who took them. He'd already tried the peptide implant, back when they first tested it in humans. After losing only ten pounds, he quickly gained it back. His second implant had been even less effective. It just didn't work with his genetic structure. But fortunately, enough people in the clinical trials had benefitted, so it was approved and marketable.

Don Tavakole stood too. "We have another candidate in mind, but we'll wait and see how this goes. If you can lose forty pounds in the next two months, we'll fund your TV campaign."

"Still at two million?"

"We'll see." Tavakole reached out his hand.

Prick. Jonas shook it, smiling. "You *will* see. I'll get this set up immediately and do the implant and video in a few days."

Tavakole breezed out, taking his potent cologne with him. Jonas plopped down, sweat pooling in his armpits and soaking the back of his pressed white shirt. He yanked off his jacket and forced himself to breath slowly. He'd just committed to losing five pounds a week for eight weeks. The only way to make it happen was to cut out the carbs and live on protein and vegetables. And exercise every day. Oh god, he'd have to get up early and start swimming laps again.

He was about to become the public face of SlimPro, and its success was dependent on his success. Now his political future was dependent on him losing weight too. Something he hadn't been able to do in the decade since he'd gained it all. *Fuck!*

Jonas opened his top drawer and reached for a small flask of scotch he kept for occasional stress. He'd have to be careful and not let small sips become long gulps. His thoughts turned to Cheryl. She and her TecLife team were working on a new weight-loss product, but damned if he could find out anything. The freelancer he'd hired to steal their files had brought back a thumb drive full of data, but none of it was that useful. The target—for him and Cheryl, first as a team, then as competitors—had always been a widely effective weight-loss product. The peptide implant had resulted from her research, and she had to be gleeful that it hadn't worked for him personally. He wouldn't blame her, except that the bitch had set fire to his warehouse, costing him thousands in lost sales. He couldn't prove she'd done it, but who else?

The intercom interrupted his thoughts. Jonas shoved the flask away and pressed the respond button. "Yes?"

"Dominic Prill is here to see you. He says it's important."

For a moment, he didn't place the name.

"From R&D," his assistant prompted.

"Yes. Send him in." *Please let it be good news.* He started to reach for his jacket, then changed his mind. He didn't need to impress his employees.

The scientist was in his late twenties, ridiculously thin, and not smiling.

"Have a seat."

Dominic perched on the edge of a chair and repeatedly clicked the pen in his hand.

Jonas resisted the urge to snatch it away. "Just relax and tell me what's going on."

"Someone took three SlimPros from the sample batch."

No! "How is that possible? Unless it was an employee."

"A woman drugged me at the gym." A pink flush spread over Dominic's cheeks, and he cast his eyes down. "I think she put me in a wheelchair and used my palm-pass to get into the vault. I barely remember any of it. I woke up in my car about three in the morning, feeling drugged and confused."

Oh hell. Cheryl again? It had to be. But why did she want the SlimPro? Was her own product failing? "What did the kidnapper look like?"

"I'm not sure. I have a vague memory of a tall blond woman waiting at the front of the gym."

Not Cheryl, but maybe someone she hired. "You say she took three?"

"I counted our supply this morning, and that's what's missing."

"Thank you for telling me." He couldn't bring himself to let the researcher off the hook. "We'll have to increase our security. And you should be more vigilant."

"Yes, sir." Dominic blinked a few times. "Are you going to report the incident to the authorities? I'd prefer not to."

What did his employee have to hide from law enforcement? "I don't think they can help us. But I'll have our security team check the video footage and see if the cameras caught her." Jonas was torn. He desperately wanted to stop Cheryl and find out what the hell she had in development. But he didn't want the FBI coming around again. Things had been too weird lately.

Yet now that Cheryl had the SlimPro and could start reverse engineering, his company had to fast-track the launch. Instead of producing a small test batch this week, the manufacturing plant needed to scale-up and produce a full run—so they could get the product on trucks and out to as many clinics as possible.

He reached for his desk phone, temples pounding. He'd never felt so much pressure.

Chapter 23

Monday, July 14, 3:20 p.m.

Cortez waited in a conference room in the massive downtown headquarters, where all six homicide teams worked. He drank his coffee, studied his notes, and practiced his presentation. He wanted to sound professional, with an excellent command of the terminology. A flutter in his stomach, as he realized he had nothing significant to report. Would Hawthorne start giving Harris the legwork and make him comb through the paper trail?

This would be the first time the three had met together to discuss the case. Hawthorne had been in the hospital until Saturday, keeping everyone updated by phone, then had come into headquarters that morning to get caught up. He'd been abrupt when he'd called Cortez to set up the meeting. Maybe Hawthorne had run out of pain meds.

A moment later, the older detective crutched through the open door, his canvas briefcase slung around his neck. Following him was Detective Harris, a matronly woman in her early forties with a long, horse-like face. She had a reputation for sharp analysis, and Cortez hoped to learn from her.

"Good afternoon." He stood to show respect for both.

"Not really." Hawthorne lowered himself into a chair and set his crutches on the floor. "Sergeant Riggs will join us shortly wanting an update. He scheduled a press conference for this afternoon and wants something to report."

"We may have a lead." Harris went to the case board and began mapping out the evidence. "We should have done this on Friday," she mumbled as she wrote. "But the College Killer case still takes priority over a B-list actor."

B-list? "James Avery was a classy Hollywood star," Cortez argued. "Those designations are not just about how much money a movie earns."

"Don't hyperventilate. Hawthorne told me to say that." She gave him a wicked grin. "I'm a James Avery fan too, but only a few actors past fifty are still a big box office draw."

Hawthorne cut in. "Let's focus please." He turned to Cortez. "What did you learn this morning about Avery's appointment at ProLabs?"

"Not much." He cleared his throat. "The victim arrived at four-thirty for a DNA analysis. He was probably under a court order because of the paternity suit filed by Alicia Freison. Blood was taken and submitted to their in-house lab analysts, but they won't have results until later this week." Cortez paused, forgetting what else he wanted to say.

"When did the victim leave?" Harris asked.

That was it. "I don't know. The appointment should have only taken five or ten minutes, but the receptionist doesn't remember seeing him walk out the door."

"What does that mean?" Hawthorne's tone had an edge.

"Probably nothing. She could have been away from her station." Had he failed to ask the right questions? "But no one saw him or heard from Avery after that. The lab doesn't have any security cameras inside the building, but they monitor the front door from outside. I asked the manager to send me the video for late that afternoon."

"Let us know what you find out."

"What about his family?" Harris asked. "I'm sure Avery has a sizable estate."

"His widow has a solid alibi until about ten with her yoga instructor, and his son lives in Oceanside. Julian Avery says he was home with his family, and his wife corroborates that."'

Harris turned from the case board. "Who stands to inherit? Have you read the will?"

Heat rushed to Cortez's cheeks. "His wife thinks the money will be divided between her and his son. But she hasn't seen the last version of the will. Avery's lawyer was out of town last week, but I left messages for him to call me. I'll stop at his office first thing tomorrow."

"What about the paternity suit? Did you find the woman?"

Sergeant Riggs strode through the door. "What have you got for me? The press conference is in twenty minutes. Most of the questions will be about the College Killer, and the lieutenant will take those, but someone will ask about James Avery."

Hawthorne gestured. "Cortez was going to tell us about a lawsuit he's following up on."

All eyes were on him, so he sat up straight. "Her name is Alicia Freison, and I questioned her Saturday morning. She claims James Avery is the father of her four-year-old son and that the DNA test will prove it. She has an alibi for Tuesday night, but it's her sister, so I don't have much faith in it." Cortez hesitated. Should he offer his opinion? It seemed important. "Whoever killed Avery either transported him out to the cannery or met him there. Then they punched him in the face repeatedly and gave him an overdose of barbiturates.

Freison doesn't seem physically big enough to do that by herself, and she had nothing to gain by killing Avery."

A moment of silence.

Harris spoke up. "Unless she thinks his heirs are more likely to settle with her now that he's dead. Instead of going to court, I mean. We need to bring her in for questioning. She probably has a thug boyfriend."

"I agree." Hawthorne glared at Cortez. "Make it a priority."

Cortez thought it was a waste of time, but he wasn't running the case. "Copy that."

"Is that all you've got?" Riggs gestured with impatience.

What was he forgetting? Cortez glanced at his notes. The truth serum. "The medical examiner's office called this morning and said Avery had sodium thiopental in his blood. It's a barbiturate that's sometimes used by psychiatrists to relax patients or get them to tell the truth."

"What the hell?" Hawthorne stared, open-mouthed. "Was that the only drug in his system?"

"He also had high levels of phenobarbital, which is what killed him. There was only a trace amount of the thiopental, but I think someone wanted information. That would explain the beating and the drug."

Riggs shook his head. "I can't tell the media that. They'll go nuts with speculation."

"Why didn't I get a copy of the toxicology report?" Hawthorne demanded.

Cortez didn't know and refused to feel guilty. He had enjoyed delivering that revelation. "The full blood-work analysis hasn't been done, and the assistant ME was returning my call."

"I have to go prep," Riggs said. "I'm sorry I can't get more people on the team, but the College Killer is still out there preying on young women, so that has to be our priority." He turned and left.

Hawthorne glanced back and forth between the two detectives. "What else have we learned?" His eyes settled on Harris.

"The paper trail wasn't helpful." She gave a small shrug. "Avery's phone records revealed nothing of value. The day of his death, he took a call from his manager around noon, and made a call to a cosmetic clinic to set up appointments for laser treatments. That's it. Except for all the calls from his wife, asking where he was and when he'd be home. There isn't anything unusual in the days leading up to his death either."

"His bank and credit cards?" Hawthorne tapped his cast, his jaw set.

"Nothing interesting," Harris said. "No large deposits or withdrawals. No unusual purchases."

Hawthorne turned to Cortez. "Where was Avery between the time he left his house and the time he reached Prolabs?"

"Playing golf. I checked it out on Friday. He was with two friends. Nothing unusual."

"Oh, hell. We have to be missing something." Hawthorne looked pained and shifted his cast to a new position.

Harris paced in front of the board. "If the killer wanted information, it was probably about money or valuables. Maybe Avery has a stockpile of cash, and they wanted the combination to his safe."

"Why not take him to his house?" Cortez countered.

"What if Avery screwed somebody over?" Harris asked. "Maybe a producer or somebody who'd invested money in a film project."

"It's possible. But I talked to his agent and his friends. He wasn't involved in any films. Everyone is mystified."

Another silence.

Finally, Cortez said, "I'll pick up Alicia Freison for questioning tomorrow and canvas the businesses around ProLabs again to see if anyone witnessed anything in the parking lot."

"ProLabs." Harris' eyes lit up. "Who owns the company?"

Cortez checked his notes. "An investment group called Biomed Holdings."

Harris snapped her thick fingers. "Avery is one of the investors. I saw an earnings report that was included in the financial information his accountant gave me." She jotted the firm's name on the board.

"So Avery is a partial owner of the business where he was seen last?" Hawthorne squinted at the board. "I don't know what it means, but we have to follow up." He looked at Cortez again. "Go back to ProLabs and get a look at their books."

As Hawthorne grabbed his crutches and struggled to his feet, he gestured at Harris. "You pick up the Freison woman and question her. She might open up better for a woman." He slung his briefcase around his neck. "I'm heading home."

"You might wait in your office until the reporters are gone," Harris called after him.

Hawthorne groaned and kept moving.

Cortez grabbed his satchel and strode to the front of the department, where several distressed civilians waited their turn to talk to the desk clerk. He wanted to see how Riggs was handling the press conference. The desk clerk spotted him and warned, "It's a circus out there."

Cortez nodded. "I want to see how it's handled."

He pushed out the doors, surprised by the crowd. At least ten reporters, plus camera guys were gathered. The sun beat down, and one older man in the back wore a sun-brella on his hat.

A young female reporter asked, "What about James Avery? Can you tell us how he died?"

Riggs wiped his dark brow. "We know two things from the autopsy: Avery died of an overdose of barbiturates. But he also experienced blows to his head prior to his death, so the medical examiner's office has ruled it a homicide."

The crowd stirred with excitement, and a different young woman called out, "Do you have a suspect?" It was Risa Rispoli, who he'd had a crush on for years. But today, he didn't feel it. Adie had called Saturday, they'd had dinner, and she'd won over his heart.

The sergeant spotted Cortez and motioned for him to come over. "We're following several leads, but we haven't made any arrests."

"What about motive?" Risa asked. "Who would want to kill a well-known actor?"

"We're not at liberty to talk about it yet. But Detective Cortez—" Sergeant Riggs turned and nodded at him—"is a member of the homicide team and is looking into a legal matter that Avery had pending. We'll know more soon."

A little red meat for the wolves with microphones and notepads. A few of the reporters might be industrious enough to track down Avery's lawyer or call the court and see what they could discover. Cortez had to get there first.

Risa took three quick steps to where he was standing. She shoved the microphone at him. "The rumor is that James Avery had a paternity lawsuit pending. Is that connected to his death?"

His throat closed up and he caught himself blinking. Finally he squeaked out, "I'm still looking into that." She started to ask another question, but he cut her off. "We need the public's help. Mr. Avery was last seen at four-thirty Tuesday afternoon. But he didn't die until after eight that evening. We need to know where he was in between. If anyone saw him during that time, please call our tip line immediately."

Chapter 24

Monday, July 14, 5:25 p.m.

Dallas watched the clock, waiting for employees to leave the building. Her boss would probably work late, but she didn't know Decker's pattern yet. The bacteria samples in the lab called to Dallas. Grabbing one and sending it to the CDC seemed critical. If the pathogen matched Palmer's wound samples, that would give the bureau what it needed for a comprehensive search warrant. How late would the lab people stay? She would wait them out if she had to.

Decker stepped out of her office, looking surprised. "You're still here?"

"I wanted to finish this project. You said the FDA needed it right away."

"Thanks." Decker gave her first tiny smile. "But don't work too late. As long as we send it tomorrow." She stepped toward the outer door. "I'm going down for coffee. Want some?"

"Sure. Thanks."

Decker strode out.

Had the boss forgotten to lock her office door? Dallas waited until the footsteps in the hall faded, then jumped up and scooted around her desk. The inner doorknob turned easily. *Yes!* She hurried in. How much time did she have? Seven or eight minutes for Decker to make two cups of coffee and climb a flight of stairs. What could she accomplish? She had already accessed Decker's email and could do it again. Her cell phone. Dallas trotted to the big desk and scanned the surface. Stacked folders covered most of it, but a small space by her mouse pad was clear, and the phone was there. Dallas picked it up, not caring about fingerprints, and pressed the active button. The screen lit up, but asked for a password. She keyed in *AmDeck9,* but it failed. *Damn.* She tried a couple more, then gave up, and put the phone back exactly how it had been. The bureau had probably requested Decker's tracking information, but since government surveillance had become a public issue, the phone companies had been hesitant to supply customer information without a subpoena.

Knowing she had little time, Dallas scooted back into the outer office and grabbed her purse. She found the bottom flap, unzipped her secret compartment, and pulled out a tiny recording device. It surprised her they'd had enough probable cause to get the affidavit signed. But federal judges tended to be sympathetic about dead law enforcement personnel. Dallas touched her Kel-Tec out of habit, then zipped it back out of sight. Maybe three minutes left. She rushed into Decker's office and placed the self-adhering bug under the desk, far enough back that it wouldn't be discovered.

Dallas raced out of the main office and closed the door behind her. Footsteps echoed by the outer door. She plopped into her chair and stared at her monitor. Decker came in, and Dallas looked up. "That coffee smells great."

"I hope you like it black."

"I do." She reached out for the paper cup. "Thanks." After

taking a small sip, she asked, "Are we the only ones working late, or is it pretty common for employees?"

"It varies, but it's Monday so I think it's just us. I'm leaving by six-thirty and so should you."

"Do you have children at home?"

"Just one. But she's with a caregiver." Decker flinched, as if in pain, then spun and strode into her office.

Dallas worked just long enough to drink half the coffee, then slung her bag across her chest—in case she had to move quickly—and headed out. The building was silent as she took the elevator down and walked the hallways to the back exit. The administrative and sales people all seemed to have gone home. Outside the back door, the R&D lab loomed across the grassy expanse, but the sun was still so bright she couldn't tell how many lights were still on. She hurried across to the other building, the heat making her skin moist before she got there.

As she stood at the entrance, Dallas slipped her hand into the outside pocket of her bag and rubbed the familiar scrap of cloth. She wanted to pull it out and sniff, but wouldn't risk someone witnessing it.

Feeling confident, she flashed her badge at the camera, the door clicked and Dallas stepped in. A beeping noise startled her. An alarm? *Oh hell.* She glanced around for a place to shut it down and spotted a small silver box on a side wall. She rushed over, pressed the most-prominent button, and held her breath. The beeping stopped.

But what had it activated? She'd used a badge, but clearly the company wanted to know when an employee entered the building after hours. She remembered the morning meeting about stepping up security. They'd acted very quickly. She waited for a few minutes to see if a lab worker would come to the front in response to the alarm. When no one did, she made her way back to the research area she'd visited that morning, walking quietly and listening for the sound of others. Lights were on everywhere, but the building was quiet except for the hum of air conditioning.

At the end of the hall, the door to the lab was closed this time. And probably locked. *Damn.* Would her badge open it or did she need special access? Dread tickled the back of her neck. She spotted the security box on the wall and reached for her badge. A sneeze welled up, and she suppressed it, letting out only a small harsh-breath sound. *Please let that be the only one.* Dallas slid her badge into the slot. The locking mechanism clicked. She grabbed the handle and pushed into the room. The researchers had left for the day, their stainless-steel work benches cleared-off and shiny, the microscopes all lined up for the next round of slides in the morning.

Feeling a sense of urgency, Dallas crossed the room, heading straight for the cold vault the lab worker had accessed after Santera yelled at him. She reached for the handle on the bottom, then hesitated. Should she put on latex first? Dallas glanced around, looking for a box or dispenser full of gloves.

Footsteps pounded in the hallway, making her heart jump. *Someone was coming!* She yanked open the bottom drawer, feeling a cold blast, then grabbed a handle and pulled out a tray of vials and Petri dishes. She took one of each, slid them into evidence bags, and shoved them to the bottom of her purse. She was about to be caught, but at least she had the bacteria samples to walk away with. She might even be able to bullshit her way out of this and not lose the job.

The door opened and Curtis Santera call out, "What are

you doing in here?"

"I wanted to talk to the lab worker who was here earlier today. I thought he might be working late."

"Clearly, he's not, and you have no business in this building after hours."

"I'm sorry." Dallas gave him her best innocent, about-to-cry look. "I didn't know it was off limits. This is only my second day at TecLife."

"What did you want to see Josh about?"

"His name's Josh?" She let her face fall in disappointment. "I only got a glimpse of him this morning, but he looked like someone I went to high school with. An old boyfriend. But I guess it's not him." She let out a small sigh. "I would have talked to him then, but you were mad, and it seemed like a bad time."

"It's still a bad time." Santera gave an angry shake of his head. "Get out and stay out, unless Cheryl sends you." He stepped aside to let her pass.

"Okay. I said I was sorry." Dallas started for the door. A tiny clinking sound in her purse filled the quiet room.

"Stop." Santera grabbed her arm. "Did you take something from the lab?"

Dallas fought to calm her thumping heart. "Why would I? Let go of me." She pulled free and started walking again.

"Stop or I'm calling security."

Shit! She turned back and gave him her best smile. "I'm sorry you're having a bad day. Please don't take it out on me."

"Let me see what's in your purse."

Her pulse pounded in her ears as she tried to come up with a believable explanation for having bacteria vials in her purse. *Oh fuck it.* Santera was either part of the criminal activity and could be turned to bust the others, or possibly a source of insider information. She glanced up and down Santera's body to see if he was carrying a gun. Not that she could tell.

"I'm an FBI agent. And I have taken bacteria samples that likely match a pathogen that killed another agent."

His mouth fell open and he blinked rapidly. A moment later, he scoffed loudly. "No you're not. You're a spy from ProtoCell. I'm calling the police." He reached for his cell phone.

Dallas lunged forward, grabbed both his wrists, and squeezed the pressure points until he dropped the phone.

"Ow! Shit. That hurt." His expression was a mix of pain and confusion.

She eased up, but didn't let go. His body language didn't show any sign of aggression, so she released her grip and stepped out of striking range. "You need to come with me to the bureau and answer questions. But first, kick the phone over here."

For a long moment, he didn't move, his eyes twitching as he calculated his options.

"I have a gun in my purse, but I can put you on the floor faster than you can say 'What the fuck?' So push the cell phone over with your foot and turn around." With one hand, she reached in and unzipped the pocket, not taking her eyes off him.

He kicked the phone. "Prove you're an FBI Agent. Call the bureau or something. We had a spy in here on Friday." His eyes widened. "The first day you started. What a coincidence."

She finally had the compartment open and the plastic-tie cuffs in her fingers. The gun was accessible now too. "We suspect you in the murder of Agent Joe Palmer. Cooperate and turn around."

Santera bolted through the door.

Dallas sprinted after him. She caught him mid-point in the hall and grabbed the back of his shirt. After looping a foot around his ankle, she shoved his back with her free hand. Santera went down hard, barely getting his hands under him. Knees on his back, she jerked his left arm up, looped the plastic cuff over a wrist, and grabbed his other arm. When he was secured, she started working through the cover-up. "Are there cameras in this hall?"

"No." He rolled over and struggled to sit up. "This isn't necessary. I'm not a criminal. But I'm convinced you're with the FBI."

"Good. Think of this as protective custody. Are there cameras in the lab where I took the samples?"

"Yes."

Shit. "Let's find the footage and destroy it."

Then what? She needed River's help to get him into the bureau. Her cover was still intact, and she had to keep it that way.

Chapter 25

Monday, July 14, 7:40 p.m.

Watching Grissom to see if he would meet anyone made River's nerves jangle. The big-screen TVs and loud music were not her scene, and she was restless to get moving. She glanced over again. The man was off his stool and reaching for his briefcase. *Finally.* He'd been drinking at the bar for an hour without so much as a trip to the urinal. Should she watch to see where he went? The text he'd received the week before, from someone asking him to bring cash, flashed in her mind. The screenshot Dallas had captured said *our usual spot at 8.* River checked her phone: 7:42. Was Grissom meeting his contact again? She needed to stay with him and find out.

River sat back down and turned away from the door. Grissom would have to pass behind her, then she'd pick him up outside. Not ideal, but it was too late to do anything else. He wasn't likely to notice a strong-jawed, middle-age woman in jeans and a T-shirt.

After he pushed out the door, she counted to five, then followed. On the sidewalk, she spotted him heading to the right. The sun was sinking in the sky, but people were still clipping down the sidewalk, in search of something—food, entertainment, or maybe just escape.

Ahead, Grissom disappeared behind a young couple coming her way. River quickened her pace. After the couple passed, she spotted her target veering off into a building. A moment later, the Sunset Motel came into view, surprising her. The neighborhood was otherwise a mix of industry and apartments, but not an area she was familiar with. She'd grown up north in the university area and hadn't ventured out much as a teenager.

Why a hotel? Was he meeting the hired saboteur? It didn't look like an establishment with a drink lounge for conversations. River hurried to the front door, made of solid wood that kept her from seeing inside. She hesitated to go in. If the lobby was small and Grissom was the only person at the counter, he might turn and get a good look at her, compromising her ability to tail him. A deep breath calmed her. She would wait a minute for him to register, then take a peek. If he'd disappeared, she'd question the clerk.

A woman in high heels strode noisily up the sidewalk. She looked like a tall Dolly Parton, with a bouncy blond wig and breasts that were significantly larger than her tight red dress. The woman headed inside the motel, and River stuck her foot in the door before it closed, catching a glimpse of the interior. Dimly lit with dark wood-paneled walls. But her focus was on the counter, where Grissom stood with his back to her. The blonde stepped up next to him, their bodies only inches apart.

The clerk greeted her, calling her *Tasha*. Grissom didn't speak or look at the woman, but before he walked toward the stairs, he gave her a pat on the ass.

A hooker. Grissom's eight o'clock cash meetings were about sex—or some other private need. Tasha *could* be a well-disguised corporate-thief/arsonist, but that seemed unlikely. River let the door close.

On her way back, her phone beeped. A text from Dallas: *Things went south, and I have Santera in custody. Need you to pick him up.*

Oh dear. River wanted to call and ask questions, but texting was safer, in case there were other employees in the building and Dallas wasn't free to speak. She keyed: *Be there in six minutes. Where should I meet you?*

A block later, Dallas texted back: *Side parking lot, next to the R&D building. Dumpster.*

The image made her smile. River jogged for two blocks, then had to walk again. Her morning yoga kept her flexible but didn't do a damn thing for her stamina. The thought of taking up running to get in shape distressed her, so she quickly let it go. This assignment was unusual and personal, and her typical work in Eugene didn't require her to be an athlete.

Her rental car was on a now-empty block, and she made a last-minute decision to drive it over. Less risk of someone in the company spotting the head of R&D being walked away in cuffs, then alerting someone that they were under investigation. She cruised to the back of the R&D parking lot and spotted the dark dumpster. River waited in the car, windows open, assuming that less activity was better. A moment later, Dallas came around the metal container, leading Santera, who was cuffed behind his back. Dallas opened the passenger door, and the R&D man climbed in, smelling like a clove-flavored e-cigarette.

"You don't have to leave me cuffed. I'm not a criminal." Whiny and irritated.

Dallas shut the door and came around to River's side. "He

tried to run, so we have to assume he has something to hide."

"I thought you were a ProtoCell spy." Santera leaned toward them, angry now. "You never showed me a badge."

River pushed his shoulder and forced him back into his own space. She displayed her badge. "When we put you into an interrogation room, it will seem more real." She turned to Dallas, who was dressed in a short skirt and sleeveless blouse and didn't look like an agent. "What have we got on him?"

"Nothing." Dallas grimaced. "He caught me taking bacteria from the lab, so I had to do something." She pulled two plastic bags from her oversized purse. "But we finally have samples to compare to Palmer's tissue."

River felt her first real hope that her friend and mentor would get justice. "Do you feel compromised? Do you need to get out?"

"I don't think so. But that depends on Santera and how long we can hold him. Or if he's willing to work with us."

And whether they could trust him not to warn the others, River thought. She had to find a reason to hold him. "We'll do our part."

"We'd better both get out of here." Dallas gave a little mock salute. "Keep me posted."

River nodded, rolled up the windows and cranked the air conditioning. This would be a long night, but they might finally get some answers.

The interrogation room in the San Diego bureau was much like the one in every other FBI office she'd been in— windowless and oppressive. But that was the point. She uncuffed Santera and sat down. Agent King joined them moments later, carrying a mug of coffee. They'd agreed that he would take a harsh lead, then River would follow up with a softer approach.

Santera leaned toward King, eager for a new audience. "This episode is beyond acceptable. I will sue the bureau for false arrest if you don't let me out of here immediately."

"Have you ever heard of anyone winning such a suit against the FBI?" King's tone was dry and amused.

Santera's mouth tightened. "What is this about?"

"The death of an FBI agent from a toxic bacteria. An agent who was looking into TecLife's activities." King stayed on his feet, one step away from their suspect.

"What activities?"

"We'll ask the questions," King said. "Did you meet Agent Palmer?"

"No."

"Where were you on April tenth?"

Santera blinked. "I'd have to check my calendar. Why?"

"A warehouse owned by ProtoCell burned down and a security guard died. What do you know about that?"

"Just what I read in the news." A look of alarm flashed in Santera's eyes. "You think I had something to do with that?"

"We know someone at TecLife is sabotaging its competitors." King hit the table for effect. "How much stock do you own in the company?"

"I have a twenty percent share. So?"

"You have a lot to gain from a billion-dollar product about to launch. Why not take out the competition?"

Santera shook his head. "I'm a medical scientist. That means I've spent years in the lab pursuing a new chemical or mechanism of action. I'm patient and passive. I had nothing to do with any of this."

Chest forward, Santera's body language was open,

pleading. He also glanced back and forth, meeting both their eyes. River thought he might be telling the truth. She spoke up. "Someone in your company committed arson and murder. Who do you think it was?"

"I find that hard to believe. The two founders are also scientists. I just can't see either of them doing anything criminal."

River took over, keeping her tone pleasant. "The bacteria samples will go to the CDC. If they match Agent Palmer's tissue, we'll get a search warrant for everything—your computers, product data, financial information, and cell phones. You might as well tell us what you know now and cut a deal."

"I don't know anything!" Panic in his voice now.

"Then you have to work with us to find out."

"What do you mean?"

"For starters, keep our agent's presence at TecLife confidential."

King broke in. "Excuse us for a moment."

River stood and followed him out. In the hallway, King turned to her. "I don't want to let him go until we can get a search warrant."

River didn't either, but she didn't see a way to hold him. "What will we charge him with?"

"Didn't you say he resisted arrest?"

"That won't hold. Dallas was undercover and taking something from the lab."

"Do you want to let him go back to work?"

"No. Dallas could be compromised. I wish we had something on him."

"Our guys are digging for that now."

"Let's press him about Grissom and Decker and see if he

knows more about their activities."

King looked skeptical. "Then what?"

"We let him go, tell him to call in sick for a few days, and park an agent on his doorstep."

"He could still make calls and warn the others."

"We tap into his conversations and he leads us to them. Let's use him if we can."

A young analyst hurried up the hallway. "I just found something. Santera was investigated for a stock-swap scheme six months ago, but the SEC couldn't make a case."

King gave a sly smile. "Let's go break him."

Chapter 26

Tuesday, July 15, 5:45 a.m.

Cortez made two bowls of oatmeal with banana slices and put one down for Grumpy. "Sorry, I'm out of apples." He petted the pig's head, knowing Grumpy would finish his breakfast before he could sit down with his. Cortez turned on the television to catch the morning news, then snapped his fingers at Grumpy to leave the room. He didn't like being eyeballed or bothered while he ate.

The TV newscaster reminded him of Adie, and he wondered what she was having for breakfast. She'd ordered pork tenderloin with a chile relleno on their date and had eaten with gusto. He'd liked that. No pretending to be delicate. Adie had also mentioned playing basketball three times a week to keep in shape. Cortez had wanted to ask her if she liked dancing, but wasn't ready to admit to her that he did. Their date had ended early, with her kissing him on the cheek, but they'd agreed to go out again this weekend.

What would she think of Grumpy? Dread filled his stomach and ruined his breakfast. Was that why he was still single? Because he was afraid to bring women home? He'd rescued Grumpy from an abusive scene after booking a Puerto Rican couple into jail, both on assault charges. The plan had been to find the pig a permanent home elsewhere, but the longer he stayed, the less Cortez had looked for a new caregiver.

He cleared the breakfast dishes, took Grumpy for a walk around the block, then strapped on his weapon and headed out. He wanted to be at ProLabs before it opened. His sense that it was the key to solving Avery's homicide had only grown. It could be coincidence that Avery had gone to a lab where he was an investor—the day he turned up dead—but the video surveillance made that unlikely. Cortez had watched it at the department the evening before, and during the span of four to six p.m., the actor had not walked out the front door. Either someone had doctored the footage, or Avery had stayed inside the facility after it had closed. Or possibly had left out a back door. All of which seemed odd for a man with a simple blood test appointment. Cortez planned to obtain and view more footage of later in the evening, but he needed to ask a lot more questions of the people who worked there.

The same receptionist was on duty, and her smile collapsed when she saw him. "You're back."

"And more determined than ever." Cortez smiled. "I'd like a list of everyone who was in the building between four and six last Tuesday."

"I'll see if I can figure that out." She sighed and clicked her keyboard. "I heard that James Avery was beaten and drugged. What makes you think someone here knows anything about that?"

A young couple came in the door, and Cortez stepped aside. The receptionist excused herself, checked them in, and led the clients to a blood-draw station.

When she came back, she said, "I think it's a short list. Just me, two phlebotomists, the manager, and a bookkeeper. The lab people come in early and leave by four." She wrote down the names. "They're all here now except Wilona. She comes in at ten."

Cortez took the list and decided to start with the bookkeeper. He wanted financial information.

"You never answered my question," the receptionist said. "Why do you think someone here was involved in his murder?"

"The security video shows that he didn't leave out the front door after his appointment, so Avery stayed in the building after hours or left some other way."

She made a face. "That's weird. The back door is an emergency exit only, and the alarm didn't go off."

Had Avery been drugged and carried out after hours? Had the perp been stupid enough to leave the evidence on the video footage? "Call the security company please. I need the rest of the file from six to ten."

"I'll have to ask my boss."

"Call now and tell him to send it immediately. If he argues, hand the phone to me."

She did as instructed and didn't seem to get any flak.

"I'll start with the bookkeeper," Cortez said, when she'd hung up. "Where can I find him or her?"

"Zurie's in the back office." She pointed down the opposite hallway from the blood-draw rooms.

The manager was in the office with the bookkeeper, and Cortez could hear their voices through the closed door. They were arguing about a quarterly report, but he couldn't hear everything or process the information fast enough. He knocked on the door, but they ignored him and continued arguing. He tried the doorknob, but it was locked. *Weird.*

On impulse, he decided to check out the back exit. A metal door at the end of the hall with a red push-bar handle and a sign warning that an alarm would sound. No window indicating what was behind the building. To the right was a door that said *Testing Lab.* Cortez walked in, hoping to ask questions, even though the technicians had supposedly left before Avery arrived. Equipment filled a back wall, and two young men in blue scrubs and hairnets hunched over microscopes.

"Excuse me." Cortez waited for their attention. They looked up, one seeming irritated, while the other was hard to read behind thick glasses. "I'm Detective Cortez with SDPD, and I'd like to ask a few questions."

"Like what?"

"Did you see the actor James Avery in the building last Tuesday afternoon?"

Blank looks. "We don't see clients," Glasses guy said. "Just the *ple-bots* who bring us the blood to analyze."

Cortez stepped toward them and pulled out his notepad. "When did you leave that day?"

"Three-thirty, as always." The annoyed one spoke this time.

Cortez asked their names and jotted them down, but it seemed pointless. "Thanks." He started to leave, then had a funny thought and turned back. "Is there another way out of the building besides the front door and the emergency door?"

"Sort of." Irritated lab guy cracked a small smile.

"What do you mean?"

"There's an old enclosed walkway between here and the building behind us, but no one uses it."

A tremor of excitement raced up his spine. "What

building is it connected to?"

"ProtoCell. We're owned by the same company."

In which Avery was an investor. "Show me the entrance."

The technician led him to a storage area with a metal door in the corner.

"Is it locked?" Cortez asked.

"Usually. We keep the key on the window shelf." The technician reached up and located it. "Do you want to go in?"

"Not yet." Cortez was trying to visualize Avery taking this route. "Did you see a client, an older man, enter the walkway last Tuesday?"

They both shook their heads. Cortez slipped on gloves, held out his hand for the key, and unlocked the door. It opened into a narrow passage that reminded him of a walkway in a small airport. Heart thumping, he turned back to the technicians. "Where does this come out in the other building?"

Glasses guy said, "In the R&D wing."

"Does everyone who works here know about it?"

"I think so."

"Thank you." He would explore the passage, but not just yet. First, he needed to get the team's specialist to come out and take fingerprints from the doorknob. Right now, it was time to see what the heck was going on at ProtoCell.

Once he was outside, doubts flooded him, and he stood on the sidewalk, uncertain. How would James Avery have known about the passage and why would he use it? Cortez could hear Hawthorne asking in a tone that implied his protégé was either stupid or crazy. But he had to trust his instincts. He called Hawthorne and left a message, asking him to start reviewing the new chunk of ProLabs' surveillance video as soon as it came. "I don't think Avery walked out the front door after his appointment," he added. "Something weird is going on, and I'm headed to ProtoCell to find out."

He went around to the back of the building to view the walkway from the exterior. It was about half the length of a football field and crossed a patch of wild grass before connecting with an older, metal-sided structure attached to the back of the newer building. The siding on the walkway had faded to an ugly sage green, indicating it had been there for decades.

Cortez jogged along a strip of cropped lawn to reach the front of the other building. From the street perspective, the ProtoCell offices—three stories of tinted glass and sandstone-colored concrete—sat around the block from ProLabs. The corner between them was occupied by a coffee shop and specialty bookstore that shared some of the parking space in the middle of the block.

Cortez approached the front door, pressed the buzzer, and asked to be let in. A receptionist, spoke through the intercom on the security plate. "Show me your badge and tell me who you want to see."

Cortez complied. "I'll start with Jonas Brickman, the CEO."

"I'll see if he's in."

Her lack of cooperation annoyed him. "I'm investigating a murder. Open the door."

Footsteps behind him made him turn. A big man in a white button-down shirt approached. At six-two, he carried the extra weight better than most people would. Cortez recognized him right away. The ProtoCell CEO had a political website promoting his run for mayor, and Cortez had found him online soon after learning Avery owned part of his company. His size and broadly handsome face made him easily identifiable.

"Jonas Brickman?"

"Yes. Who are you?"

"Detective Cortez, SDPD. I need to ask some questions."

"About what?"

Cortez straightened his spine and pulled his shoulders back to give himself more height. Brickman made him feel like a kid. "The death of James Avery."

A pause. "You mean the actor?"

"Yes. Let's go inside."

"I don't know why you could possibly want to talk to me." Brickman slid his ID card into the security slot. "But come in and let's get this over with. I'm a busy man."

"When do you start running for the mayor's race?" Cortez followed him into the cool building, as the receptionist's voice buzzed behind them.

"In the fall, but I'm gearing up now."

"What happens with your company while you're campaigning?"

"We have many capable people here, and I plan to win and give up my leadership role."

They crossed a lobby encased in shiny silver-and-white tiles and boarded the elevator. Cortez wondered about Brickman's net worth. He'd founded the company, so he owned much of the stock, in addition to drawing a nice salary.

Another man in a suit scurried on the elevator with them, so Cortez held his questions. If necessary, he would interrogate everyone who was in the building the day Avery was killed. So far, no one credible had come forward to say they'd seen James Avery after he entered ProLabs. Whatever happened to him that day had started here on this medical-research campus.

Inside Brickman's office, the sweat on Cortez's body

cooled so quickly it made him uncomfortable. What did the heavy man have the AC set to? Brickman closed the blinds, blocking out the daylight, then took a seat behind his massive desk. Cortez set out his recorder and asked his main question. "When was the last time you saw James Avery?"

"At a fundraiser for the animal shelter three years ago. That was the only time I've seen him in person."

"Was he ever in this building?"

"Not that I know of. Why would he be?"

"The last place he was seen alive was the ProLabs clinic around the corner. The video surveillance doesn't show him leaving the building, yet five hours later, he was drugged, beaten, and murdered. Tell me what you know about it."

Brickman's eyes flashed with anger and his jaw tightened. "I have no idea, and I resent the implication. Even the suggestion that I'm under investigation could ruin my campaign."

That wasn't his concern. "I believe Avery came through the walkway that connects the two buildings. Why would he do that?"

"I don't know. This is so bizarre."

"Where is the access?"

"In the R&D facility."

"Do you have video surveillance in that area?"

Exasperation seeped into Brickman's voice. "Why would there be? The walkway is only for employees, and no one uses it."

"Did you know James Avery was an investor in BioMed Holdings?"

"No. When I sold ProtoCell to BioMed last year, I stepped back from the financial management. I'm transitioning into politics."

"But you understand why I'm here?"

"Yes, but I'm baffled and don't know how to help you."

"I need you and your employees to cooperate with my investigation."

"Of course."

"I want the surveillance footage from both buildings for Tuesday, July eighth, everything from four o'clock until ten." He would have to get help to view the files, but Cortez was confident he'd find something.

"I'll talk to security and have them assist you."

"Where were you Tuesday evening between eight and ten?"

Brickman's mouth dropped open. "You suspect me?"

Cortez thought the reaction seemed a little put on. "We suspect everyone until we have solid evidence. Where were you?"

"Let me check my calendar." Brickman reached for his computer mouse.

Cortez glanced at his list of questions while he waited. He still needed more financial information.

"I didn't have any engagements that evening," the CEO finally said. "So I must have been home with my wife."

"What's her name and phone number?"

Brickman sighed. "Do you really have to bring her into this?"

"I have to check your alibi. And question everyone who was in the building on that day. So I need a list of those employees as well."

"I'll get that to you later today."

"I need it now while I'm here. And your wife's phone number."

Brickman rattled it off, his voice tight. "There has to be some rational explanation for all this. Maybe Avery had a sexual encounter with one of the women at ProLabs. Maybe her husband caught them and killed him. Then he doctored the video to cover it up. I can't image why James Avery would access this building."

The suggestion filled him with more doubt. An affair, followed by a jealousy killing, made much more sense. Cortez made a note to follow up. But it didn't explain the financial connection. "As an investor, what would Avery be worried about?"

"I don't know."

"I want access to your financial records for the last three months."

Brickman let out a snort. "That's ridiculous."

"Then I'll get a warrant."

"Good luck."

"Is ProtoCell making a profit?"

"Of course. It has been for years."

"Why did you sell to BioMed?"

"I wanted more time to pursue my political ambitions."

"Any financial concerns?"

"We're in great shape. In fact, we're launching a product this week that will make our stockholders rich."

"What is it?"

"A weight-loss implant called SlimPro."

Cortez tried to hide his surprise. Why was Brickman still overweight if he had developed an effective diet product? More important, was there any possible connection between a blockbuster product and the murder? "As an investor, did Avery know about SlimPro?"

Brickman shrugged. "He probably saw it in the report we filed for BioMed. *If* he read the report. I don't see how it's relevant."

Cortez decided to move on. "Will you show me where the walkway connects?"

"My assistant can do that. I'm expecting an important call."

Cortez felt as if he'd been dismissed. "While you wait for it, don't forget to create the list of employees who were in the building last Tuesday." He stood and leaned over the desk. "I hope you'll reconsider giving me access to your books. Cooperation is how innocent people handle investigations."

Brickman stood, his mouth twisted in a smirk. "Our competitors are out for blood. We can't release sensitive information without a court order."

"Out for blood? What do you mean?"

The CEO grimaced with regret. "It's just an expression. They would use our sales projections and pipeline information against us if they got their hands on it. We have to be careful, that's all."

"Who are your competitors?"

"Other medical device companies, such as TecLife. But there are dozens of startups hoping for a break."

As he walked out, Cortez had an odd thought. Had Avery been looking for proprietary information?

Chapter 27

Jonas pushed the detective out of his mind. He had more important concerns. After promising the wealthy campaign donor he'd lose five pounds a week, he'd learned that Cheryl—who'd become a backstabbing bitch—had probably sent someone to steal SlimPros. Then yesterday afternoon, HR informed him that his lead scientist had committed suicide. His work on their next product, a peptide-based diabetes treatment, was critical, and Michael Pence would be impossible to replace.

The timing was devastating. And suspicious. Could Cheryl have been involved? Arson and theft, yes. But driving a man to suicide? Jonas couldn't rule it out. She seemed ruthless in her campaign to take him and his company down. Or maybe it was all about grabbing her share of the sixty-six-billion-dollar weight-loss market. He couldn't blame her for that. It's what they all wanted.

The SlimPro theft was more puzzling. Why now? They were so close to launching it was too late for TecLife to beat them to market with a similar product. What was Cheryl up to? The possibilities unnerved him. Even though she'd been extremely cautious and secretive, he knew she was testing her own appetite-suppressant device in a Phase Three study.

It was her life's work and Cheryl never gave up. His operative had managed to copy some files from Max Grissom's computer at TecLife, but it was all clinical trial data. Still, from reading the results, Jonas had been able to determine that Cheryl was working with digestive-friendly microbiota and having great success. But the mechanism of action eluded him. Maybe he needed to send the freelancer to Costa Rica to bribe the clinical trial doctors for information.

What if Cheryl's product rolled out six months from now and obliterated the SlimPro? He'd been worrying about that scenario for years and had finally sold the company to detach himself. Cheryl was an amazing and determined scientist, and he'd never doubted her ability. But she'd been humorless and sexually repressed. When he'd finally broken off their affair, she'd become too difficult to work with and he'd had no choice but to force her out. But he had paid for it dearly. Having her for an enemy had become far worse than having her as a bitter and uncooperative research partner.

Would she stop punishing him now that he was getting out of medical devices and into politics—or would it only get worse?

Jonas shelved his worry and spun away from the window. He had to stay focused on launching SlimPro earlier than planned and getting his media initiative set up. He called his executive assistant and his PR director, and they showed up minutes later. Keyed up, he stayed on his feet, pacing in a short circle.

"I've decided to be the first person to get the SlimPro implant," he announced. *Except for the hundreds in clinical trials,* he mentally corrected. "The first post-approval customer, I mean. And I want it done immediately." He turned to his assistant, a loyal woman in her late twenties.

"Book me into the Pacific Family clinic, and let them know we'll be filming."

She opened her mouth to protest, but he cut her off. "I'm running for mayor, and I plan to put their clinic on the news. They'll make room in their schedule. The sooner the better."

His next missive was for his public relations director. "We'll film the entire procedure and use it for marketing. Line up a crew, probably from the Taylor Agency, as soon as we have the appointment time. The idea is to show the world how easy and painless the procedure is. Doing it live with a real person will be so much more effective than the commercials we had planned."

"I love it." Rashad pointed at him, a youthful gesture of admiration. "Not just a real person, but the CEO of the company that makes the product. What better testimony to our faith in the medicine?"

Nobody in the pharmaceutical or device industries used the word *drug*. They produced remedies, treatments, medicines, biologicals, and devices. Never drugs. "Let the media know about the event, including print journalists and magazine editors. We'll hold a press conference and get some news coverage too."

Rashad's leg vibrated, filling the room with nervous tension. "I'll tweet the event live and upload the video to You Tube when we have the edited version. This is brilliant."

Jonas was on a roll. "Let's get a copywriter started on the script and find a narrator. We have to be ready by tomorrow, in case the clinic can accommodate us that quickly."

His assistant jumped up. "I'll call now."

"I'd like to get started too," Rashad said, "unless you have something else for me."

"I'm sure I will, but let's get everything rolling, then meet again tomorrow with updates." Jonas gestured for him to go.

When he was alone again, dread set in. Making a public commitment to lose weight terrified him. He'd tried and failed many times, but at least those failures were private. He'd never talked about his diets to anyone but his wife and his brother. But now if he failed, everyone would know, and his blockbuster product would look bad. Yet, more than anything, he wanted to be mayor and beat Cheryl to market. This was the only way.

He picked up the phone to call his factory manager and ask if they'd been successful in producing a full product run. He wanted SlimPros in clinics around the country by the time his procedure went on the air. Customers would start making appointments immediately. Everyone wanted to lose weight.

Chapter 28

Tuesday, July 15, 2:35 p.m.
Dallas worked diligently on the task she'd been assigned, knowing Decker wanted to send the file to the FDA by the end of the day. This was part of the undercover assignment—doing the administrative job well enough to stay employed until she gathered enough intel. But holy crap she was bored. How did people do this kind of tedious work day after day?

She thought about the FBI analysts in the San Diego bureau who were currently listening to the audio being transmitted from Decker's office. An even more boring job. Dallas felt grateful for her career and would never take it for granted. The data she was sorting, copying, and pasting, was intriguing in its own way. Decker's weight-loss product might be weird, but it was also effective. Some of the subjects had lost fifteen percent of their body weight in six months. Others had lost less, but still ended up with healthier indexes. Decker might turn out to be a criminal, even a killer, but she was clearly a brilliant medical researcher.

Dallas finished the project by three and uploaded the files. Should she snoop in Decker's messages again while she had the chance? Why not? She backtracked into the main email program and keyed in *AmDeck9*. An error message popped up, indicating Decker had her software open. Dallas backed out, intending to try again in a few minutes.

Impulsively, she pushed to her feet. Time to get out of the boxy little office for a minute. Maybe even step outside, if it wasn't too hot. Or at least stand in the atrium for a few minutes where she could see the sky.

Decker stepped through their adjoining door, locking hers behind her. "Thanks for finishing the project so quickly. I'll look over your work in a few minutes." The boss kept moving out into the hall.

Where was she headed? Dallas grabbed her bag, waited two seconds, then followed her out. Decker was turning into Grissom's office down the hall. Too bad she had no way to eavesdrop on that conversation. Dallas passed the door to the conference room between the two executive offices. Could she hear from there? She ducked into the room, which contained a sleek metal table and matching chairs. Scooting along the left wall to the back, she pressed her ear to the surface.

Raised voices sent a rush of anticipation across her chest. Grissom was speaking. "Santera has never called in sick before, and now he says he'll be out all week. What the hell is going on?"

"What are you saying? That you don't trust him?" Decker was harder to hear.

"On Friday, we had a breach of security and someone stole files. Now this week, our head of R&D is suddenly absent from work for the first time in five years." Grissom paused, then seemed to lower his voice. "We have a mole at ProtoCell. Why wouldn't they have a spy here as well?"

"But why would Santera stay home? What is he avoiding?"

"I don't know, but something is very wrong. I can tell."

"I trust Santera," Decker insisted. "And if Prickman had a mole working for us, why would he need to send in a thief during a fire alarm?"

"I don't know. But Santera didn't sound like himself when he called. And he said something odd."

"What?"

Dallas strained to hear.

"I had just asked him for an update on the extended version, and he said it would take longer than we'd expected and that the ends never justify the means."

"Maybe he's just burned out," Decker mumbled. "But once this last batch of data is submitted to FDA, there's no stopping Slimbiotic."

The conversation turned to data, so Dallas ducked back out of the conference room. The Santera discussion had reminded her not to push her luck. She'd already been discovered once. She trotted down to the atrium, bought a flavored water from the vending machine, and texted River about Grissom's suspicion. The bureau had to keep Santera under wraps and monitor his communication better.

She chatted with a sales rep who came in but didn't learn anything from her. Dallas headed back up to her desk, planning to spend more time digging around in Decker's email—if she could get in.

Her office phone rang as she entered, surprising her. She'd only taken two calls, both from the FDA. "Cheryl Decker's assistant."

"This is Tara Smith, a business reporter from the *San Diego Union Tribune*. I'd like to speak to Cheryl Decker."

Not a chance. Decker had been clear about no calls from the media. "I'm sorry. She's not available. Can I help you with something?"

"Can you answer some questions about a product release?"

Probably not. "I'll try."

"ProtoCell just accelerated its launch of SlimPro, and it's rumored that TecLife has its own weight-loss product about to launch. How does your competitor's early entry into the market affect your earnings projections?"

An accelerated launch? Was that significant? "Did ProtoCell put out a press release?"

"They called and invited me to a clinical demonstration tomorrow."

"What clinic? We'll probably want to send someone."

"Pacific Family. But hey, I'm the one who's supposed to be asking questions."

Dallas laughed. "I'm just trying to do my job too." She jotted down the name of the reporter and the clinic. As an agent, she wouldn't forget either, but as a secretary, it seemed appropriate. "What else can you tell me about the event?"

"Not a thing. Can you connect me to your public relations person?"

"I'll try."

"Thanks. Please have Cheryl Decker call me."

Dallas made the connection for her and hung up. Then she googled the clinic's name, noted the location, and called their number. "This is Tara Smith again from the *Union Tribune.* I wanted to confirm the time of the clinical demonstration tomorrow."

"Mr. Brickman is scheduled for two-thirty, and the press conference is at two."

The CEO of ProtoCell? "Thank you." Dallas hung up.

The head of the company was having his own device

implanted and had invited the press. What a publicity stunt. A tremor of excitement rushed over her. The device war had just heated up again. She dug out her burner phone and texted the intel to River. If the competitor's move forced the TecLife mastermind to engage in another, bolder act of sabotage, they might have an opportunity to catch them in the act.

Dallas opened the email software and keyed in Decker's password. The files opened, and three emails landed while Dallas stared at the screen. One from the FDA, one from someone named Marta that looked personal, and one from Curtis Santera. *Shit!* Was he warning Decker about her?

Dallas clicked the email.

The door between the offices opened, and Decker stepped in, her expression grim. "I know this is unexpected, but I have to fire you."

Chapter 29

Oh shit. "Why?" Dallas kept her eyes on Decker, who looked more distressed than angry.

"Mr. Grissom and my previous assistant aren't working out, and Holly wants to come back to my office. I have to accommodate her. She's a long-term employee and very valuable."

Relief washed over Dallas. At least she hadn't been caught spying. "I can transfer to Mr. Grissom. I don't mind."

"But his wife does." Decker stepped forward and whispered, "He's not allowed to have beautiful young women as assistants. I wish we could find you another place in the company, but we just don't have anything right now. I'm sorry."

Oh hell. "Can you give me some time to find another job?"

"We'll pay you for the week, but it's best if you leave at the end of the day. I have another important project tomorrow, and I might as well get Holly started on it instead."

The rejection riled her. She'd never been fired before. More important, she would lose access.

What else could she accomplish in a few short hours? She decided to tell Decker about the phone call from the *Tribune*. As she reported the conversation, Decker's expression kept changing, but Dallas couldn't read it. Decker thanked her for the information with a tight smile.

Dallas added, "I'm very disappointed to leave this job." She focused on that day long ago when her dad ran over her dog and blinked her eyes until they misted over.

"I'm sorry." Decker retreated, as predicted.

With only an hour left, Dallas had to move quickly. She scanned the open email from Santera: *I'm sorry to miss work this week. I wanted you to know that Phase I of the extended version is going well. Maybe your new assistant can look at the data.*

Was that a warning? She'd just heard the founders expressing concern about Santera and the possibility of a spy in their midst. So the timing of the message could be damaging. Or maybe Santera was trying to get her more access. She couldn't tell. Dallas quickly scanned through a dozen more previously opened emails. Most of the addresses looked like typical business correspondence. Nervous that Decker would come back into the office with termination instructions, Dallas decided to close it up. At the last second, she opened the Sent folder for a quick peek. Decker had messaged Marta, whose email had come in earlier. A message she hadn't opened.

The outgoing email was brief: *Something came up and I have a meeting after work. Can you pick up Amber and give her dinner? I'll be home by eight.*

That was interesting. Decker could be seeing a lover or a shrink, but whoever it was, the meet had supposedly just come up. Dallas would tail her boss and see where she went. She logged out of email and accessed the server. She might as well snoop for as long as she could.

At four-thirty, she closed her computer, grabbed her personal things, and headed out. She had no intention of turning in her badge yet or letting anyone escort her from the building. Downstairs, she nodded at Adrian behind the front desk, and kept moving. Outside, the sun beat down, a bright relentless weight in the sky. But it still wasn't Phoenix heat.

She drove around the block and parked on the street in front of Saber's, the restaurant/lounge across the street from TecLife. Decker wasn't likely to leave until five-thirty or six, but Dallas would keep an eye on the front of the building. Decker's car was the silver Optima in the reserved space up front, but watching the vehicle wasn't enough. Her target might leave on foot.

Still in the car, Dallas pulled her hair up into a bun, put on oversize sunglasses, and changed into the T-shirt, shorts, and sandals she'd stashed just for this purpose. Another full set of clothes, including a jacket, was on the floor in back. Undercover work had taught her to be prepared.

A man walking by stopped to watch her pull on the new shirt, and she resisted the urge to give him a mock-shock look. She was on duty, so she ignored him and he moved on. Dallas left the AC running and called River, who picked up and asked, "What have you got? It's been a busy day already."

Where to start? "They just fired me. But my cover wasn't compromised. It's just a personnel thing."

"That's a tough break. Thank goodness you got the bacteria samples last night. What else?"

"Santera emailed Decker and mentioned me. But in a weird way, so I don't know what it means. Still, he communicated with our targets. Have you cleared him of suspicion?"

"Not officially. I didn't think he was the saboteur. But then we saw that email go out and didn't know what to make of it."

Dallas let it go. "We may get a break tonight. I found out that ProtoCell just accelerated its product launch and is doing a big media demonstration with their CEO. I'm not sure what it means to our investigation, but right after I told Decker about it, she set up a meeting with someone after work. I'll tail her and see who she contacts."

"You'll get photos, of course." River let out a rare sound of nervousness. "I get the sense that this rivalry has reached a boiling point. Something big could go down."

"I had the same feeling today. Do we need to bring in more people to watch all the players?"

"I'll call King and see what resources he can drum up."

"Anything new on Grissom?"

"I followed him to a meeting with a hooker last night, but otherwise no."

Dallas laughed. "He's a horny beast. That's part of why they let me go. Grissom's wife won't let him work with pretty young assistants."

"Poor woman."

"Any word on the bacteria samples?"

"Not yet. Analysis takes time."

"I'd better go. I'm watching the building for Decker to leave."

"Be careful."

"Always." Dallas hung up and headed inside the lounge where it was cooler and she could sip a beer.

Decker didn't come out of TecLife until six-thirty. At the sight of her, Dallas bolted out of her seat, so restless she'd resorted to drawing on napkins for the last half hour just to keep from exploding. She started for the door, passing a group of TecLife employees, and forced herself to slow down. Hanging back and looking casual was the secret to a successful tail. Outside, she watched Decker get into her Optima and leave the now-empty parking lot.

Dallas bolted to her rental car, fifty yards away. Keeping her eye on the silver sedan, she cut into traffic and sped toward the intersection. The sedan turned right, and with two cars between them, Dallas followed. After a ten-minute drive, Decker pulled into a corner strip mall. Dallas sensed they were near the bay. She cruised past the mall, glancing back to see where the sedan had parked. Near a small Latin diner. She circled the block, parked on the outer edge of the lot, and trotted toward the cafe, which had outdoor seating. She suspected Decker and whoever she was meeting would be inside.

She passed the Optima and stopped in her tracks. Decker had taken a seat at an outside bar counter. Dallas headed for the seating in front of the ice-cream parlor across the open space. She chose a table behind a potted palm, where she could keep Decker in sight without being spotted.

After a few minutes, a woman approached and sat on the stool next to Decker. At least the person seemed to walk like a woman. Thirty or so, with a slim build on a five-eight frame. She wore a baseball cap with no hair showing, sunglasses, and a baggy shirt. Her skin tone suggested an Indian or Middle Eastern background, but Dallas was too far away to know for sure. After a moment, the woman reached over and tapped Decker's arm, then said something Dallas couldn't hear. She tried to read the woman's lips. She'd taken the training, but hadn't used it enough to be skilled. She thought she made out the word *job*.

The woman gestured at the newspaper on the counter, and Decker handed it to her. Dallas' nerves pinged and she went into high alert. This looked like a clandestine meet with someone who didn't want to be recognized or remembered. And Decker had likely just passed her something. A payment? Should she move in for an arrest? No, it was too soon. What if it had just been a newspaper? And the two were complete strangers? The meeting might not be happening yet. A friend or lover could show up any minute and give Decker a hug. Dallas grabbed her BioTech phone and set the camera to zoom. Could she capture their faces from here?

Probably not. She moved closer, keeping her own face averted, and snapped two shots. The bureau would use facial recognition software and, if the operative was in the database, they would identify her. *If* the photos were good enough. She needed to get closer. *Damn.* She wished she had a high-powered camera. But she was an undercover agent, not a spook. She had to travel light and realistic to the assignment.

A young man carrying a skateboard approached. He looked clean and drug free. Was he trustworthy? If she handed him her cell phone and a twenty and asked him to discreetly take their picture, would he take off with the money and her phone? A small loss that was worth the risk.

"Excuse me?" She stood and stepped in front of him. "Will you do me a favor? It's very important."

He shook his head and kept walking. "Sorry, I'm late for something."

Jerk. Dallas glanced back at her targets. Decker was getting up. *Shit.* She needed a better shot of them together. Dallas lifted her camera as if taking a picture of the art structure in the plaza's center, then started backing toward them. Four steps later, she turned and snapped a shot of the bar counter. Just another tourist documenting everything. As she spun back around, she saw Decker grab her purse from the counter and leave. *Good.* The target had still been in the photo frame. Dallas walked away from the outdoor tables and stopped at a nearby stand that sold souvenirs.

Now what? Instinct told her Decker would head home to her daughter. Dallas decided to stay with the operative and see where she led. Learning something about her would help the bureau put someone on her full time, maybe get a tap on her communications.

She glanced over at the Latin diner again, and the operative was gone. *Shit!* Instinctively, Dallas started toward the bar counter, scanning the sidewalk. Decker, in her black-and-white clothes, was easy to spot in the distance. A group of young people moved together, taking up a chunk of the walkway. Where was the woman in the baseball cap? Had she passed behind her while Dallas pretended to be a tourist looking at T-shirts?

She spun back around. Another group of boys with skateboards surged toward her. A nearby event must have recently ended. She strode through the crowd, with mumbled apologies. Near the end of the row of shops, she spotted a person of about the right size—but no baseball cap. This woman had a straight-black ponytail and carried a large bag that could be worn as a backpack. Could that be her? The pink sun, low on the horizon, wasn't casting enough light to distinguish the shirt color at that distance. Had the woman altered her appearance as she scurried away? Dallas charged forward, remembering her own quick change in the car. Who was this operative? Most for-hire criminals were men, especially if arson or murder was involved. But the bureau had a database full of deadly women too, and this unsub was crafty enough to be an ex-agent.

The ponytailed woman ducked between two small shops and disappeared. Dallas broke into a run. At the break in the shops, she slowed and approached the alley from a wide angle. Just in case the unsub had spotted her and was lying in wait.

The short alley was empty. *Damn,* her new target was fast. Dallas raced to the end of the alley, which opened into another courtyard. A few couples and families with teenagers were eating at tables, but the operative was nowhere to be seen. The shops surrounding the courtyard were all open, and the woman could have ducked into any of them. Dallas checked the closest two but didn't see her. *Oh fuck.* She'd lost their best lead. Frustration made her head pound, but she tried to appear casual. She left the clothing store and headed for her car. Where had she gone wrong? By turning her back on Decker after the meeting? By moving too slowly after finally spotting the operative? But charging after the unsub too soon could have blown her cover. *What cover?* She was no longer a TecLife employee. But she also didn't want the arsonist, and maybe killer, identifying her either. Another thought hit her. Would the bureau take her off the case now? She hated leaving an assignment with a sense of failure. It didn't happen often, but she was hoping to become a Special Agent eventually.

In her car, Dallas accessed the last photo she'd taken. A little blurry, but Decker's face was recognizable, so the bureau techs should be able to isolate the other image, clean it up, and hopefully ID the unsub. She sent the file to River, put in her earpiece, and started her car. Dallas called twice more on the drive home before River finally answered.

"Sorry, I was tailing Grissom. What's happening?"

"Decker met with a woman who was careful to disguise herself. Decker also passed her something under a newspaper. I tried to follow the unsub after the meet, but she's damn good."

"Did she know you were watching?"

"Maybe. But I got a photo of the meet and sent it to you. Let's see if the unsub is in our files."

"If she saw you, maybe we should pull you out completely. Especially now that you've lost your access to TecLife."

She'd known River would say that. "I can tail Decker when she's not at work."

River was quiet for a moment. Dallas took the freeway exit and headed north to her condo.

"Don't beat yourself up. You got a photo of their meeting and brought us a bacteria sample. We can probably get a search warrant now."

"What about Santera? I think his email got me fired, so I don't trust him."

"The team will meet tomorrow morning and make some decisions. I'll talk to King and ask if you should be there."

"Let me know if you ID the unsub. She's about five-eight and slender, maybe one-thirty-five with Middle Eastern skin and hair. Or the hair could have been a wig. She carries a backpack-style bag and changes appearance on the move."

"Age?"

"Younger than thirty-five."

"She sounds like an anomaly. But we'll get the info out to the companies she's reportedly sabotaged and see if anyone recognizes her."

Dallas wasn't ready to give up, but she didn't know if she should share her plan.

"What are you thinking?" River asked.

"'I still have my TecLife badge, and I'm tempted to go back in after midnight and poke around some more."

"I thought they beefed up their security."

"They already fired me. What's the worst that could happen?"

"You could get killed, remember? An agent, a warehouse worker, and a scientist are already dead."

"I'm too hyper to sit around until Decker gets off work tomorrow."

"Go for another run on the beach. I've got to call Agent King and get this photo to the bureau."

"Keep me updated." Dallas hung up. A run was a good idea, but it wouldn't keep her busy tomorrow. She'd have to brainstorm ideas while she pounded along the sand.

Chapter 30

Kiya watched the pretty woman with reddish-blond hair get into her car. Who the hell was she? A federal agent? The woman had definitely taken a picture of the counter where she'd met Cheryl Decker. Who was the operative's target? Decker or herself? Kiya climbed on her motorcycle and waited. She wanted to go back and find the knife she'd lost leaping over the wide plant container in the mall, but couldn't risk losing sight of the operative.

She seemed to be texting someone. A contact at the FBI? Or did the woman work for Kiya's ex-husband, who was now a captain in the Uzbekistan army, with access to international information? Had the bastard tracked down Martel in jail, bribed him to get her location, and sent someone out to kill or kidnap her? Kiya had shamed her husband—and her father—by escaping the marriage. In keeping with tribal tradition, either could have sworn to find her and kill her. But she didn't believe it. They wouldn't waste the resources. No, she was the one who'd sworn revenge. As much as she hated the man she'd been forced to marry as a child, her father was to blame. And she would soon make him suffer.

Kiya forced herself to focus on the moment. The spying woman was likely a federal agent, which meant Decker had been stupid somehow and attracted the authorities' attention. Until the moment that picture had been taken, Kiya had been completely in the clear on the work she'd done for Decker. Even the ProtoCell scientist she'd kidnapped couldn't identify her. And the U.S. federal government probably wouldn't be able to ID her either. The hat and sunglasses she'd worn would get in the way. More important, she didn't think she was in their system, because she'd never been caught or questioned. Still, the agent had seen her and followed, and if Decker caved under questioning, the feds would come after her. It was time to get out of San Diego and follow through on her personal goal. Good thing she had a ticket already. But she wasn't leaving any loose ends.

The gray midsize car—purposefully nondescript— backed out of its parking space and headed for the exit. Kiya started her motorcycle, glad she'd modified her muffler to make the bike quieter. She tucked her ponytail inside her shirt, pulled on her helmet, and exited a side street, watching over her shoulder as the other vehicle headed north. Her best guess was the freeway, so she hung back, knowing she could make bold moves on the cycle to catch up if her quarry took a sudden change of direction.

But she didn't. Kiya followed the agent uneventfully to a complex in the Pacific Beach area. Darkness had nearly fallen, but she could tell by the location and landscaping that they were upscale apartments. A waste of money. She parked a block away, and from across the street, watched with binoculars as the woman entered an upstairs apartment. Breaking into it wouldn't be challenging, but the agent probably slept with a gun nearby. She would have to plan this carefully, with the limited time she had. She didn't owe Decker anything, but keeping the federal agent from questioning her client was the best way to protect herself.

Kiya had only killed one other person, and he'd deserved it. The stupid bastard had slammed her against the wall and squeezed between her legs, not realizing she carried a knife and the attitude that sexual predators were subhuman. Too bad she didn't have the blade with her now. Killing the agent would be unpleasant, but Kiya would do what she needed for survival. She was tempted to warn Decker about the feds but wouldn't risk contacting her again. They might be monitoring Decker's phone and email.

After a few minutes, she climbed off the bike and started to take a quick tour of the complex. The soft sound of a door opening caught her attention. She glanced up, and in the dark, saw movement at the target's door. The woman came out, wearing what looked like shorts and running shoes. Kiya turned away, walked back to the sidewalk, then strode down the street.

She ducked behind a palm tree and waited, trying to predict where her target would go. To the beach, of course. The boardwalk was only six blocks away, and now that it was dark, the crowd would thin out, making it a lovely place for a seaside run. The slapping sounds of a jogger indicated the agent had crossed over and was running west. Kiya waited two minutes, took a parallel side street, and parked when she neared Mission Boulevard. The rest of the job would require her to stay on foot and scout out the perfect spot for an attack.

Trotting up Mission to where she expected the agent to cross, Kiya tried to visualize this section of the boardwalk along the beach. She remembered something big. A pier with little cottages for tourists. Perfect. She would wait under the pier, hiding in the dark behind one of the massive support beams until her quarry came along. Kiya retrieved a heavy flashlight from her saddlebag. A few hard blows to the back of her head, then drag her into the ocean and let the tide do the rest.

Chapter 31

River pulled on slacks and a button-up shirt—her androgynous work clothes. After sixteen years on the job as Carl, she would probably never wear feminine clothes around other FBI agents. She'd only been back to the apartment long enough to eat and shower, then Dallas had called with the update about Decker's meet-up. River had contacted Agent King to strategize their next move but he hadn't answered. She strapped on her Glock, knowing he would get back to her in a moment. That was the nature of their jobs. They were never really off duty, and a ringing work phone made them jump with a mix of dread and adrenaline. She walked to the window, where the sun had set, taking her picturesque view with it. A sense that the case was about to break wide open disrupted her inner peace. They needed to bring in more agents and get a spook team over to keep watch on Decker.

River felt too keyed up now to wait longer. It was time to interrogate Santera again. The suspect had emailed Decker and subtly warned her not to trust Dallas, costing their UC her access to TecLife. River had picked up Santera earlier and left him in the interrogation room at the bureau. A few hours alone in the hole should have made him nervous enough to cooperate. River planned to question him until he gave her something. Their session with him the day before had proved fruitless. He'd maintained that he had no knowledge of the sabotage or Agent Palmer. But warning Decker this afternoon made him look like a conspirator, and the paper-pushers at the bureau were crafting a stack of search warrants that would be submitted to a judge as soon as they found one willing to work after hours. The only piece not in place yet was the bacteria analysis, and she expected that in the morning.

River grabbed two bottles of water from the freezer and headed out. Despite the darkness, the heat was still oppressive. She would never get used to it again. In Eugene, even the hottest days in August cooled off after the sun set.

In the car, King finally returned her call. "What's happening?"

"Decker met with a female unsub and passed something to her. Dallas captured a photo of the meet and followed the unsub, but then lost her. Dallas plans to keep an eye on Decker until this breaks open, but I think we need 24/7 surveillance."

"I wish I could get more agents, but the police department asked for our help with a serial killer, so we're stretched thin."

Good glory. "This case is about to break wide open. We can't shortchange it."

"If Decker just met with the saboteur, then I wouldn't expect anything else from her tonight." He sounded tired and defensive. "Where are you now?"

"Headed into the bureau to interrogate Santera. He sent Decker an email this afternoon that cautioned her about Dallas. Minutes later, they fired her. We need a task force meeting to regroup now that we've lost our access."

"We'll meet at eight tomorrow, then go serve the papers and confiscate everything."

"We have a photo of the saboteur, and I'll upload it as soon I get into the office."

"Keep me posted." King hung up.

Was he taking this case as seriously as he should? Three people connected to TecLife and its competitors were dead. Although none looked like murder on the surface, those deaths couldn't be coincidence. River took deep breaths and willed herself to be calm. *I can only do my best and control my part in this.*

Despite the AC, sweat dripped from her forehead. San Diego was the last place she wanted to be in July, except maybe Phoenix...or Iraq. She missed cool evenings on the deck with Jared, in her garden back home. But until she arrested someone for Joe's death, she would sweat it out.

Santera's head was on the table when she walked into the interrogation room. He jerked upright, revealing a face that had gone slack and lost some of its robust color.

"What is going on?" he whined. "I want to see my lawyer."

She had purposefully not spoken to him earlier. Not knowing was more unnerving than having someone shout in your face. People could shut down when confronted with stress. Silence tended to grow and undermine one's confidence.

River made a point to cuff him to the table before she sat down. "We saw Cheryl Decker meet with a known criminal this evening, so we have the search warrants we need to look at every file in your company. We plan to charge you personally with conspiracy."

"I don't know what you're talking about."

"You sent Decker an email today after we told you not to communicate with anyone at TecLife."

"I had research information she needed. The work we do is important."

"You mentioned her new assistant, and minutes later, Decker fired our undercover agent. You sent a coded warning."

Santera yanked at the cuffs, wanting to gesture. "No. I told my boss I was out sick and gave her an update on my research. I haven't done anything criminal."

"Why mention her assistant?"

"I was trying to give her access to more data."

River didn't know if she believed him, but decided to move on. "We're watching Decker. If you're involved in sabotage or product tampering, we will find out very soon. You might as well cooperate and get a plea deal."

"What product tampering?" He seemed genuinely surprised. "Are consumers at risk?"

"You tell me."

"Are you talking about ProtoCell's new implant? That's the only one we consider a threat to our pipeline."

"Tell me everything you know about Decker's competition with ProtoCell."

A long pause while his eyes went through a series of stressful calculations. "It's personal for Cheryl. She used to work for Jonas Brickman, back when ProtoCell was first founded. He fired her and stole her product research. The SlimPro is based on her work with peptides."

The research probably belonged to the company. That's just how it worked. "How did Brickman steal it from her? Did she sue him?"

"Technically, the data belonged to ProtoCell, so Cheryl didn't have a lawsuit. But Brickman forced her out and gave her no credit for her discovery."

"So she bears a personal grudge."

"Yes. They used to be lovers too."

A woman scorned *and* ripped off. "Is that why Decker is developing a competing product?"

"It's one reason."

"What are the others?"

"The weight-loss market is huge and still untapped." He sighed. "But it's more than that for Cheryl. Her daughter has Prader-Willi Syndrome, which gives her a voracious appetite. Cheryl is determined to help her have a normal life."

"Why didn't you tell me this last time?"

"It's very personal for her, and it didn't seem relevant. And you were mostly accusing me."

River still thought Santera might have seen or heard something important. "Did you know about the fire at ProtoCell's warehouse?"

"Afterward, yes. Everyone in the industry heard about it."

"Did Decker ever talk about the warehouse? Or mention sabotage?"

"No. I'm a scientist. I can't even stand the marketing meetings they make me attend."

River stood and crossed her arms. "After the fire, did you ever suspect Decker or anyone at your company?"

His jaw tightened and he glanced away.

In the silence, River heard him think *We all did.*

The whole company thought their president had committed arson?

"Of course not," Santera lied. "Decker isn't capable of that kind of thing."

"She hired someone to do it for her, and a warehouse guard died. Conspiracy charges could send you to prison for a decade."

"I didn't know about it."

"But you suspected her. I can see it in your eyes. Why not go to the authorities?"

Santera was silent for a long moment. "I still don't believe Cheryl would hurt anyone on purpose."

"Let me remind you that an FBI agent who was looking into TecLife's activities is also dead. And a ProtoCell scientist conveniently committed suicide over the weekend. Why would he do that?"

"How would I know?"

River locked eyes with him and waited him out.

Finally, Santera asked, "What was the scientist working on?"

"An improved SlimPro device."

"Oh, god." Santera wouldn't look at her.

"Tell me what you know. More lives could be at stake."

"I don't know anything. But I fear Cheryl Decker may have gone off the deep end."

Chapter 32

Dallas jogged along the boardwalk, enjoying the warm air and tangy ocean scent. The pounding surf soothed her rattled nerves, helping her make peace with her failure that evening. She finally stopped obsessing about what she could have done differently with the unsub and shifted to strategizing about what she could do next to assist the investigation. The undercover part of her assignment was over—unless she could get into ProtoCell, maybe posing as a reporter doing an in-depth story. Someone had sent a data thief into TecLife on Friday, and the competitor seemed to be a logical source. Why wouldn't they retaliate against their competitor's aggressive tactics? Someone in authority had orchestrated the theft, and it seemed likely that it was Decker's ex-partner, Jonas Brickman.

Dallas planned to re-read her background information on Brickman and show up at the Pacific Family Clinic tomorrow when he underwent his implant. She might be able to intercept him beforehand and ask a few questions. Or, if the bureau analysts identified the female unsub, Dallas might be assigned to help track her down. She wasn't ready to be sent home. San Diego was pleasant—especially compared to Phoenix—and she loved being near the ocean. She knew there was more to it though. Such as avoiding another encounter with Cameron until she could figure out if she really wanted a relationship with him. But how would she know until they spent more time together? He claimed he wouldn't pressure her or be needy, but she'd heard that from several boyfriends.

There was also her dying father. If she stayed in California long enough, his funeral would be held before she returned to Arizona.

The boardwalk ended when the hotels, restaurants, and bars gave way to condos and private homes, so Dallas jogged toward the ocean. She turned and headed back north, running along the water's edge, whitecaps glinting under the moonlight. Jogging in the sand made her winded, and she had to slow her pace. A moment later, she passed a couple stretched out on the beach, kissing. A pang of loneliness crept in, and the sound of the surf was suddenly ominous—a relentless pounding force that couldn't be trusted. She eased away from the surf, and the sand under her feet became softer and harder to run in.

Up ahead, the pier loomed in the dark, a long platform sticking out into the ocean. Rental cottages lined the sides with interior lights glowing. Or she assumed they were rentals. Would anyone want to live out there year round, surrounded by the constant pounding of waves?

Dallas shifted to the right again, heading for the opening in the braces under the pier. About a half mile left to go, she calculated. As she entered the covered space, the air temperature dropped and the moon disappeared. Thick beams with X-shaped cross supports were evenly spaced on both sides. She quickened her pace, eager to exit the dark passage. Dallas passed another post and sensed movement to her right. A faint fruity scent caught her attention. She reached for her pepper spray and spun, instinctively bringing up her other arm.

But she was too late. Something hard smashed into the back of her head and she collapsed to her knees. Yellow pinpoints of light danced around her eyes. Before she could think or turn or use her spray, another blow slammed into her temple. The lights blinked off and her brain shut down.

Chapter 33

Wednesday, July 16, 8:55 a.m.

The crowded briefing room reeked of sweat. At home, the temperature gauge had hit eighty-five, and Cortez had left his air conditioning on high for Grumpy. Still, the detectives—even the few women—were all wearing suits, leather shoes, and weapon holsters. Hawthorne sat on the end of the back row, looking miserable, his cast extended into the aisle. Cortez was glad they were meeting now, instead of at four this afternoon after a long day in the field.

Sergeant Riggs called the meeting to order. "I'm filling in for the lieutenant, so we'll make this brief. I know you're all swamped with work, and this heat will only make things worse. But we've asked the FBI to help with the College Killer, so we hope to make an arrest soon." The sergeant called on the lead detective for that case and asked for an update. Cortez tuned out, rehearsing what he would say if asked to report. But it would most likely be Hawthorne who gave the update.

Riggs gave new assignments on the serial killer investigation, then asked Detective Ricci to update his case. Ricci, always a bit egotistical, stood and talked without notes. "The medical examiner hasn't made a ruling, but all the physical evidence indicates Michael Pence committed suicide. His wife is adamant that he was murdered, so I'm still looking into his personal computer files. But the FBI has essentially taken over the investigation."

"Why does the wife think he was murdered?" Riggs asked.

"Because he was on the verge of a research breakthrough on a billion-dollar product."

A charge of energy shot up Cortez's spine, and he interrupted his coworker. "Who did the suicide victim work for?"

Ricci turned slowly, giving him a look. "ProtoCell. It's a medical device company."

"Holy mother." Cortez blushed at his outburst. "Our murder victim, James Avery, had financial ties to ProtoCell. And it may have been the last place he was seen alive. We should meet and compare notes." He started to say *and combine the cases*, then hesitated.

Riggs cut in. "What else do you have?"

Cortez looked at Hawthorne, who nodded, giving him the go ahead to speak for their team. Cortez summarized everything they'd learned and only had to check his notes once.

"What is your next move?" the sergeant asked.

"We'll bring in Jonas Brickman, the CEO of ProtoCell, for questioning."

The sergeant scowled. "He's running for mayor. Why would he kill a famous actor? Why would he kill one of his own scientists?"

Good questions. Cortez doubted himself again.

Hawthorne spoke up. "It's about money, of course. ProtoCell is launching a blockbuster product. Brickman may not be our main suspect, but someone in the company is. We have to start somewhere."

"Get together with Ricci and write subpoenas," Riggs ordered. "We need to see who benefits from their deaths." The sergeant moved on to the next case.

The meeting with Detective Ricci took longer than expected, then Cortez had to spend an hour writing a subpoena, then another hour driving back and forth to the court because the judge wanted to narrow the scope of their financial probe. Cortez grabbed a quick lunch, and by the time he arrived at ProtoCell, it was after one o'clock. The receptionist let him in, and he went straight upstairs to Brickman's office. The CEO's assistant told him her boss wasn't in the building.

Cortez didn't believe her. "This is a homicide investigation, and I need information." He reached for the inner door, but it was locked.

"I told you. You're wasting your time."

Cortez turned back. "Where is he?"

"I'm not supposed to say. Jonas will be back in a couple of hours."

"I could bring you in for questioning instead." Cortez couldn't believe he'd just said that to a pretty young woman.

Her eyes went wide, then her mouth tightened in irritation. "Fine, then. He's at the Pacific Family Clinic on Broadway in Chula Vista. They're implanting a SlimPro and filming it for marketing purposes. This is a really bad time to ask him questions about a murder."

"I'll be discreet. Who in this company would benefit from the death of James Avery?"

"Who's that?"

Did anyone under thirty watch his movies? "He was a famous actor."

She looked annoyed. "What does he have to do with our company?"

"He's an investor."

"Then our competitors are more likely to want him out of the way than anyone here. We like to keep the money coming in."

It made sense—unless Avery had discovered something irregular. "Who would want Michael Pence dead?"

"The same competitor. Michael was our lead scientist. Without him, our pipeline could dry up."

"Which competitor?"

She shrugged. "Most likely TecLife. They're working on some secret product to rival the SlimPro."

"Thank you." Cortez hurried back downstairs, wondering if he should bother Brickman at the clinic or drive to TecLife instead.

Chapter 34

Wednesday, July 16, 5:55 a.m.

Cheryl woke sweating and trembling. In the nightmare, she'd been trapped inside a burning building and couldn't get out because she was too big to fit through the exit. The third time this month. Guilt about the death of the warehouse guard surfaced in her dreams no matter how much she repressed it during the day. She headed straight for a cool shower, dreading another hot day. *The dead man had been near retirement,* she told herself. And he hadn't burned; he'd died of smoke inhalation. K had claimed the watchman wasn't supposed to be in the building on the weekend, and Cheryl had tried to let it go. The important work she was doing far outweighed the risks of bringing the product to market. People sometimes died in clinical trials too, but that didn't stop the industry from developing new, life-saving medicine. No pain, no gain.

She pulled on her favorite sleeveless black dress, white pumps, and pearl necklace. Today was special. Brickman—the fat, rat bastard—would finally get what was coming to him. She'd looked forward to this moment for a long time. Hearing that he was having a SlimPro implanted had made her nearly giddy. The tainted device would give him an infection and make him pull the product from the market. It served him right for stealing her research and pretending it was his own. With his family history of heart disease, the infection might even kill him. But she probably wouldn't get that lucky.

Cheryl took her meds, then drank a cup of coffee while checking her email. When it was time, she went to Amber's room and gently shook her daughter's shoulder. "Wake up sweetie, it's time for school."

Still half asleep, Amber mumbled, "I don't want to go."

Like every other day. Cheryl had become numb to it. "I know, but you have to. An education is important."

"But someone always picks on me. Let Marta come live here and teach me at home."

Cheryl held back a sigh. She'd tried homeschooling with a qualified nanny. But the woman had quit in four days. The next one had lasted nearly two weeks. Cheryl felt sorry for Amber's teachers at the private school, but at least Amber controlled her behavior better in public. It was hard for her to be pleasant and cooperative. The poor girl was always starving.

"I'll talk to the principal again. Just get up, please. You have to go. And you have to learn to deal with things."

Cheryl didn't bring up the SlimPro implant, which seemed to be helping. She'd inserted it on Saturday, and by Monday, her daughter's appetite had started to decline. But not enough. Still, Cheryl was cautiously optimistic it would give Amber some peace. But for how long? She only had two more implants, but they would last until ProtoCell could sanitize its facilities, have them inspected, and produce another batch.

As she helped Amber to her feet, Cheryl had a stressful

thought. What if K hadn't sabotaged the SlimPro product line? The proof—a cell phone picture of an unconscious watchman outside the building—could have been staged. Or maybe the quality control person at the factory had discovered the contaminant and they'd halted production.

In either case, Brickman's implant wasn't tainted, and he wouldn't even suffer personally, let alone financially. *Unacceptable!* Hands shaking, she started to text K, then realized the pointlessness. Keeping busy while her mind whirled, Cheryl pulled her paperwork into her briefcase, tucked her gun into her purse, and packed a lunchbox for Amber.

Then it hit her. The only way to ensure that Brickman's implant was contaminated was to sabotage it herself. Her father had always said it was the only way to ensure that things were done correctly. Maybe she could simply swap out the one the clinic had ready with one that contained the infectious bacteria. But that would mean one less implant for Amber. No, she would have to inject the clinic's device with a syringe of bacteria. The idea intimidated her. She'd never done anything clandestine in person. But she'd intended to show up at the clinic anyway and witness the spectacle the asshole had planned. She wanted to watch him walk out the door, thinking he was on the path to better health, all the while breeding bacteria and heading toward financial and political ruin.

Cheryl went back to her bedroom and dug out the ProtoCell employee badge from the back of her closet. Her spy—a sales rep that used to work for her—had stolen the badge six months earlier when Cheryl had decided to escalate her plan to cripple ProtoCell. She'd never used it until now.

On impulse, she took the last of her cash from the floor safe, stuffed it into an envelope, and shoved the money to the bottom of her purse. Her fingers touched the gun, and she checked to make sure it was loaded. It always was. She might run into Brickman today, and if he went into one of his rage-generated meltdowns, she needed to be ready.

Chapter 35

Wednesday, July 16, 7:09 a.m.
River woke to the sound of Jared's ringtone. The sweetness of hearing from him was quickly pushed aside by the sense that she'd slept late and something bad had happened while she snored, oblivious to everything. She sat up and reached for her personal phone, which she kept on the nightstand next to her work phone and Glock—just as she did at home.

"Good morning." River blinked and squinted at the clock. It wasn't that late.

"I woke you, didn't I? Sorry."

"It's okay. I needed to get up. Is everything all right?"

"Things are fine. I just want to know what color to use on the base molding. I'm finishing the dining room today." The remodeling project had been going on for months, and she was in no hurry to wrap it up. His warm and handsome presence had stirred her first real sexual longing in years. But she would never let him know. The follow-up conversation about her body would be too painful. "What are my color choices again?"

"You brought home two samples, one labeled warm taupe, whatever the hell that is. And the other is sandstone."

"Which gives more contrast with the paint?"

"The taupe."

"Let's use it." River felt a flash of impatience. Not with Jared, but with having to make mundane decisions while involved in such a high-stakes case. But her life had to go on. She didn't want to be like Dallas, living out of rentals and never forming long-term relationships.

"You seem distracted," Jared said. "I'll let you go."

"I'm sorry. This case is escalating, and I need to check in with someone."

"When will you be back? I miss you."

Her heart fluttered, and River had to take a moment to respond. "Another week or so. I miss you too." Embarrassed and flustered, she added, "I haven't had a good bacon breakfast since I left."

Jared laughed. "Good. Save your appetite for me, and I'll whip up something special for your return."

"Thanks. I have to go." She hung up before he could say anything else. What did he mean? Did he miss her as a roommate and someone to talk to? Or did he have feelings for her? *Good glory.* What was next? She either had to send him on his way or tell him the truth about her past. *Every decision will be correct in the moment,* she reminded herself.

River pushed Jared gently out of her mind and picked up her BioTech phone. No texts from Dallas. That was unusual. But it was early, and they'd both had a late night. River keyed in a message, asking her to come for a task force meeting at ten, then headed for the shower.

Dallas wasn't in the conference room when River arrived at the bureau, and her pulse quickened. Dallas hadn't responded to her earlier text. River calmed herself with another mantra, then took a seat.

Agent King, at the head of the table, looked up. "I have a warrant prepared and a supportive judge ready to sign. We should be able to confiscate Cheryl Decker's computer this afternoon."

"Good news. Any luck identifying the unsub?"

"We got nowhere with facial recognition software. She's never been arrested or detained by any law enforcement agency in the U.S. We'll reach out to the international community next."

Agent Kohl came in, his face animated, and announced a finding. "The CDC called, and the bacteria from TecLife is the same thing they found in Palmer's wound. Now we can get a warrant to seize everything in the R&D department too, effectively shutting it down."

Another worry wormed into River's gut. Dallas had been exposed to the bacteria, and now she wasn't communicating. "Has anyone heard from Agent Dallas?"

Three heads snapped toward her.

"She was fired yesterday and witnessed a meet-up last night," River explained. "But now she's not responding to my texts or calls."

"Do you have a key to her place?" King asked.

"Yes, and I'll check on her after our meeting." River took a long slow breath. "She was exposed to the bacteria when she took it from their lab. Can we get someone to start calling hospitals?"

"What name would she be under?" King asked.

"Her current ID says Jamie C. Hunter."

"I'll get someone on it." King's tone was worried. "Update us on recent activities."

River summarized the meeting between Decker and the unsub, then reported her conversation with Santera.

"Is he still in custody?"

"I released him last night after he gave us permission to search his personal phone and email. I picked up his home computer this morning, and it's with the tech people." She felt certain now that Santera wasn't involved.

Agent King stood, signaling a wrap. "Let's wait to move on TecLife until we have the warrant for the lab too, which should be soon. We don't want to spook anyone at the company until we're ready."

"What's the plan for this morning?" Agent Kohl asked.

"Get the unsub's photo out to local law enforcement and to airports and train stations. We think Decker passed her a pile of cash last night, so she could be on the move."

River stood, her worry mounting. "I'll try to find Dallas."

Chapter 36

Wednesday, July 16, 12:05 p.m.

Jonas bit into the meat lovers' pizza and moaned in pleasure. He'd eaten many pizzas right here at his desk, by himself, but this was the last one before starting his new life as a physically fit politician. The sacrifice would be worth it. He couldn't let food get in the way of his ambitions. He chewed slowly, enjoying every bite, then surprised himself by tossing the last two slices when he got full. Jonas took it as an omen that this time would be different. And not because of the SlimPro. He already knew the product didn't work well for him. He simply had to become a different person. And eventually, Cheryl's product would be on the market—either from TecLife or ProtoCell, however it worked out—and he would be the first customer again.

After washing his hands, he stepped into his assistant's office. "I'm heading over to the clinic now. Is everything in place?"

"It should be, but I'll check with Rashad. He's already there, working with the film crew and staff to set up."

"Thanks for making this happen so quickly."

"My pleasure."

Should he invite her to attend the event? No, it would be

a circus already with the reporters. And possibly some of his competitors, if someone had inadvertently leaked the news. He hoped not. Cheryl was the last person he wanted to see today.

As a commitment to his new program, he took the stairs for the first time. His phone rang on the way to his car, and he recognized Detective Cortez's number. Jonas let it go to voicemail. No one was going to ruin this day for him.

Chapter 37

Cheryl stopped in her office long enough to check her voicemail and return phone calls, then crossed the walkway to the R&D building. She hurried back to the main lab, a sense of excitement building. She'd missed working under the bright lights where anything was possible and her coworkers shared her passion. Two young scientists greeted her, with only a hint of surprise. She gave them a rare smile, feeling more upbeat than she had in years. After a decade of plotting, waiting, and working seventy-hour weeks to develop a superior product—*Prickman* was finally going down.

She strode to the stainless steel refrigeration drawers and looked for a vial of STA-2014. The cultures were gone. A shimmer of panic darkened her mood. The vials had been here last Friday when she'd taken one for K to use in the sabotage. Cheryl turned to the closest young man, whose name she couldn't remember. "Where is the STA-2014?"

"We moved it to the isolated unit in the storage area this morning."

"Why?"

"We had a contamination issue last Friday, and Curtis asked us to."

"Why didn't anyone tell me?" Her heart raced. Was Santera working against her? Or spying for ProtoCell? She recognized her paranoia, but it seemed warranted.

"It was a minor thing." The young scientist's voice wavered.

"Contamination is never minor. Is the next wave of research compromised?" They were already working on a better version of Slimbiotic, one that lasted longer.

"Everything is fine, I assure you."

She would investigate the incident more thoroughly when she had time. Right now she needed to grab the bacteria culture from the other storage area, fill a syringe, and drive down to the clinic before anyone from ProtoCell arrived.

Cheryl pulled into the L-shaped parking lot, surprised to find it half empty. Pacific Family included a chain of medical facilities around the San Diego area, but the Chula Vista branch was near ProtoCell and contained an urgent care center for its clients. She drove around to the back, not wanting Brickman to see her car, and parked near the ambulance bay.

She slipped on a white lab coat, a black scarf, and dark glasses, then checked herself in the mirror. Not easily recognizable. A quick glance into her bag to make sure the plastic gloves and syringe were still on top. She grabbed a clipboard, then climbed from the car. Cheryl hurried across the parking lot, eager to get out of the hot sun. Her skin was pale and burned easily. Once she was under the shade of the entryway, she paused. Could she do this? Her heart pounded with anxiety. What was the worst that could happen if she were caught? Scientists were expected to be a little eccentric, and she could say she'd forgotten to take her meds. And if she ever faced a jury, they would side with her over Brickman, any day.

Cheryl forced herself to move forward. Her daughter's health, plus a billion in profits, could be riding on this. Once inside, she strode calmly to the waiting area and called the clinic. She watched a chubby young woman pick up the phone at the third check-in counter.

"This is Jonas Brickman's assistant," Cheryl said. "He asked me to make sure the SlimPro device was ready for his procedure. Will you please check to see if it has white packaging? We want to ensure that you use an implant from the current batch. This is important."

"Uhh." The receptionist hesitated. "Sure. Can you hold a minute?"

"Of course."

The girl stood and excused herself from the patient at the counter.

Clicking off her phone, Cheryl scooted to the open hallway leading to the center of the clinic and waited for the receptionist to enter it from the counter area. When she did, Cheryl slipped into the medical area and followed the girl to a procedure room. A middle-age woman in pink scrubs approached in an intersecting hallway, and Cheryl turned away, glancing down at her clipboard. The nurse passed and Cheryl turned back. The receptionist had gone inside to look at the device. Cheryl walked into another hallway, counted to five, and hurried back. The receptionist was already headed back to her check-in station.

Cheryl ducked into the procedure room, which held a narrow surgical table in the center. She hurried to the prepped, stainless-steel tray on the counter. Hands shaking, she pulled on latex gloves and slipped the syringe out of its plastic bag. She lifted the SlimPro package from the tray and carefully pressed the needle into the end-seal where it wouldn't be noticed. Feeling with her other hand, she pushed the small cylindrical device up against the tip of the needle and injected a tiny drop of solution into the package. A microscopic amount of bacteria would do the job. And if K had done the factory sabotage, the device would also have STA-2014 inside its magnesium-and-silk exterior. Cheryl had a moment of uncertainty. Had she gone too far? Would the infection overwhelm his system and kill him? She almost laughed. Others had already died for this cause, but Brickman was the one who deserved to.

Cheryl placed the device on the tray exactly where it had been, shoved the syringe back in her purse, and hurried out of the room. In the hallway, she spotted a man with a big camera and a tripod talking to a woman in a white doctor's coat. They were setting up for the video already. Relieved that she'd completed her task just in time, Cheryl walked in the opposite direction, then made her way toward a back exit. Too nervous to wait in the clinic lobby, she went back to her car and pulled off the white coat. She was tempted to drive around until her nerves settled, but decided she didn't want to lose her parking spot. The lot was already filling up, and once the reporters arrived, it would only get more crowded.

A small sandwich shop next door proved to be a perfect place to wait. The large spans of glass gave her a view of the clinic, and the shop served a decent cup of coffee. She ordered a bagel too, but couldn't eat it. Twenty minutes later, Brickman's SUV pulled into the lot. When he climbed out, she blinked in surprise. She hadn't seen him in a few years and was surprised at how much weight he'd gained. No wonder he was getting the SlimPro implant.

Cheryl tossed her bagel in the trash, left the sandwich shop, and crossed back over to the clinic. An attractive woman in a red suit entered the building just ahead of her. Was she a reporter? Sometimes not watching television or any news made her feel disconnected, but most of the time she was glad to not be bothered with the distraction.

Inside the clinic, she found an empty chair in the corner about twenty feet from where Brickman and another man were staging for a press conference. They'd moved a tall lectern into place, and the fat bastard stood behind it, his hands on the top. Brickman had dressed well for the occasion in a charcoal-gray suit with a light-blue shirt, but neither concealed his girth. The lectern would hide most of his belly from the cameras, but it wouldn't do anything for his upper body. Jonas had been so handsome when they were together, but his face was now buried under a thick layer of insulation.

More reporters gathered around the lectern. Brickman was too busy checking his tie and his notes to look over and notice her. Ten minutes later, he announced that he was ready to take questions.

The woman in red spoke louder than the rest. "Is this weight-loss effort connected to your run for mayor? And what if it fails?"

Cheryl nearly choked on her coffee. He was running for mayor? How did she not know this? More important, how could she stop it? Even though she hated politics, she wanted to protect her town from this heartless thief.

Brickman gave a tight smile. "I expect the people of San Diego to judge me on my platform and success as an entrepreneur, not my body. I'm getting the SlimPro because it's effective, and I want to improve my health. I also want to show consumers that the product is safe and that the insertion is easy and nearly painless."

Another reporter, a middle-aged man, cut in. "The product's clinic trials indicate that only fifty-eight percent of the participants experienced a significant weight loss, and another twenty percent had some weight loss. What if this doesn't work for you?"

"I'll try something else. I've never given up on anything important."

The woman in red asked about people gaining weight back when they stopped using the implant.

Cheryl was no longer listening. The bastard was running for mayor and gaining voters' sympathy with this publicity stunt. He was shameless. She had to stop him. Should she finally go public with his treatment of her? Maybe sue him for her share of the SlimPro profits—just to give him some negative publicity?

Cheryl tried to tune back into his press conference, but her phone rang.

"It's Holly." Her assistant was whispering.

"Speak up please."

"I can't. The FBI is here. They have a search warrant, and they're taking everything."

Cheryl's heart skipped a beat. How much did the feds know? "What are they looking for?" Cheryl tried to sound calm.

"I don't know. I didn't read the warrant."

Was it real or another attempt by Brickman to steal her product? "How many agents?"

"Four."

Good god, it was real. Panic gripped her and she couldn't think straight. What if they had caught K and offered her a plea deal in exchange for testimony? Had the feds already searched her records? Cheryl was good about deleting texts, but the information could still exist at the phone company somewhere. Heart hammering, she tried to plan for the worst. If she went to prison, what would happen to her research? Would Santera abandon it? He'd never fully supported the idea.

And what about Amber? Her daughter would not only lose her mother, she might never get a treatment for her disease.

Cheryl stood, legs shaking so badly she had to grip the chair for support. She couldn't go to prison. It was that simple. She wouldn't survive in a cell, surrounded by idiots and criminals, with no access to a lab. A better option was to go into hiding and conduct her research in private. That life wouldn't be much different than how she lived now. Amber might even be happier. Saul would take her daughter in. From there, Cheryl could cross into Mexico if she had to.

As she stepped toward the door, she heard Brickman say, "This product is the result of years of research and dedication. I have great compassion for people who struggle to maintain their weight, and I'm thrilled to finally be able to help them."

Lying motherfucker! She couldn't let him get away with saying that. Not any more. Cheryl rushed toward the group, ready to grab a microphone.

Another reporter stepped toward Brickman. "One of your employees said you'd been questioned about the murder of James Avery. What's your connection?"

Cheryl's heart seemed to stop. Then her thoughts shattered into sharp pieces that rained down, each one cutting into her soul. Her father was dead? When? And the bastard had killed him? Confused, she froze in place. Why hadn't her father's wife told her? That jealous little cunt. Just because Cheryl had cut her father out of her life long ago didn't mean she didn't deserve to know he was dead. How dare Veronica keep it from her? Another sharp thought: How had she let herself become so isolated?

Grief and rage engulfed her—dark, sucking pain like she'd never experienced. Cheryl couldn't bear the grief, so she focused on the rage.

Jonas Brickman had done this, and she would make the bastard pay.

The reporter's question hung there, while Brickman's face tightened and his eyes narrowed into slits. He spun around and walked toward the center of the clinic. Cheryl hurried after him. Someone grabbed her arm and tried to stop her. She shook them off and reached into her purse for her gun.

Chapter 38

Dallas opened her eyes and glimpsed blocks of white and silver. But everything else was blurry, and the back of her head hurt like hell.

A voice in the distance said, "She's coming around."

Where was she? She tried to sit up, but a gentle hand pushed against her shoulder.

"Not yet. Take it slow."

The room came into focus. Medical equipment, a partitioning curtain, and a man in a white coat. She was in a hospital. Her eyes closed again as she tried to remember what had happened. She'd been running on the beach and had passed under the pier. Someone had smashed her on the head. Dallas sat up, pushing the hand off her shoulder.

"How did I get here?"

"Two drunk young men brought you in around five this morning. They said they found you on the beach near the pier."

"I don't remember anything."

"You were hypothermic. We spent hours warming you up." He smiled. "But the cold water kept your brain from swelling, and we think you'll make a full recovery."

She shivered, instantly aware that she was still cold. "I

have to get going. Where are my clothes?"

"Slow down. We need to know who you are before we let you go."

"Jace Hunter." She inched toward the edge of the hospital bed.

"It looks like you were assaulted and left to die. A police officer wants to question you."

Left to die. The phrase scared her. And she hated to be scared. But she was still alive, so dwelling on it was pointless. "What time is it?"

"Around one o'clock. In the afternoon."

Oh fuck! She'd lost more than half a day. River was probably freaking out. And Brickman's procedure was scheduled at the clinic in an hour. It seemed important to be there. Dallas pulled out her IV line and swung her legs down to the floor, unconcerned about the flapping hospital gown. "I have to go."

"You haven't finished your antibiotics. Your white-blood count is high, so we assume you have an infection."

"Just give me some sample packs to go. Where are my shoes? And my key and phone?"

"Your shoes are on the shelf over there, but I don't know about your key or your phone. You were on the beach with waves washing over you." The doctor's voice was gentle. "You could have died."

"I'm sure that's what she had in mind." Decker's slick little operative must have circled back and followed her. Boy, she'd really blown that encounter.

"Who attacked you?"

"Don't worry, my people will handle this." Habit made her keep her agent status to herself.

"You should talk to the police officer."

255

She didn't have time for that. "Please bring my clothes." Maybe the cop would give her a ride home, so she could retrieve her bag with her other phone and weapon.

"They were wet and bloody, so we threw them away. But a nurse will find you something in the lost and found."

Bloody? Dallas felt the back of her head and came in contact with a gauze bandage. "How much hair did you shave off?"

The doctor gave a sympathetic smile. "A couple of small patches that you can cover with the rest of your hair. And eight stitches."

Not that she cared about her hair. She would shave her head if an assignment called for it. "Thanks for patching me up."

"Take it easy for a while." The doctor left the room.

Dallas stood and took a few steps. Yep, she was fine. She made a trip to the bathroom and was startled by how haunted she looked without makeup and proper body temperature. As she waited for a nurse to bring clothes, she realized her hair smelled like seaweed. None of that mattered. She had to call River. But the hospital room didn't have a landline, just a call button for the nurse's desk. Everyone used cell phones now.

A nurse brought her a baggy brown skirt and a lime-green T-shirt with a surfboard logo. "It's all I could find in your size."

They could have been worse. "Thanks. I had a house key in a zipped pocket in my shorts. Do you know if it's still around?"

The nurse turned to a shelf on the wall and handed her the key.

"My cell phone?" It had been in an open back pocket.

She shook her head. "Sorry."

Dallas dressed in the borrowed clothes, ignored her blinding headache, and pulled on her still-damp running shoes. Out in the hall, she found a young male officer waiting in a chair. "Hello." She grinned at him. "Will you give me a ride home?"

"I'm glad you're okay, but I need to get a statement from you."

Dallas leaned in and whispered, "I'm a federal agent on an undercover assignment. We know who assaulted me, and we'll nail her on several charges."

The officer looked her over, skeptical. The lime-green shirt obviously wasn't helping.

"You can call the bureau on the way. Let's go." Dallas started down the hall, and he got up and followed. She turned back. "But first, I need to use your cell phone and let my contact know I'm alive."

River tried to talk her into sitting out for a while and taking it easy, but Dallas ignored her. "I'm going home to change and pick up necessities, then I'll drive over to the clinic." She glanced at the officer, not sure if she should use sensitive names out loud. At this point, it probably didn't matter. "What if Decker shows up there? Can I arrest her?"

"Not yet. The team is serving search warrants at TecLife. As soon as we find anything solid, we'll bring her in."

"I saw Decker meet with someone who later tried to kill me. Isn't that enough?"

"You said the unsub hit you from behind, so you can't really ID her. Be patient, we're almost there."

"Did you find the perp in the database?"

"No, but we've got law enforcement all over the state

looking for her."

"Good luck. She's a chameleon. Anything else?"

"The TecLife bacteria killed Palmer, which is why we're getting the warrants. Good work."

"It'll stand up in court?"

"Curtis Santera gave you permission to take the sample."

A version of the truth that was close enough. "Keep me posted."

River started to speak, stopped, then finally said, "You had me very worried this morning, and I didn't like it. Please be careful."

Dallas chuckled. "It's a medical clinic, where an overweight man is having a minor procedure. What could possibly happen?"

Chapter 39

As Cortez drove toward the clinic, he kept second guessing himself and almost turned around. Maybe it was more important to question the scientists in the building where Avery had likely exited the walkway. Brickman's wife had claimed her husband was home the evening Avery died, and as a mayoral candidate, the man had everything to lose by involving himself in a murder. Unless Avery knew something about Brickman that could derail his political career. Cortez still thought it was someone else in the company. Or two lower-level employees working together. It had probably taken more than one person to drag Avery into the cannery and bind him to the chair. Unless he'd been drugged first. Yet Brickman was a big man who could have pulled it off by himself.

His mind more settled, Cortez pulled off the interstate and turned on Broadway. A few blocks later, he spotted the clinic and its packed parking lot, including a couple of TV news vans. *Dang.* He didn't want this to become a public spectacle. If he was wrong about Brickman, the man might sue him. Should he wait? He could go back to ProtoCell's R&D facility and question everyone. Brickman wasn't going anywhere and wouldn't be hard to find later. Cortez pulled into the parking lot and sat, trying to make up his mind.

His phone rang and he glanced at the ID. The evidence facility. About time. He picked up, praying for something he could use. "It's Cortez."

"DeMarco at the processing center. I went back over the Avery vehicle to see if I could pull more fingerprints. I found one on the inside of the steering wheel, and you're not going to believe who it belongs to."

Cortez's breath caught. "Who?"

"Jonas Brickman. He was printed twenty years ago on a DUI, so he's in the system."

Yes! A solid break. "Thanks. I'm about to pick him up for questioning." Cortez started to get out of the car, then stopped and called Harris. He might as well have backup. Brickman was a big man, and this could get ugly.

Chapter 40

Dallas promised the officer she'd give a full statement the next day and hurried into her condo. She headed straight for the kitchen, gulped three aspirin for the pain in her head, and brewed a strong pot of coffee. The saltwater had made her skin itchy, so she took a quick shower. The water made her think about herself lying there on the beach in the dark, with waves washing over her body. She'd almost disappeared into the nothingness of death. Like her father would soon do. Cold pain gripped her torso. She jumped out of the shower, pulled on a robe, and had to sit on the bed for a moment and just breathe.

It wasn't the closest she'd ever come to death, but this time it scared her more. She reminded herself that death was only painful when you looked at it too hard. Once it happened, there was no more to think or feel or regret. Still, she was lucky to be alive. Lucky that someone had found her and given her help. She wished she could thank the young men. But her father wouldn't get a second chance. He would just be gone soon. Dallas found her lucky cloth and rubbed it between her fingers, but it brought her no comfort.

Shaking it off, she dressed in work clothes—lightweight pants and a short-sleeved shirt—then grabbed her bag. No longer undercover, she pulled her gun out of its zippered compartment and strapped it to her ankle.

The lot at the clinic was full, so Dallas had to circle the block and park at the sandwich shop next door. Before she got out, she put her hair up and donned sunglasses in case Decker was around. She would hang back and keep a magazine in front of her face too. She was curious to see how Decker and Brickman would interact. But more important, she wanted to scout the crowd for the unsub who'd tried to kill her. If Decker was determined to sabotage ProtoCell, she might have planned something for today. The meet-up last night could have been about this last-minute opportunity.

Dallas looked over at the medical building. Larger than she expected, with an urgent care entrance that accommodated emergency arrivals. There was Decker's silver car, parked in the back by the ambulance bay. Feeling better about being here—instead of searching computer files with the rest of the team—she headed into the clinic, each step causing a fresh wave of pain in her head.

The cool air inside the clinic eased her distress. She stood near the entrance and took in the scene. A tall man with the weight of an aging linebacker stood behind a podium, taking questions from a group of reporters—while patients waited and clerks went about their business. A strange juxtaposition and too many people to keep track of. She scanned the patients in the chairs against the wall. No one who looked like the unsub. One woman was the right size and skin coloring, but she had a little boy in her lap. Where was Decker?

Brickman held up his hand to the reporters, gave a parting smile, and turned toward the nearby hallway. As he walked into the medical back area, a woman in a black dress and white shoes darted out from behind an L-shaped bend. *Decker!* The scientist headed straight for the group of reporters and pushed her way through. What the hell was she up to?

Dallas crossed the huge waiting area, no longer concerned with whether Decker would spot her. She followed the woman down the hall and watched her push past a nurse in pink scrubs. Brickman turned a corner and so did Decker. Dallas started to run. A male doctor stepped out of the back office and blocked her path.

"Please leave this area immediately."

"I'm FBI. Move!"

She pushed past him and rounded the corner. In front of a procedure room, Decker had a gun to Brickman's head and a syringe in her other hand. A fifty-something woman in a doctor's coat was against the wall, about five feet away. *Holy shit!* Decker had snapped. Dallas itched to grab the weapon in her ankle holster, but feared that the sudden move could get her or Brickman killed.

"Back off!" Decker yelled. "Or I'll kill him and inject the doctor." Decker turned briefly to the woman against the wall. "Take this scarf and tie his hands. Now!"

The doctor followed orders, making short work of it, and stepped back.

What was in the syringe? "Don't do this," Dallas pleaded. "He's not worth life in prison."

Decker didn't seem to hear or recognize her. The crazy woman's eyes were glazed over, like someone on meth. She began to step backward and yelled at Brickman to do the same. He hesitated, frozen in fear.

"I will shoot you in the head!"

No one doubted her. Brickman began to walk backward too, his body shielding Decker. Ten feet behind them, sunlight burned through a glass-door exit.

"Do not call the police!" Decker shouted. "If I see a squad car, I'll kill him!"

Dallas scrambled through her options. She could rush them and use Brickman's body to take down Decker. No. Risking the civilian's life to save him wouldn't fly. She could keep moving forward, hoping for a chance to shoot or knock down Decker before she made her next move. Another risk to Brickman. The needle worried Dallas even more than the gun. People survived gunshot wounds all the time. Gangbangers sometimes survived multiple GSWs. But whatever was in the syringe could kill instantly. Dallas was leery of getting too close to the crazy woman until she had parted with her lethal injection.

Decker reached behind her back and opened the door. She was talking to Brickman, but Dallas couldn't hear what she said. She made a decision. The best thing she could do was follow Decker, watch for an opening, and be there when this scenario played out. She turned and bolted for the front door, a faster way to reach her car. On the way, she passed a man in a dark suit asking a clerk what was going on. Was he law enforcement? She didn't stop to find out. Someone at the clinic had probably called 911 already. Decker wouldn't get away. But she might kill Brickman before they arrested her.

Dallas sprinted toward her car, glancing to the right as she ran. A paramedic was climbing into the driver's seat of an ambulance. Nearby, Decker shoved Brickman toward the vehicle. The big man went along, probably terrified of the syringe. Or maybe Decker had already drugged him with it. The crazy woman shouted something at her captive, and he opened the back of the ambulance and climbed in. Decker followed, slamming the door closed.

Dallas finally reached her car. She fired up the engine, grabbed her weapon out of its holster, and called River. As the phone rang, she put in her earpiece and looked over at the clinic. The ambulance was rolling toward the street.

Chapter 41

Cheryl's heart had been thundering like a freight train, but as soon as the ambulance rolled forward, she felt calm. At least she would get some answers before the FBI arrested her. And if she were smart—and caught a break—she might make it to Saul's house where she could pick up necessities, then cross the border into Mexico. Saul would send a guide with her, and she would be safe. From there, she could continue south until she reached Costa Rica, where the Slimbiotic trials had been conducted. Cheryl knew doctors who would give her access to labs and help her continue her research. She had ten grand in her purse and could buy another ID, plus she had an offshore bank account the feds wouldn't be able to find or freeze. Giving Amber unapproved medications was illegal, and she'd been doing it for years. So she'd prepared long ago to be ready to flee to a less-restrictive country. Marta could take Amber to Saul's, and he'd eventually help them reconnect.

"What do you want, Cheryl?" Brickman kept his voice even, as if dealing with a crazy person. "Continuing this is insane." He had sat on the floor, wedged between a gurney and a stainless steel medical cabinet.

She moved past him and tapped the plexi-glass between

her and the driver. The man glanced over his shoulder, his expression surprisingly calm. "Head south toward Ocean View Hills," Decker directed. "Stay off the main roads. No sirens, no radio. Just keep making turns and drive fast. This bastard's life is in your hands."

The paramedic lurched the ambulance into traffic, forcing drivers to brake. He gunned the gas and sped toward Palomar Street.

Cheryl turned back to her captive. "What did you do to my father? You bastard!"

"Come on, I had nothing to do with that. The police are just making wild accusations." Brickman gave her his best you-know-me look.

She did know him. He had the same driving ambition she did, only he was capable of hurting people on purpose. Cheryl inched toward him, checking his hands to ensure that his wrists were still tied. The scarf wasn't ideal, but it would hold long enough.

"You're a lying pile of shit." She still couldn't believe her father was dead. Even though she'd been mad at him, she still loved him. And she'd been hurt when he'd finally given up contacting her. Apparently, he'd cut her out of his will too. Otherwise, his lawyer would have contacted her.

Brickman was still unresponsive, so she prodded. "Did you go to James for campaign money?"

No response.

"Did he threaten to sell his shares in ProtoCell and plunge the stock price? What happened?"

"You're wrong. And this is only making it worse."

Cheryl stabbed the tip of the syringe into his arm, just above the elbow, and gave a tiny push.

Brickman let out a squawk.

"It's a MRSA-related bacteria, in case you're wondering." Cheryl gave him a wicked smile. "An accidental byproduct." He'd been dying to know what new research she'd pursued all these years, and now he would find out just as it invaded his body. "That dose probably won't kill you if you take antibiotics in the next hour, but if I hit you with the whole syringe, you're a goner no matter what. Septic shock is what they'll write on your chart." She laughed. It felt so good to hurt him back.

"You're bluffing." His natural pink cheeks lost their glow.

"You know me better than that. Tell me what happened to my father!" She glanced over her shoulder at the driver. He had his eyes on the road and didn't seem to be doing anything but driving. The next turn was only a half-mile away. But the cops had to be looking for the ambulance by now.

Brickman swallowed hard. "Your father snuck into the R&D building, and I caught him. His death was an accident."

What? That made no sense. She would have given anything to know what the media had reported, but she knew Brickman was lying. "That's not what the police think. He's my father. I deserve to know the truth." She decided to play on his natural cockiness. "The FBI are probably following us, and I'm not likely to survive this day. It can't hurt you to tell me. Why was James at ProtoCell?"

A smile played on the bastard's rubbery lips. "He came to steal the SlimPro. It took me a while to get that information out of him."

She still didn't understand. "But why?"

"The idiot was trying to win you back. He had an appointment at our affiliated lab and saw a chance to get into our facility. So he took it."

James had wanted her forgiveness? Had her father tried

to steal a cure for Amber?

Brickman's eyes narrowed. "It was such a bizarre thing to find him there. And I was having a really bad day. You can blame yourself for that."

She knew he meant her sabotage campaign, but she didn't rise to the bait. "So you killed him? To get back at me?"

"I wanted to send you a message. To get you to back off. There's room in the market for both our products." Brickman shook his head in disbelief. "But you don't watch the damn news, so you didn't hear about his death." Another half smile. "His new wife must really hate you. No surprise."

Rage engulfed her. "You're a sick bastard." She held up the syringe. "You won't be around to see the disaster, so I'll tell you a little more about this bacteria." She leaned forward, as if sharing a secret. "I infected your product line. Every SlimPro on the delivery trucks is contaminated. Every patient who gets an implant this week will develop a fever and pain in the incision. Their devices will be removed, and their doctors will file Adverse Reaction Reports with the FDA. Your company will voluntarily pull it from the market until it's been investigated. And my product will launch in the mean time."

Cheryl laughed again, a full bitter outpouring. "These things will happen whether you and I are here or not." She had started to doubt her ability to survive this incident. Poor Amber. But her daughter could live with Saul and be homeschooled. The girl might even be happier.

Brickman's jaw trembled and his eyes jumped with panic. "You selfish bitch! When did you get so greedy?"

She gave him a rueful smile. "It's not about the money. Not directly."

"Why then? Revenge? Because I didn't love you? Because

I continued the product development without you?"

Cheryl decided to tell him the truth before she killed him. "Not just revenge. I did it for Amber. Our daughter. She has Prader-Willi Syndrome, and I need the money to continue the research. In case neither of *my* products works this round."

She readied the syringe and plunged a large dose into his arm.

Chapter 42

The ambulance blew through the intersection, and Dallas tried to follow. An SUV making a right turn cut in front. She laid on her horn, cursing the idiot driver. Behind her, an engine roared. She looked in the rearview mirror and spotted a dark blue sedan. The guy in the suit *had* been a cop. Great news. He'd likely called for reinforcement. But what was protocol in this situation? A civilian's life was in jeopardy if they moved too aggressively. Dallas tried to put herself inside Decker's head. What did she want with Brickman? Revenge for his old betrayal? Decker had already tried to ruin his company, so maybe she simply wanted to kill him and had taken him hostage to buy herself time. Decker seemed smart enough to realize she had to ditch the ambulance.

Ahead, the vehicle turned right and Dallas spotted a sign for the 805 freeway. Was Decker making a run for the border? That would be stupid. Even an ambulance would have to stop and deal with customs. With her earpiece in, Dallas pressed re-dial. River finally picked up. "What's the report from the clinic?"

"Decker took Jonas Brickman hostage, and they're in an ambulance heading south on Picador. I'm about four blocks behind."

"Good glory. Do you have backup?"

"Some guy in a dark sedan is behind me. I think he's with the PD." Dallas swerved around a slow-moving mini-van. She'd taken high-speed driver training, but dealing with real traffic was far more challenging. "Decker threatened to kill Brickman if anyone called the cops, but someone probably did anyway."

"What kind of weapon does she have?"

"A small handgun and a syringe that she says is deadly."

River drew in a sharp breath. "It's bacteria. Maybe she killed Palmer with it too."

"I think Decker snapped and is unpredictable, but instinct tells me she'll kill Brickman, then take off on foot. Any idea where she'll go?" River knew the San Diego area and would have a better guess.

"The border isn't far, but that area is open with nowhere to hide."

"Decker is smart, so she might grab another vehicle and go in another direction."

"Don't let her out of your sight. We can't let her drop that syringe into a food or water supply. I'm hanging up now to make some calls."

Cars kept pulling off the road for the ambulance, then darting back into traffic in front of her rental, creating more distance between her and Decker. Up ahead, she caught sight of the ambulance as it took another left turn. Dallas honked at the car in front of her, hoping it would let her around. The driver flipped her off and slowed down. *Prick.* A glance in the rearview mirror told her the cop was still behind her. She was curious about his presence at the clinic, but couldn't focus on it.

After she was able to make the next turn, she spotted the

ambulance parked on a side street. The driver was still in the cab, and the back doors were open. Decker was not in sight. The crazy woman was either still inside with Brickman or she'd fled on foot. *Damn, damn, damn.*

The traffic in front of her came to a dead stop. *What the hell?* Dallas kept her eyes on the ambulance. Half a block from it, a figure in black disappeared into an alley. Yanking the wheel left, she careened into the corner parking lot and cut across, honking at pedestrians who lumbered into her path. At the perimeter, she slammed the car into park and scurried out. First, she had to check on Brickman. When she approached, the paramedic in the driver's seat gave her an OK gesture through the window. Brakes screeched, and to her right, the dark sedan went over the curb and blocked the street in front of the ambulance. Dallas ran for the back of the vehicle.

Brickman sat on the floor, his hands still tied. Alive, but breathing hard, as if his oxygen had been cut off for a while. "I need to go to the hospital," he gasped. "For intravenous antibiotics."

River had been right. But at least Brickman still had a chance and didn't have a bullet in the head. "Where did Decker go?"

With bound hands, Brickman pointed across the street, where Dallas had seen the person run into the alley. She sensed someone behind her and spun around. The guy in the suit.

"Detective Cortez," he shouted. "I need to arrest Jonas Brickman for murder."

What? "He needs antibiotics or he'll probably die." She started to run toward the alley.

"Wait," Brickman called. "You have to stop the SlimPro

273

deliveries." He gulped for air. "The bitch infected the product run. Our customers will get sick."

Dallas nodded at Cortez. "Call the FBI. Tell Agent Carla River. I have to go after Decker." She bolted for the alley, ignoring the car coming up the street. It honked but braked. She sprinted down the concrete strip between the back walls of the shops, but didn't see anyone. Had Decker ducked into a store the way the unsub had the night before? The back doors were all closed, and Dallas figured that Decker had kept moving. The woman had to be looking for transportation. A car to steal. Or a bus to jump on.

The alley opened into another street, then continued on the next block. Dallas slowed and scanned in both directions. A group of teenage girls took up the sidewalk nearby, talking animatedly.

"Hey," she shouted. "Have you seen a woman in a black dress?"

They ignored her. A moment later, she realized they were speaking Spanish. She repeated her question in their language. Two of the girls turned, startled.

Dallas dropped her gun to her side.

One scowled. "Tomó mi coche. Quiso comprarlo, luego señaló un arma."

Decker had stolen a car from her. "What color? What make?"

The young girl pointed up the one-way street. "Toyota plata."

The most common car on the road. "Gracias."

Dallas ran in the direction of the traffic and tried to guess what Decker would do. She needed a main artery to get out of town. That meant circling the block and heading back to the street they'd been on before. Dallas spun around and charged down the alley on the next block. With any luck, she'd hit the street before Decker drove by. Her earpiece was still in and her phone was in her pocket. She tried to call River using voice commands, but she was breathing too hard.

Bursting out of the alley, she spotted the silver Toyota coming up the street. Decker was driving, and seemed to have both hands on the wheel. Where was her gun? Dallas raised her weapon and aimed at the vehicle.

A family with young kids came out of the sporting goods store across the street, and other pedestrians stopped and stared. Afraid of hitting a bystander, Dallas wouldn't take the shot. What now? The Toyota was about to pass by. On impulse, she charged at the oncoming car. At the last moment, she leapt and threw herself on the hood, landing on her belly. "FBI! Stop the vehicle!"

Decker's mouth dropped open in shock.

Dallas pounded the windshield with the butt of her gun, hoping to rattle Decker enough to make her pull over.

The engine roared under her belly, and the car sped forward. Gripping a wiper with her free hand, Dallas pounded the windshield again. In the distance, she heard a siren. "FBI! We have you surrounded. Stop the car and get on the ground."

Decker hit the brakes. Dallas slid off the hood, scraping her stomach on the way. She landed on her feet and aimed her weapon at the driver. Decker shut off the car, then fumbled with something in her lap. The crazy woman closed her eyes for a moment, then climbed out with her hands up. "Don't shoot me. I want to see my daughter again." Her voice held a trembling fatality, a woman resigned to a dead-end future.

Dallas rounded the car and shouted, "Get on the ground!"

She didn't have handcuffs with her, but backup would arrive any moment.

Decker sunk to her knees. "I did more good than harm," she said softly.

Dallas stepped toward the open door of the car, looking to secure Decker's gun. It lay on the passenger's seat. Next to it was an empty syringe. Brickman had been right to call for a trip to the hospital. The siren got louder, then a black-and-white patrol car careered around the corner and stopped. Dallas stepped back, waiting for help.

She glanced at Decker, wanting to say something, but couldn't find words. A drop of red on the scientist's bare white arm caught her eye. Blood. From a pinprick. Decker had injected herself with the bacteria too.

Chapter 43

Cortez followed the ambulance carrying Brickman to the Sharp Medical Center. Apparently, his suspect had been infected with deadly bacteria and might die. Cortez didn't care about the man personally, but he wanted closure for James Avery. He just needed a few minutes with Brickman. Confronted with the fingerprint evidence—and his own mortality—Brickman might confess. Or at least reveal enough information for Cortez to have a sense of resolution.

His phone rang, and he pressed his earpiece. The call could be critical to this case or to the tainted products on the trucks. "Detective Cortez."

"This is Rollin Fisher, attorney for James Avery." His voice was pleasant, but clipped. "Sorry for the delay in calling. I was out of town with my own family crisis, then had to deal with James' family when I learned of his death."

Finally. "This isn't a good time to talk, but I'd like to set up a meeting with you."

"What is this about?"

"Avery's will." Now that he knew Brickman was the killer, Avery's estate no longer seemed important. But he still had some unanswered questions, particularly about finances and motive.

"His death is devastating." A little catch in the lawyer's voice. "Especially since James had made an appointment to change his will and testament, then was killed and couldn't keep it."

Was that why he was murdered? "Do you know what change he planned to make?" Cortez saw the ambulance change lanes and followed.

"James wanted to re-instate his estranged daughter and leave her a reasonable share. He'd cut her out years ago, but that was before I worked with him."

Avery had a daughter? "What's her name? And why didn't his wife mention her?"

"Cheryl Decker. She's president of TecLife." A pause. "As for Avery's wife, I don't know her motive, but my understanding is that she's not fond of either of James' children."

Was Decker the woman who'd taken Brickman hostage? "Do you know anything about Jonas Brickman?"

"No. Sorry. Let's meet Friday at two."

Cortez agreed, and they hung up. The mystery daughter only added to his confusion about Brickman's motives. He hoped the man would live long enough to tell him something.

Cortez arrived at the hospital minutes after the ambulance. He pushed through the swinging door into the treatment area and quickly found a group of people in blue scrubs surrounding his suspect, who was still handcuffed to the gurney. He stood back and let them get Brickman hooked up to antibiotics. He would question him as soon as the medical people stepped back.

Moments later, the blond woman came into the treatment center, pulling along the crazy kidnapper in the black dress. *Cheryl Decker?*

"I'm Agent Dallas with the FBI," she shouted. "This woman needs the same antibiotics you're giving Jonas Brickman."

An older male doctor rushed from Brickman's area to the handcuffed woman, and Cortez followed. "Let's get you into a bed," the doctor said, reaching for the suspect's arm.

She jerked away. "I don't want treatment."

"Give it to her anyway," Dallas insisted. "She's suspected of product tampering. I need to question her."

Decker vehemently shook her head. "I'll sue any doctor who lays a hand on me. The fourteenth amendment guarantees my right to refuse treatment."

Cortez spoke up. "This is about public safety. Tampered products are going out to patients right now. We need information that could save them."

The doctor shook his head. "I can't treat her without consent."

"Goddammit." Dallas stamped her foot.

A big woman in a dark suit barged into the area. Older than him, she seemed to command authority. "I'm Agent River. This is my case." She turned to her fellow agent. "What's the update?"

Dallas gave a brief rundown, then Cortez cut in to introduce himself. "I called you about the product tampering at ProtoCell. What's the situation?"

"We're handling it." River turned back to Dallas. "Let's get Decker into an interrogation room while we seek a court order for treatment." She grabbed the kidnapper's arm and spun her around. Dallas latched onto Decker's other elbow and they practically carried her down the hall.

"Why did she kidnap Jonas Brickman?" Cortez asked,

following them.

"I'll call you after we've questioned her," River said.

"Just tell me her connection to Brickman."

"Ex-lover and current competitor."

That explained a few things. He started to ask another question, but Dallas turned back and said, "Who did Brickman allegedly murder?"

"James Avery. I just found out he's Cheryl Decker's father."

River stopped and turned, her expression both curious and distressed. "Why?"

"I don't know yet. But Avery snuck into ProtoCell, then Brickman drugged him and beat him, so maybe it was about proprietary information." Cortez gestured at Decker. "Please ask your suspect and get back to me."

"I will." River turned, and they barged through the crowded waiting area and out the door. Cortez headed back to Brickman.

He tried to get the remaining doctor at the bedside to give him a best guess about Brickman's fate, but she refused, claiming it could go either way. She also tried to discourage him from questioning her patient, but Cortez persisted.

Brickman's face was pink and damp, and his eyes were worried.

Cortez got right to the heart of it. "Your fingerprint is on James Avery's steering wheel. You drove his car, and I know you were involved in his death. Tell me what happened."

"I don't know anything about it." Brickman sounded weak.

"You're probably going to die. You'll feel better if you confess. It's good for the soul."

"I have nothing to say." The infected man closed his eyes.

Cortez wished he'd had more time to confer with River

and Dallas, but Brickman was his priority. He owed it to James Avery to get closure.

"I know Cheryl Decker is Avery's daughter." He leaned toward his suspect. "Why did she kidnap you? And try to kill you? Because you killed her father?"

Brickman let out a soft laugh. "Cheryl's crazy." He grimaced in pain. "Get the doctor please. Something is happening in my intestines."

Disappointed and conflicted, Cortez went to summon medical help. Brickman had to live long enough to be charged with murder.

Chapter 44

River entered the interrogation room at the SD bureau, hoping it was the last time. She wanted to be on a plane headed home Friday morning. Decker was cuffed to the table, looking oddly out of place in her black, cocktail-party dress. But her disheveled hair and tear-stained face were a common combination for people in her situation. The bacteria invading the suspect's body as they interrogated her would be a first though.

River took a seat and her stomach growled. She hadn't eaten since breakfast and her body was tired. She was ready for Agent King to get in here so they could wrap this up. Dallas was watching on a monitor, but she planned to fly home the next day. River had sent her back into the ER for a bottle of antibiotics, and Dallas claimed to feel fine. If Decker didn't plead out—and survived the infection—Dallas would have to come back for her trial. River doubted that would be necessary.

King came in, carrying a stack of thick folders and sat down. The paper was a show of mounting evidence, and his not staying on his feet meant he expected a soft interview. So did she. People facing death liked to get things off their chest, and egotistical perpetrators like Decker, couldn't resist bragging or at least revealing how clever or effective they'd been.

King let her take the lead. Another expression of his gratitude for her insistence on pursuing the TecLife investigation and bringing closure for the Palmers.

Which is where she would start. "Agent Palmer died from an infected wound on his hand. The bacteria was unique and came from your lab. Did you expose him to it on purpose?"

Decker's face was expressionless. "He exposed himself to it. He was snooping around in the lab without permission."

Accidental? River's hopes plunged. "As far as we're concerned, you killed him. And if you die, that's how our case report will read. Why not tell us the truth?"

"I just did. I'm not stupid enough to cause the death of a federal agent who'd just questioned me. I got lucky on that one."

Everything in Decker's tone and body language signaled honesty, and the PulseTat found in Palmer's pocket had come up clean. But River would come back to the subject. She feared she had little time and needed to extract as much information as she could. "Who did you hire to set the ProtoCell warehouse fire?"

"A woman named K. That's all I know about her."

"Come on. We need to find her. She's a dangerous criminal."

"Good luck. She's very elusive, and I really don't know anything about her."

"How did you first contact her?"

"She came to me. She said one of my competitors had tried to hire her to steal my Slimbiotic data, but they hadn't offered her enough money. K wanted to know if I would pay her more to work against them. I couldn't resist the opportunity to give Brickman what he deserved." A grim smile.

"Was Brickman the one who tried to hire K?"

"She wouldn't name her client, but I suspected it was him." Decker slumped in her chair. "I'm not telling you anything else until I see my daughter. I feel feverish already, and I don't know how long I'll be coherent."

King cut in. "We have an agent picking her up now. So she's on her way. Keep talking and we'll let you visit with her in another room. No cuffs."

Decker's eyes squinted, trying to assess who had the most leverage, but she didn't respond.

River pressed on. "Did you kill Michael Pence? A neighbor saw a car that matches yours outside his house the night he died."

Decker shook her head, angry. "I'm not a killer. I went to see Michael because I wanted to bribe him to come work for me. But he'd been drinking and was belligerent. Then I realized he had a gun sitting there on the couch." Her expression shifted to regret. "I decided to leave, but he grabbed the gun and threatened me. He said he'd been thinking about suicide but that he might kill me instead."

River didn't buy it. "Why would he threaten you?"

"He was drunk, suicidal, and angry. My offer of employment offended him. He aimed his gun at me and threatened to shoot me."

"How did he end up dead?"

"He wanted to kill himself and frame me for it. He grabbed my hand and tried to wrap it around his gun. It was so bizarre." A watery mist came into her eyes. "But I got away and pulled out my own handgun. I had no intention of using it. I just wanted to get out. I started backing toward the door and he shot himself."

"Why would he kill himself? His wife and friends all said he was happy."

"Is anyone really happy?" Decker's voice had softened and her cheeks were flushed. "When I offered Michael a job at TecLife, he scoffed. He said one lab was the same as another, that they were all prisons." She rolled her eyes. "He said scientists were all slaves to their research and that it was no way to live. Did I mention that he was drunk and depressed?"

River had to accept her version. The autopsy had been ruled a suicide, and all the physical evidence indicated Pence had put the gun to his own head. "What about Jace Hunter? Someone bashed her on the head and dragged her into the ocean. That clearly wasn't an accident."

Decker sighed. "I told you I'm not a killer. And I liked Jace. I'm upset to find out she was spying on me, but I didn't know she was a federal agent until she jumped on the hood of the car and pointed a gun at me."

Dallas was certain the for-hire saboteur had attacked her, and River was inclined to think so too. It was good to get information about the other deaths, but she felt disappointed.

Decker's eyes started to look glassy. "I'll sign a confession for the acts of sabotage, but only if you let me see Amber. This bacteria will probably kill me in twenty-four hours, and it won't be pretty."

River looked at King and he nodded. She stood to uncuff their suspect. "Do you know why Brickman might have killed your father?"

"He's an asshole and wanted to get back at me," Decker said, sounding exhausted. "Brickman confessed to the murder when we were in the ambulance. The bastard is going to die, but I want the public to know the truth about him."

"But why was James Avery at ProtoCell?" River was still confused about that scenario.

"He was trying to help me and Amber." Decker shook her head. "Please don't smear his name in public. Let his fans remember him as their hero."

As River uncuffed Decker and let her stand, the suspect said, "One more thing. I want to call Curtis Santera. He has to continue looking for a cure for Prader-Willi syndrome since I won't be here to do it. It's my dying wish."

King escorted Decker to another, *softer* interrogation room, and River went in search of Dallas. She found her in the break room pouring coffee.

"What's the update on the SlimPro delivery trucks?" River asked. Agents and police officers had descended on the ProtoCell factory earlier, but the trucks had already gone out. The bureau was coordinating a statewide search to stop them and confiscate the product.

"We've got all but one, and we think it crossed into Nevada. Their state patrol is searching for it. And the FDA and CDC are working together to warn doctors and clinics that SlimPro is lethal and should be treated as a bio-hazard."

Relieved, River said, "So other than Brickman and Decker, no one was infected?"

"Except me." Dallas grinned. "But my exposure was minimal, and since I didn't have an open wound, I'll be fine."

"How's your head?"

"Painful, but I'll live." The young agent gave a sad smile. "Decker's nuts, isn't she? The agents who searched her house said she had seventeen kinds of medication. Some of it was for paranoia and anxiety, but the rest was all appetite suppressants and weight-loss drugs. I think her daughter will be better off in the care of someone else."

"I wonder what the state will do with her."

"That depends on who the father is and whether Child Services approves of Decker's friend Saul Ortega to be her caregiver."

A moment of silence. They were both exhausted.

"I'm going home," River said. "By that, I mean my rental. So should you. The local guys can do all the grunt work."

Dallas grinned again. "That's what I like best about undercover work. They always send me home just as the investigation gets boring."

"Let's get out of here."

Dallas didn't argue and they headed out of the bureau into another dark warm evening.

On the drive to her apartment, River called Jana Palmer, who picked up right away. "What's going on? Agents were all over TecLife today, but no one would tell me anything."

"We arrested Cheryl Decker and she confessed to the sabotage." River paused, knowing this would be hard for Jana. "Decker says Joe's contamination was an accident. He handled the bacteria with a wound on his hand."

"So he died from a scratch?" Jana let out a small sob. "How unfitting for his career."

"His death wasn't in vain. If you two hadn't initiated this investigation, thousands of innocent customers might have died from tainted SlimPro products." It was mostly true, and Jana needed closure. "Decker also infected herself and refused treatment."

"She's going to die?" Jana's voice was quiet.

"Yes. She was facing life in prison."

"What about her daughter?"

"We don't know yet."

"Thanks, River." Jana started to cry. "I can't talk anymore right now. Come see me before you leave town." She hung up.

River vowed to keep in better touch with her. And in the next few minutes, she made two important decisions. The first was easy. She would not go see her father in prison. She'd said goodbye to him long ago. And a visit would be distressful, with nothing to gain.

Her relationship with Jared was a conundrum though. If she only thought of him as a friend, she probably would have told him about her past already, and let the chips fall. A true friend would be supportive. But since she'd been attracted to him from the beginning, she hadn't been able to bring it up. Yet, if they were going to have a sexual relationship, he needed to know.

River made a decision. She would tell him as soon as she got home. Not only that she used to be a man, but that she wanted more from their relationship. She expected him to be polite and supportive, then gone the next day.

Every decision was correct in the moment.

Chapter 45

Kiya took a cab to the airport, thinking the jobs she'd done for Decker had paid nicely and brought her closer to her goal of retiring to Greece to paint and be happy. The day before, she'd sold her motorcycle and rented a moving truck. Then packed her few possessions, driven them to a storage unit in Silicon Valley, and come straight back. A long tedious day, but vital to her survival. She wouldn't risk coming back to San Diego.

Kiya climbed from the cab, tipped the driver, and hauled her two carry-on bags inside. Her first flight was to Hungary. It was never a good idea to fly direct to a Middle Eastern country from the United States. The TSA scrutinized those passengers more closely. Even with her fake passport and adopted American name, her skin color was still suspicious to security people. The bright-blue contacts and dyed-blond hair would help though. From Hungary, she would fly to southern Uzbekistan and meet with Abdul. After she paid the councilman, her father would be arrested and imprisoned. Once she was certain of his fate, she'd fly back and set up in her new home. In Silicon Valley, she could probably make money in intellectual theft and sabotage for quite a while.

An hour later, she stepped up to a customs counter and

handed the man her passport and boarding pass.

"Who are you visiting in Hungary?"

A routine question. They always asked something just to see who began to sweat. "My sister. She's getting married."

He stared at her face for a long moment, then picked up a clipboard and checked a list of names. Were they looking for her? Kiya fought to stay calm. If they searched her, she was screwed. How would she explain the thirty thousand hidden in the back panel of her coat? Not to mention the fake passport. The customs agent flipped through the papers on the clipboard and stared at a new page. He studied her face again, as if comparing.

Had the federal agent taken an identifiable picture of her? And shared it with transportation hubs? *Dashat!* She gave the man a small smile. "I'm not crazy about weddings, but she's my sister. You know?"

"I know." He set down the clipboard, handed back her ID, and waved her through.

Her muscles relaxed as she walked away, and a strange sadness came over her. She wished she'd come up with some other reason for visiting Hungary. Mentioning her sister had messed with her head. Now she couldn't stop thinking about an eight-year-old girl she'd never met. A child with her genes living the same horrific life she'd been subjected to.

Her gate was just ahead, so Kiya sat down to wait for her flight. Maybe she would use her cash to buy the girl's freedom instead of taking revenge on her father. She could teach her sister everything she knew and put her to work. Together they could make a great team. They could earn another fortune—and move to Greece together.

* * *

Dallas sat on the terrace in the dark, drinking a beer and staring at the phone in her lap. It was her personal cell, and the last caller had been her mother. The little icon in the corner indicated her mother had left a message. She didn't want to play it. Yet, she had to know.

She finished her beer, fetched another, and sat back down. Cameron had texted her too, and she read his message again: *I'm in Phoenix, looking for a place to live. When will you be back?*

Her brush with death, plus her failure to apprehend K, had left her feeling eager to get away from San Diego. She keyed *Soon* into a text message and pressed Send. It wasn't a commitment to see him. Just the courtesy of a response.

Halfway through her beer, she listened to the voicemail from her mother: "Your father died this morning. The funeral is Saturday. I hope you'll come."

Dallas visualized the old man in a casket, and an unexpected grief overwhelmed her. A moment later, she was sobbing. She didn't try to hold back or talk herself out of it. She let the tears flow.

But the outburst was brief, and another longing took over. She keyed in a second text to Cameron: *I'll be on a plane Friday. Let's hook up for the weekend and see how it goes.*

L.J. Sellers is an award-winning journalist and the author of the bestselling **Detective Jackson mystery/thriller series:**

    The Sex Club
    Secrets to Die For
    Thrilled to Death
    Passions of the Dead
    Dying for Justice
    Liars, Cheaters & Thieves
    Rules of Crime
    Crimes of Memory
    Deadly Bonds

Agent Dallas novels:
    The Trigger
    The Target

Standalone thrillers:
    The Baby Thief
    The Gauntlet Assassin
    The Lethal Effect

When not plotting murders, L.J. enjoys performing standup comedy, cycling, social networking, and attending mystery conferences. She's also been known to jump out of airplanes.

Thanks for reading my novel. If you enjoyed it, please leave a review or rating online. Find out more about my work at ljsellers.com, where you can sign up to hear about new releases.
—L.J.

Made in the USA
Coppell, TX
10 October 2021